CHOICE OF STRAWS

In *To Sir, With Love* and *Paid Servant*, E. R. Braithwaite recalled his experiences as a teacher in the East End of London and as the first coloured child-welfare officer for the L.C.C. These two books brought him immense fame as a writer. *Choice of Straws* is his first novel.

Dave and Jack Bennett were twins, and inseparable. They worked side by side at the factory bench, they chased girls together, often they used their identical appearance to play practical jokes. A happy-go-lucky, rootless pair, popular in their neighbourhood, they were not unlike many young Londoners of today. If they did occasionally rough up a Negro, it was not from conscious race hatred. They may have had a confused idea that they were avenging an attack on their father by a group of coloured men. But it was just a game, really.

Then one evening they picked a tough one, who showed himself a determined fighter. In a moment of panic Dave drew a knife. The Negro was killed, and Dave himself was seriously wounded. Later that night, far from the scene of the struggle, Dave died in a car crash.

Choice of Straws is Jack's own account of these events and of the weeks that follow. Grief-stricken and disorientated by the death of his brother, deeply ashamed of their attack on the Negro, and always in fear that the police will discover his part in the murder, his confusion deepens when he meets a lovely coloured girl. Mr Braithwaite has drawn a memorable portrait of a young man forced by circumstances to come to terms with the shifting, multi-racial society he lives in.

Choice *of* Straws

E. R. BRAITHWAITE

THE BOBBS-MERRILL COMPANY, INC.
A Subsidiary of Howard W. Sams & Co., Inc.
PUBLISHERS/Indianapolis Kansas City New York

For Michelle
With Love

1

WE'D BEEN LIKE that for nearly an hour. Just waiting. The cold, damp, bitter-sweet stink of the place was beginning to get on my nerves, but I said nothing, waiting for Dave to make the first move about leaving. Outside, the shadows of evening had thickened with the persistent drizzle which occasionally slanted in through the paneless window of our hiding-place, to add to my discomfort. My legs were beginning to feel numb. I wanted a smoke, badly. This waiting had taken the edge off the thing as far as I was concerned, and if Dave had said let's call it off, he'd have had no argument from me. But I didn't think he would. Not Dave. Once he got on to something he'd never back out.

I thought of the people who might have lived in the very room where we were waiting. It looked out on to the street through two huge windows from which the glass had long ago been shattered by bomb blast or the marksmanship of small boys, and may have been the best room where friends were received for Sunday tea. Dead and gone, perhaps. Mother and children with father off to the wars to make Britain safe for heroes. Heroes hell! So many black buggers about the place, the ruddy heroes couldn't get a fair crack at the jobs or their own ruddy women. Bloody Spades.

Near me I could hear Dave with that faint, tuneless, whistling sound he always made when excited, more like a long breath indrawn through his teeth. I couldn't see anything of his face the way he was leaning against the wall to have a clear view of the street as far as the pub at the corner.

'Seen anything?' I asked him.

'Not yet.'

'Think he'll come?'

'He'll come.'

'Then he'd better ruddy well hurry.'

'Why, what's up.'

'Cramp in my legs.'.

'Quit nagging. You'll survive.'

I was squatted on my heels beside him, to be out of the way of anyone glancing in from the street. It was Dave's idea, though I couldn't imagine who'd want to waste time looking into any of those dead houses. We'd come in here to wait because the place was open, the main door not boarded up or anything, just a huge, gaping hole in the front of the house. Even the woodwork had been ripped off. The floor was thick with dust and garbage.

'I still don't get it, how you're so sure about him.' I said it, not to start an argument, but just to show him my attitude to the whole thing, this waiting for something that might not happen.

'Look, Jack.' There was in his voice that schoolmasterish tone which always got under my skin, that way he had of making the thing seem simple and me as stupid as hell. 'Look, when we were coming to that pub at the corner, didn't you see the fellow come out, heading this way? Right. Then someone stuck his head out of the door and called him back, Doc or Jock or something like that? Okay, so it stands to reason that when he's ready he'll come out again and head this way.'

I looked up at him while he talked. Never once did he take his eyes off the road outside.

'It had better be soon.' I couldn't give him a broader hint than that.

'Oh, wrap up.'

'But how do you know he's a Spade? I didn't even get a look at his face.'

'I know. He's a Spade all right.'

'Dave.'

'What?'

'I feel funny about this one.'

'Scared?'

I didn't answer. The truth is I wasn't really scared. At least that's not the word for what I felt. After all, it wasn't the first time we'd done something like this, but always it had been done

8

on the spur of the moment. No waiting around. We'd go up where we knew some of them lived, Brixton, Goldhawk Road, places like that, and wander around, keeping an eye out till we saw one by himself. Then we'd have a little fun with him if we thought we could risk it. Knock him about a bit, then push off. Always at night, when there wouldn't be any nosey people trying to interfere. But this was different, hiding here for more than half an hour, the place stinking as if the whole neighbourhood had been relieving themselves in it. Dave nudged me and I stood up alongside him. Over his shoulder the houses opposite were glued together in a faceless dark mass all the way down to the corner.

The door of the pub was open and someone was framed in the broad patch of light, moving, as if talking with another inside. Then the light was cut off.

'That's him. He's heading this way,' Dave whispered, the excitement tight in his voice. It was too dark to see his face clearly, but I could well imagine the grey-green eyes shining with anticipation, the thin mouth half open for breathing, pulling away from the teeth. I often wondered if, all the time, I looked exactly like him. Often wished there was some way of seeing myself when watching him, to find out if the resemblance between him and me extended to every look, every smile, everything. True, nobody but our Mum could tell us apart, but that was on the outside, and I know I didn't always feel the same way as he did about things. At least, I didn't always want to; especially with everybody expecting us to even think alike, just because we were identical twins. Sometimes I only went along with doing something with him just because, well, just because we were always together. Since we were little it was always the Twins or Dave and Jack. Always Dave and Jack, even at school. Never Jack and Dave. Kids would call to us, hey Dave and Jack, never knowing which was which.

The man from the pub came along the far pavement. From where we hid we could hear the tap, tap of his shoes, as if he had metal tips on his heels.

'We'll wait till he's a little ahead, then we'll cross over and come up behind him,' Dave whispered, pushing me towards the doorway, where we stood, one on each side. As the man came nearer there was a clinking from something he was carrying, loud in the silent night as he came abreast and went past. We left the house and crossed the street, our jeans, black sweaters and suède jackets mixing into the dingy wetness, silent as ghosts in our rubber-soled chukka boots. He was laughing and singing to himself, the words trailing behind him . . . She's a whole lot of woman and she sure needs a whole lot of man . . . fading away into laughter. Probably half stewed. He stopped to shift the parcel and was moving on when we reached him, one on each side.

'Hey, Spade,' Dave whispered.

The man stopped and turned.

'What the . . .' The words were cut off as Dave hit him. Dave was right. A bloody Spade. In the gloom all you could see was the dark head shape. I hit at it and heard him grunt, then we were hitting him and suddenly the crash as his parcel fell and broke and the strong smell of rum or whisky or something. I kicked him and he doubled forward, grabbing Dave and falling on top of him. I kicked him, the excitement so strong in me I wanted to shout, this was so different from the other times. The Spade was fighting, silently, like a madman. Suddenly he sprang away from Dave and came at me, hitting me in the stomach. I could hardly breathe, but Dave pulled him and they were on the ground again, the Spade hitting Dave and muttering, 'I'll kill you, you lousy fuckers, I'll kill you.'

Then Dave screamed. 'Get him off me, Jack. Get him off.' I grabbed the Spade's coat, pulling him backwards, but he flung me off and I fell. He was strong as a horse, and I was suddenly frightened. We couldn't cope with him. I got up, and the Spade was banging Dave's hand on the ground. I saw the glint of the knife just as Dave let it go, snatched it and stuck it into the Spade's back. He twisted around and came at me, and I dropped the knife, frightened, turning to run. Then I heard him cry 'Aaaah,' and when I looked around there was Dave with the knife in his hand, the Spade bent over, walking out into the middle of the street. Slowly, carefully, he knelt down, his arms folded low in front of him.

'Come on, let's get out of here,' Dave said, pulling my arm. I was watching the Spade. He made an attempt to get up, gave it up, and reached forward, braced on his hands and knees like a sprinter. Then slowly he fell over sideways, coughing.

'Come on.' Dave was pulling my arm.

We ran up the street leaving the Spade.

'Come on,' Dave urged. We ran headlong away.

Keeping as much as possible to the shadows we cut through Cable Street and a maze of alleyways towards Commercial Road, and beyond it, till we came to a narrow lane behind the big mass that is London Hospital. We took a breather against some iron railings, Dave hanging on and gasping as if he'd run out of his last breath. My face was running with the drizzle and perspiration, and inside my clothes the heat was like a steam bath. Not another soul in sight, and home seemed a thousand miles away. Dave was groaning beside me.

'Take a look at my back,' he said. 'It's hurting like hell.'

'Turn around.' I couldn't see much, with the poor light from the street lamps across the road, except the shiny wetness on his jacket. I slipped my hand underneath, felt the stickiness on his sweater and withdrew my hand, covered with blood, smelling raw and awful.

'You're bleeding, Dave.'

'Fucker had me down on those ruddy bottles. Is it bad?'

'Can't tell, but your sweater's soaked. Look at my hand.'

'Suffering Christ.' We looked at each other, the fear coming over me like a thick black fog. My brother's face was like a mirror of the things inside me. I felt weak and lost. Dave rallied quickly.

'Oh, bugger it. Come on, let's get off home.'

The lane led into Whitechapel Road, diagonally across from the Underground station. We made it through a break in the traffic just as two policemen came out of the Underground, and in our rush we nearly banged into them. We waited in the dark entrance of a tobacconist's and watched them wait at the zebra crossing while the traffic rushed by. One of them looked back towards us and said something to his mate. My heart nearly stopped beating. But then the traffic halted and they crossed over and went into the hospital gate with the neon sign 'Ambulance'. Dave was leaning weakly against the shop window. Two women came along, slowed to look in our direction, then walked on.

'Want a fag?' I asked him.

'Yes. Christ, I feel sick as a dog.'

Over the flame of my lighter I watched his face, chalk-white and running with perspiration, the fine rain like tiny diamonds in his short, curly blond hair. His blue eyes looked black in the bloodless background. The feeling of sickness came up in me.

'We'd better get you home quick, Dave. Come on, let's go down the Tube.'

He straightened up suddenly. 'You raving bonkers or something? What do you think would happen if I went down there like this? Some nosey parker'd be sure to . . . Tell you what, we'd better split up. The way those coppers looked at us, let's not take any chances.'

'What are you on about, splitting up? I can't leave you to make it home by yourself. Not like this.'

'Oh, wrap up. What do you think I'll do, pass ruddy out or something?'

'But your back.'

'Bugger my back. I'm not going to bleed to ruddy death. Look, I'll catch a bus to Leytonstone and take the Central line from there, okay? One of us by himself is fine, but together we're sure to have them staring as always.'

'Okay, Dave, okay.' From the set of his mouth I knew he'd made up his mind. No shifting him.

'But I'll wait and see you on the bus.'

'What for? Go on, scarpa before those coppers come back.'

'Mum will want to know what's up if I go in alone.'

'Tell her I'm seeing a bird home and I'll be in shortly.' He grimaced with the pain, but made an attempt to smile. 'Better keep an eye out for me, though. Go on, hop it.'

He walked across to the bus shelter, stiffly, like those toy soldiers in the comics, and stood holding on to one of the shiny metal posts. I went and stood just inside the station entrance to watch until his bus arrived and he climbed on, going upstairs. Even after it rolled away I stayed there, stiff with fear and confused, the whole rotten evening a heavy lump in my stomach. Please God, just let him get home safe. Please. He looked so white and scary, like that time long ago when as kids we'd been messing about on the diving-board at the swimming baths and he'd slipped off and belly-landed on the water. The attendant had fished him out white and limp like a broken doll.

'If you're going some place you'd better hurry, mate,' someone said behind. 'There's one just in.' It was the ticket collector. I showed my ticket and rushed down the stairs to the train. Jumping on the train I nearly lost the ticket. It fell out of my hand and landed on the edge of the platform. I picked it up and put it away in my pocket. The return half Upminster to Piccadilly Circus. That's where we'd planned to go tonight and listen to some jazz, where we should have gone if we hadn't changed our minds.

I sat down between a bearded student and a fat, elderly woman with a fat little boy on her lap, and closed my eyes, wishing desperately that I could open them again to find that the night hadn't really happened and I'd only dreamed all those terrible things. But the fear and worry followed me deep inside my mind wherever I tried to hide, real as the cold sweat I could feel running down my face and neck and alongside my ribs.

'Look, mummy, the man's crying.'

I opened my eyes to see the little boy twisted around in his mother's tight grip, pointing a pudgy finger close to my face, his eyes wide with surprise. With a quick, accurate movement his mother smacked his hand down, but he continued staring, his eyes swivelled around until I thought they'd pop out. He had a tiny mole near the right side of his mouth, just like Dave's. Oh God, let him be okay. Just this once. He was always the tough one. I might even reach home to find him there ahead of me.

13

'Young man, are you all right?' The woman was speaking, pulling me back to the time and place beside her.

'Yes, thanks, I'm fine,' I told her, trying to avoid looking at the four eyes from the two fat heads which seemed perched recklessly one on top of the other. All along the opposite seat eyes seemed to be watching me, so I closed mine. Perspiration was running down my face and into my mouth. I wiped it with my handkerchief, smelt the rank smell and right away remembered I'd wiped my hands on it after feeling Dave's back. I opened my eyes to see if anyone had noticed. Seeing the wide streaks nearly made me sick. I pushed it into my pocket, thinking about Dave, wanting him to be okay, to reach home safe, even ahead of me. Oh God, oh Jesus God, please, please. Oh Dave.

'Something the matter, young man?'

I kept my eyes shut tight, not answering her. Why the hell didn't she mind her own ruddy fat-arsed business and leave me alone? God, it was only supposed to be a bit of a giggle, just knock him about a bit and push off. If the bloody fool hadn't got hold of Dave we'd have just given him a few and been out of it, but the bastard just wouldn't let go. Bloody Spades. They had it coming to them. After all, our Dad hadn't done anything to them, yet they'd jumped him and beat him up. And him always on about how they were human beings like anyone else and why shouldn't they come here, the only reason was they wanted work and why not. And if things had been different and there was plenty of work in their countries with good pay lots of English would be rushing over there. Well, what the hell good had all that talk done him? He'd had nothing to do with the riots in Notting Hill. He was coming home from the building site in Ladbroke Grove when they jumped out of a car and beat him up. Put him in hospital for nearly three weeks, and not a ruddy policeman in sight to lend a hand.

When he came home he wouldn't talk about it. Not to us, not to Mum. Funny thing, though, we were watching television one night and there was this Spade come on and right away our Dad got up and switched the set off. Didn't say anything, just switched off as if he couldn't bear the sight of that black face.

The first time we got one of them was at Brixton. We'd heard so much about them living up there, and this Saturday night we'd gone up West, having a wander around, and we saw this bus with Brixton on the front and Dave said how about it and we jumped on. There were only a few of them in the High Street but too many other people about. Perhaps as soon as it was night they disappeared into wherever they lived. We walked about for a while but it didn't look as if anything would turn up, then out of a side street this fellow came, in a hell of a hurry, his overcoat collar turned up around his ears and hands stuck in the pockets. As he passed us we noticed the black face and glasses. We waited until he'd gone a few steps then turned and followed. He turned by that big shop with the Bon Marché sign. There wasn't anyone else in sight so we caught up with him. As Dave punched him I tripped him up, flat on his face. He rolled over and then we saw he was old, with not a single tooth in the wide open hole of a mouth. Lying there squinting up at us, probably couldn't see much since his glasses had fallen off. Not saying a word.

Funny thing about them. They'd either fight back, or just be there and take it, but they'd never run or shout for help, as if they didn't expect anyone to help them anyway.

Then there was that time we'd come out of Lancaster Gate Underground and were going up Bayswater Road on the Park side when we passed this one, standing by himself as if he was waiting for somebody. Dave said let's take him and we turned back, but the Spade must have guessed what was up because just as we reached him he pulled a knife. Must have had it in his pocket. Just flicked open the blade and stood there looking at us, nobody saying a word. So we left the stupid bugger standing there and went about our business. We couldn't figure how he'd guessed.

This night after work Dave had said let's go and have a little fun. We often went up West, sometimes two or three times a week, mostly Friday or Saturday nights. Better than going to the local hop or even Romford. We'd go up to Soho to the Kaleidescope or somewhere like that, drinking coffee or cokes and listening to jazz. Sometimes we'd meet up with some birds, mostly students, chat around with them, then catch the last train home. We caught the District Line, intending to change at Charing Cross for Piccadilly, but at Aldgate East we just got off the train, not talking about it. When the train reached the station Dave got up and I just followed him out.

Mum was always talking about the way we did things together. She said we were born with caul, or something like that. We even had the toothache and colds at the same time and our Dad used to laugh and say, one sneeze and the other wipe. But even they couldn't really understand about us. Like the time at Infants' school when Dave had gone out to the toilet and cut his penis with the old razor-blade he'd found, and I'd suddenly started screaming for no reason at all and they'd gone out and found Dave, standing there in the toilet not saying a word, blood over everything . . .

At Bow Road the fat woman and her son got off and two Spades got on, both in the stiff blue Underground uniform. One of them took the seat where the fat woman had been, the other standing near him, holding the overhead strap. I didn't want to watch them, but they were whispering and laughing. I couldn't help looking. The one standing was young, strong-looking, light glinting from his eyes and teeth. I wondered if the other one looked like him, the one we left lying in the road. Funny thing, I didn't give a damn about him, or these two, but thinking of them I remembered Dave, and the cold sweat started again.

'Man, the woman bawled.' The Spade sitting near me was speaking, his voice clear, but sounding a bit strange, like the way Welsh people speak, as if they really want to sing.

'So, what happened? You stopped?'

'You kidding?'

'Well, what?'

'Put my hand over her mouth so the neighbours wouldn't hear, and the bitch bit me.'

Laughter bubbled out of them.

'Man, you're lucky.'

'Lucky? How come?'

'Might have been something else.'

Again the laughter from deep inside them. Just between them. Secret. I hated those two, remembering Dave and the way that other bastard had knocked me about. I'd like to push a knife into their backs and really give them something to laugh about. The one standing looked across at me and the smile disappeared from his face as if he could read my thoughts. I could feel the other turn to look at me. Hatred for them was like a slow trembling deep inside. At the next station some passengers left and the Spades sat together opposite me. I closed my eyes so as not to have to look at them.

2

I LET MYSELF quietly into the house, thinking perhaps I should leave the door open for Dave, but I decided not to. I could watch out for him from upstairs and come down. It was well after midnight and I knew our Dad would be asleep, but Mum would be lying there in the dark like she always did until everyone was in. Really no point in sneaking upstairs and trying to slip past their room.

I'd just reached the top of the stairs when I heard our Mum's voice call 'That you, Dave?' from through their half open door. Same as always. Dave. Two of us go out, two of us come in, but it was always the same. 'That you, Dave?' Even as kids coming in from school, when we'd nip in the back way because of muddy shoes or something, as soon as Mum'd hear the back door open she'd call out, 'That you, Dave,' even though she could hear us both. Sometimes I'd think of it and hang back to let him go in by himself, so I wouldn't have to hear it. After all, we were the same, identical, Dave and me, and, if anything, I was the older by three hours. Mum said I came out easily as if I was in a hurry to start living, but she'd had a bit of a rough time with

Dave. Perhaps that's why she was that way with him, calling him first and things like that.

Not that she gave him anything more or different from me. Nothing like that. But it was this business of always calling him first. Never forgot that time when we were kids and went on the school outing to Epping Forest and all the kids were picking these bluebells and I said to Dave, Let's get some, and he said, What for, only girls do that, but I picked some anyway and carried them back on the coach; and when we were going in our gate I let him hold them while I undid the latch, and he carried them in and Mum grabbed him and gave him a big kiss for them, and I said that it was me who'd picked them, but she didn't even hear me.

Our Dad was different. For a long time he didn't really know which was which except when he looked for the mole by the right side of Dave's mouth. Sometimes, for a giggle, I'd make one with the end of a burnt match and fox him. But it never fooled our Mum. She'd look at me with a smile and say, 'Go wash your face, Jack boy . . .'

'No, Mum, it's me, Jack. Dave will be along in a few minutes,' I answered, not stopping.

'Why, where is he?' All this whispered, so as not to disturb our Dad who was sleeping, I guess, but still loud enough with surprise because Dave wasn't with me.

'Seeing a girl home. He won't be long.' I was at our bedroom door, Dave's and mine, when her voice stopped me.

'Jack.' It sounded loud enough to wake the dead. She was standing outside their bedroom, that old dressing-gown held around her shoulders, so tiny in the semi-darkness it seemed a miracle she had produced two such hulking things as Dave and me.

'What's the matter, Mum?' I tried to sound surprised, but all of a sudden my legs began to shake and I was dead scared she would suspect something.

'Is something wrong, Son? Something happened?'

Something in her voice made me feel even worse, but I said,

'What are you on about, Mum? I told you. He's just seeing this girl home, then he'll be in.'

'Where'd you leave him?'

'Near the station. She lives down Welham Drive so it won't take him more than a few minutes.'

She stood there in the dark, quiet, as if reading my thoughts. Then she said, 'All right, Son. Good night.' And she went in, leaving the door open.

I shut my bedroom door and sat on my bed to let the shaking in my legs pass, but listening, listening. Suddenly I felt sick, and a burning over my whole body, so painful I wanted to scream, loud. Frightened, I lay down, my face buried deep in the pillow, knowing with the fear and the pain that something terrible had happened to my brother. I tried to tell myself that I was only imagining things, carrying on like some ruddy kid, but the knowing stayed, bringing the tears so that I stuffed my mouth with the pillow so our Mum wouldn't hear and come questioning. Oh Dave, Dave. I tried to pray, tried to make my mind remember those things we used to learn at Sunday school or what we said in Assembly at school, but none of it would come. Perhaps if I did it properly, kneeling down. But it was no use. All I could remember was, Our Father which art in Heaven. All I could say was, God, don't let anything happen to him, for Jesus' sake, but it sounded a bit rude, as if I was telling God what to do, kneeling there helpless, because I didn't know where he was or I wouldn't be asking anybody anything, I'd go and find him. Then there was no more pain and I thought, I'm just imagining things because of the blood. In no time Dave would be creeping up the stairs, he'd laugh his head off to see me on my knees.

I got up and changed into my pyjamas, taking my time, stretching each movement, each part of the simple routine, to make the time go, folding my jeans carefully over the back of a chair, then my sweater and string vest, then my jacket on a hanger. I noticed the dark pressed smudge near the right pocket and right away knew what it was. Blood. Then I remembered the handkerchief I'd wiped my hands with after touching Dave's back. I pulled it from my pocket, crumpled, rank-smelling and filthy. I stuffed it in a shoe. That way I wouldn't forget to flush it down the toilet later. I dumped my underwear and socks in the laundry bag for Mum to take down tomorrow, wondering about her, probably lying back there beside our Dad but hardly breathing so she'd hear the first sound Dave made coming in.

The way she'd said 'Good night, Son,' was a dead give-away she was worried. Never called me Son except when something was wrong with Dave. Those times when he got kept in at school and I'd gone home alone, it was always 'What's happened to your brother, Son,' her voice taking off high, scared, as if just because he wasn't with me he had to be dead or something. Times like that, I was always Son – and the way she said it, accusing. Three hours difference between us, yet the moment something was up she'd act as if I was the older one and should look out for Dave. Got so that if ever he got kept in I'd hang around until he came out. Better to let her think we'd both been kept in than listen to her call me Son . . .

Like that time she and our Dad went off on holiday to Cornwall and Dave and me had those two girls up to the house. We'd met them at the Romford Palais some time before and used to dance with them and chat them up every now and then. Blonde they were, both of them, though you could tell only one was real, Maureen. The other, Sandra was always a bit dark at the roots, as if she did the bleaching herself and never got it just right. Always dressed like sisters, same tight skirts and sweaters with everything packed to bursting inside. Tall, with those stiletto heels and puffed up hairstyles. Maureen – we called her Maur – had this round, chubby face with dimples whenever she smiled and was always talking in a blue streak as if she had a million and two things she had to get off her chest. That wide, red mouth going all the time, and when not talking, still open, chewing gum. But fun, always kidding. The other, Sandra, was okay too, but different. Big brown eyes in a sick-looking face. Not really sick, when you got to know her, only because she liked wearing that whitish make-up and lipstick and all that black stuff around her eyes. Didn't say much, but she had this way of looking at you as if she could see what you'd had for dinner, and not laughing right out if you made a joke, like Maur. Just sort of smiling, as if she really thought you were a bit stupid.

Anyway, this night we met up with them and at intermission we said how about something else than the tea and orange crush they served in the Palais, and they were game. So we went down to the Bull and had a beer while they had gin and limes. Then we asked them how about if we got some bottles from the off licence and went home to listen to some records, and they said fine. Dave cottoned on to Maureen. And that Sandra, so quiet-looking – I tried for a kiss on the way home in the taxi and she nearly had my tongue out by the roots.

We paired up on the sofa, the curtains drawn, drinking beer and listening to Brubeck and M.J.Q. and a Sinatra album we'd had as a birthday present. After a while we had the lights off, all except the blue shaded standard lamp way over by the television set, necking away. And then Dave and Maur got up and went off upstairs.

Funny how things happen. While we were all together everything was fine, but as soon as Dave pushed off I began to feel uncomfortable, wondering what would happen if our Dad and Mum should walk in right then. And right away I, well, cooled off. Up to then it was okay, kissing Sandra, with my hands going all over, the first time, really that I'd ever got that far with a girl, and I suppose it was the same for Dave. Usually at the flicks or seeing them home after a dance or something, they didn't mind if you gave their breast a quick feel, but as soon as you tried reaching up their leg, nothing doing. But this Sandra. Anyway, with Dave and Maur gone, I was suddenly scared to hell, and sat up.

'What's the matter? Where're you going?' she wanted to know.

'How about some beer? Or cider?' I asked her, zipping up my fly.

'I'm not thirsty. Come back here.'

The skin above her stocking tops looked yellow in the bluish light. Her head was down between the cushions, her sweater and brassière pulled up over one breast, the eyes black in her pale face. I turned away, not wanting to look.

'What's up? What's the matter with you?' Her voice was loud, quarrelsome.

'Nothing. And don't make so much row.'

'Who's making any bloody row? What's the matter with you, you sick or something?'

'Look, keep your voice down.'

'Or else what? Don't you like girls or something?' All I knew was that I didn't want any of the neighbours to hear we were having girls in the house, especially at that time of night.

'Look, you want that beer or don't you?'

She took a long time about answering, and this time her voice was nasty and spiteful.

'Might as well. Looks like it's the only thing I'm going to get around here, eh, Jackie boy?' Then the laughter, loud and screeching, as if she wanted everyone for miles around to come and join in the fun. I felt like going over and stuffing my fist into that ruddy no-lipstick hole to shut it up for good. Dave came running downstairs, a big towel wrapped around him like some crazy Indian.

'What the hell's up with you two? Trying to wake up the whole damned neighbourhood?' Holding the towel safe with both hands.

'You've got a funny brother,' she said, laughing up at him, stuffing the breast back into place.

'What do you mean, funny? And do you have to yell the ruddy house down at every corny joke you hear?' Looking from her to me. I said nothing, standing there like a drip with the empty bottle of beer in my hands. I set it down and switched on the overhead light.

'Joke?' Her open mouth was a sudden dark hole in the white face. 'Why don't you ask your funny brother to tell it to you? You'd laugh your head off.'

Dave stood there watching her. She hadn't bothered to push down her sweater; one long, half naked leg was bent at the knee to form a figure four with the other. He turned and winked at me, grinning that grin which always meant trouble for somebody. He leaned over, patted her leg, then came and gently pushed me towards the stairs, and switched the light off.

'Why don't you go up and keep Maur company for a bit,' he said, 'I'll stay here and get lover girl to tell me a few laugh-out-loud jokes.'

Funny how, with Dave back and seeing Sandra lying there like that, the excitement suddenly came back, strong and hard, and I would have liked to spread her out and get in there, hurting her till she laughed on the other side of her face. But I went up the stairs, still hearing the echo of her laughter in my head, hating the pale-faced bitch.

The only light on in our room was a tiny clip-on reading lamp Dave had on the headboard of his bed. He used it at night for scribbling in his diary when I wanted to sleep. It was a little thing, hooded so that the light could be focused on his book, leaving the room dark. Now the hood was twisted around so the light pointed towards the ceiling. Jack's and Maur's clothes were thrown across my bed, but no sign of Maur. Then I heard the toilet being flushed and knew where she was. I sat on Dave's bed, wishing that we hadn't started any of this, and that the girls would hurry up and go. If anyone had heard that Sandra shouting and said something to our Mum, there'd be hell to pay. Stupid bitch. Perhaps I should go back down there and show her. Couldn't figure out what had happened. Didn't make any sense at all. There it was waiting, all served up and ready for the taking, and I'd gone as soft as, well, no wonder the ruddy twit had begun laughing. Why the hell didn't these things ever work out the way they were supposed to, the way you read about them in books or saw them on the flicks? The nights Dave and me would lie awake on our beds, nattering away in the dark about what we'd do if we ever had the house to ourselves and a couple of willing pieces. Well, here it was, and they could feed it to the ruddy fish for all the good it did me. Funny thing was, earlier on when we'd started kissing and feeling around I was all there, excited and hard as any bull; then when the time for action came, nothing.

The hands pressed over my eyes, cool and damp, the voice full of laughter saying, 'Guess who.' Then the face warm and soft following around to kiss me before I could reply, and against my hand the soft, smooth naked skin, trembling a little, pulling away.

'No more, Dave. You're all dressed up so I'd better get dressed. What were those two yelling about down there?'

She was already picking up her clothes, her body an exciting silhouette against the light.

'Dave's downstairs,' I said.

'What?' She jumped away, snatching clothing from my bed, and flicked the switch beside the door. In the bright light she stood there staring at me, wide-eyed and open-mouthed, bent forward modestly hugging her clothes in front of her. I stood up, and immediately the mouth opened wider as if ready to scream.

'Take it easy,' I told her. 'I'm not going to touch you.'

Those wide eyes followed my every movement while she backed away towards the corner near Dave's bed. I went out, closing the door behind me, and sat on the stairs. No sound from anyone. What a hell of a damned night. Sure that damned bitch Sandra wouldn't be running away if Dave made a grab for her. Well, to hell with the lot of them. Never again, bringing any of them home.

After a while Maur came out of the bedroom, rushed past me and down the stairs. I let her disappear down before following. Dave was sitting on the sofa still wrapped in his toga like a sultan, Sandra was in the centre of the room under the lamp looking at her reflection in the mirror fixed in the flap of her handbag.

'Dave?' I heard Maur say. She stood near the sofa looking from him to Sandra.

'All set?' Dave asked, not looking at either of us. He got up and went over to the phone.

24

'What the hell's going on?' said Maur, but he paid no attention, just went on carefully dialling as if he hadn't heard her. When someone answered he asked them to send a taxi and gave our address. After he hung up he turned around and winked at me.

'Christ, Dave, you mean to say you . . . ?' Maureen cried at him, her voice full of surprise or disbelief or something, her mouth trembling as if near tears. I felt a bit sorry for her because, after all, she was okay, not like that white-faced bitch.

'I'd better get dressed before the taxi comes,' Dave said, walking around her and up the stairs.

For a moment I thought she'd hit him, but she let him pass then, looking at me, said, 'You're rotten, all of you, just rotten. That's what you are.'

She sat down on the edge of the sofa, her back turned to us. Sandra shut her handbag and began messing about with the pile of records, reading the stuff on the covers. The taxi horn sounded outside and Maur got up and walked out, Sandra following. I asked if they weren't waiting for Dave but neither of them answered and by the time I reached the door they were getting into the taxi. In another minute they were gone. Dave came down, still with the towel around him. The bugger hadn't even started to get dressed.

'Gone?' he asked.

'Yes.'

'Suits me. Saves us having to go out.'

'What happened down here?' I wanted to know.

'Don't be a nit. What do you think happened?'

'Christ, how could you? Both of them.'

'What you bellyaching about? You didn't want it. No sense in letting a good thing be wasted.'

'Boy, you're a real bastard, aren't you?'

'Why don't you ask Sandra?' Grinning his devil grin.

I don't know how Mum found out about it. Dave guessed that Old Spotty Frock, our sleepless neighbour from across the road, must have seen us bring them home or noticed them go, and said something to Mum. That woman would never miss the chance to get her own back on Dave and me for a little trick we played on her a long time ago when we were kids. You'd think anybody would forget a little thing like that, but not Spotty Frock. She has a memory like a ruddy elephant. And always in those crazy spotty dresses. Probably makes them herself, Mum says.

We were about eight years old at the time, and Uncle Andy, Mum's brother from the farm up north came to see us and as usual told Dave and me to look in his overcoat pocket and find a surprise. Always had this way of giving us things. Even at Christmas he'd not send us anything, then afterwards he'd come down, with all kinds of stuff in his pockets, sweets, motor-cars, Meccano sets, anything. And once a little box with two white mice, but Mum made him take them back. Said she wasn't having any rats in the house, no matter who brought them.

Well, this time I was first to reach his overcoat hanging in the hall and reached into a pocket to pull out the smooth thing which seemed to come alive in my hand. Yelling with fright, I dropped it and, pushing Dave, ran away from the red-spotted green snake with the long quivery black tongue. Uncle Andy began laughing, then picked the thing up, making it twist and jump in his hand. Even though we realized then it was only a toy snake it took a lot of coaxing to make either of us touch it and finally hold it. Mum was furious. She told Uncle Andy off for frightening us and wanted him to take it away. Said it was horrid and disgusting, and you could see that although she knew it was just a wooden toy she was a bit scared of it. Wouldn't touch it. Uncle Andy had to do a hell of a lot of pleading with her before she let us keep it, and even then only on condition that we kept it up in our room.

I can't rightly remember who first had the idea of trying it on Old Spotty Frock, but this day Dave and me had been watching her from our bedroom window. Every few minutes or so she'd come out of her front door, walk up the concrete path to her gate and look up and down the street, probably just to see if anything was happening that she'd hate to miss, like whether

Mrs Davis's poodle had soiled the pavement near her gate, or how long the laundryman had been in at Mrs Palfreyman's. And if nothing really breathtaking was happening, she'd pop back indoors for another ten minutes or so. Mum thinks she's always looking up the street in case her husband comes back. He left about seven years ago, went off to work as usual one morning, and she never set eyes on him again. Mum thinks she nagged him so much that he just up and ran off, but Spotty Frock still thinks he might turn up again.

I don't know who first had the idea. Perhaps we both had it at the same time. Anyway, around six o'clock that evening, while it was still light, we tied some of Mum's black sewing thread to the snake's head, then, when no one was looking, we hid it behind a little patch of weeds in Spotty Frock's garden, so that when we pulled the thread it would come skating across the path. We passed the thread through the privet hedge which separated her place and the Wilsons', then crouched down behind the hedge to wait. Before long we heard her door open. As soon as she was on the path heading for the gate we began pulling the thread, slowly, peeping at her. She didn't notice anything until she nearly stepped on it, then she let out the most God-awful scream you ever heard, but instead of rushing back indoors as we'd figured she would, she jumped high over the snake and was through her gate and into the street in a flash, yelling as if the devil himself was after her.

In no time at all everyone was at their windows to see what all the commotion was about, and there we were, Dave and me, standing behind the Wilsons' hedge with nowhere to run to. Dave went right on pulling in the thread until the snake got itself stuck in the hedge and I had to reach through and clear it. Old Spotty Frock must have rumbled what had happened, because she came at us, yelling what she'd do if she laid hands on us. But what with her screaming and everything, our Dad must have come outdoors to see what was happening, because he got to us before she did. Didn't take him long to see what the trouble was. In no time at all that little old snake was nothing but a few broken bits of wood and rubber and we'd been made to apologize to Mrs Betts, which was Spotty Frock's real name, right there in the street with all those millions of eyes looking on. And afterwards we got a real pasting from our Dad indoors.

Anyway a few days after they returned from holiday Mum caught me upstairs by myself and with no beating about the bush started in on me about how in all the years we'd lived there nobody'd been able to point a finger at any of the Bennetts, and she didn't want any goings on in her house when she wasn't there. So in future would I please not treat her house like some cheap hotel – all with her voice carefully quiet, the way it was when she was mad about something. And not a single word to Dave who'd got the most out of the evening . . .

When I had everything straight I put my jacket across my shoulders and went quietly past Mum's bedroom to the bathroom. Using a nailbrush and soapy water I carefully cleaned the blood smudge from my jacket, scrubbed my hands clean and brushed my teeth. Back in my room, I opened the window overlooking the street, pulled up a chair, lit a fag and sat down to look out for Dave. From there I could see all the way up to the church and the corner he'd have to come around whether he took the train or hitched a lift along the Southend Road. Worry had settled like a heavy weight in the pit of my stomach. It was now nearly half past one and where was Dave? If he'd caught the Central Line at Leytonstone he'd have been home long ago, unless – well, supposing he'd fainted on the train and they'd taken him to hospital or something like that? He'd have at least told them to telephone and let us know what was happening. Or perhaps he'd decided to hitch a ride, and at that time of night not many people would want to stop for a hitchhiker. Probably still waiting somewhere along the road, hoping. Or supposing he'd fallen down somewhere, in some corner where nobody'd seen him? Oh Dave! Jesus Lord, help him.

Outside everything was quiet, you could hear sounds from a long way. Not a house light anywhere, the sky black except for the edge where it met the world, which was yellowish, probably from the amber street lights over Romford way. I'd forgotten about my cigarette until I felt the heat as it burned down to my fingers; then it was a red star trailing a few sparks as it fell into the garden. Sure Mum didn't swallow that tale about a girl down Welham Drive. She knew we didn't bother much with any of the local talent. A couple of dates and they started behaving as if you were engaged to them or something. Lights flashed up and down, glinting yellow, off the church windows and the shops at the corner arcade, and a car came around the corner, slowly. I thought, Here he comes. But at the same slow pace it went on past our house. Much later came the far away slam of a door, then silence.

I was going down a long tunnel, bright as day and full of the noises of trains coming and going, though all I could see was the sparks from wheels on rails. I wanted to get off the tracks before a train came but there was nothing I could climb on, the walls were white and smooth. Then suddenly the tunnel opened out into a station crowded with people, and I ran towards it, to get on to the platform, but they all turned, pointing and staring at me, and I saw they were black, all of them. Then from the tunnel behind me came the rush of wind and the noise from a train coming fast, and I tried to climb on to the platform, but my hands were slippery with blood and none of those black people would help me up though I shouted, begging them. The noise from the train grew nearer, then there was Dave at the far end of the platform, pushing through them, shouting, I'm coming, Jack.

My fingers could find no grip on the steep, sloping platform, the black faces stared down, hating me in my helplessness, and Dave was pushing through them, calling to me as the train came nearer, nearer, then his hand was on me just before the spinning wheels caught me.

3

'JACK, JACK!'

The hand and voice were real enough as I opened my eyes
to safety and the sight of her beside me, small and frail in the
greyish light of early morning, sitting on the edge of my bed.

'Wake up, Jack.'

'What's up, Mum?' And sudden, clear remembering. I
looked around to Dave's bed, half hoping.

'Tell me, Son. Where's Dave? Where is he? Tell me.'

Echoes of the dream, the despair in her voice and the sight of
Dave's empty bed all worked together, and something gave way
inside me. I knelt beside her, my head in her lap, and wept out
the whole terrible story. Not a sound from her. Long after I'd
finished, not a sound. I looked up at her, so tiny in the frayed
old dressing-gown, her hands crossed over her chest, gripping
the lapels tightly, the grey eyes staring through the windows at
nothing. Seeing her like that I wished to God it had been me
instead of Dave, and something told me that he wasn't coming
home again, not ever.

'Get up, Son,' she said to me. I pulled myself back into the
chair by the window, not thinking, not feeling.

We sat like that, saying nothing, not even noticing that the
street lights had faded out to misty daylight, and that gentle
stirring of things waking up. Mum was the first to react when
the doorbell rang, and was half-way down the stairs before I
even realized what was happening. I wanted to rush after her,
but my whole body felt heavy and unwilling.

From the top of the stairs I heard the strange men's voices
and hers, rising with surprise and panic, saying, 'What is it,
where's my Dave? What's happened?'

Half-way down the stairs I saw them, huge beside my mother
in their khaki raincoats, two serious-faced men, each with a

rilby hat in his hand. At the sight of them I knew, in my mind, in my stomach, in my weak, trembling legs, that it was about Dave and he was dead. I went down and stood beside Mum, holding her.

One of the men said, 'We're police officers.'

'What do you want? What have you come for?' I asked them, but then Mum spoke.

'You said you wanted to know if Dave lives here. Why? He's my son.' And I could feel the trembling in her, thinking to myself how thin she was, bones like sticks. Poor little Mum.

'Could we speak with your husband, please?' one of them said.

Mum told me to call our Dad, but she was shaking so much I led her to a chair and eased her down into it, before going upstairs. Dad was half-way down, trying to get his arms into the sleeves of his dressing-gown and grumbling about what the hell was going on, his white hair sticking up all over his head. He pushed past me without listening to what I tried to say.

Downstairs he stood in front of the men, asking, 'What's all this?'

One of them, the round-faced, baldy one with the little moustache started, 'Mr Bennett.'

'Yes. What's all this about? Who are you?'

'We're police officers enquiring into an accident which occurred soon after midnight last night on the Southend road near Gallows Corner, involving a motor vehicle. There were two persons in the vehicle. We have reason to believe that one of them was a Mr Bennett of this address.'

Mum covered her face with her hands, crying softly, 'Oh God. Oh Jesus God.'

Dad walked backward from the men until he came up against the stairs and lowered himself to sit, his face slack and grey, his mouth open, moving. Then he looked up at me and the words came out.

'Your brother. Isn't he upstairs?'

'No, Dad, he didn't come in last night.'

'But how?' He was too stunned to say more.

The other detective, with the reddish face and ginger hair took something from his pocket and put it on the low tabl' near where Mum sat, a large white handkerchief which h' carefully poked open with a long yellow pencil till we could se the thing inside. Right away I recognized the handle of Dave' knife sticking out from the brown, curly piece of burnt leather I couldn't help saying 'That's Dave's,' and the man looke' quickly at me, then pushed the pencil under and turned the lo over to show the other side, and the little shiny silver shiel' with

> David Lee Bennett
> 103 Raleigh Gardens
> Upminster, Essex.

inscribed on it.

'What's that?' Dad asked.

'This was removed from one of the bodies,' the man said, an' I wanted to scream. 'The vehicle overturned while apparentl travelling at high speed towards Southend, and the two occu pants, both male, were trapped underneath when it caugh fire.'

'But why do you think it was our Dave?' Dad asked him' 'What do they look like, these two occupants or whatever yo' call them? Didn't you look in their pockets or wallets or some where to see who they were? And what the hell's this that yo' brought here?' Pointing at the table.

'I'm afraid it has not been possible to make any sort of identi fication,' the baldy one said. 'You see, the bodies were too badl' burnt. This knife has so far been our only clue. We're checkin' the car's registration to find out who the owner was. Did you son drive a car?'

'No.'

'You recognize the knife?' the ginger one asked me.

'Yes, it's Dave's.' I bent over the table and reached for i' but the man stopped me, covered it up and replaced it in hi' raincoat pocket.

From another pocket he took a black notebook, saying, 'I'

be obliged if you would give us any information at all that would help with our enquiries. A description of your son and what he was wearing when last you saw him, anything like pieces of jewellery, wrist-watch, anything done to his teeth, anything that might help.'

'He was like Jack here,' Dad interrupted, 'just like him. You see one, you see the other. They're twins, see, identical twins.'

Now they both looked me over, slowly, from head to toe, the way you scrutinize a piece of cloth when choosing a suit. At first I felt awful having them looking at me like that thinking that they were detectives and remembering about the night before and the Spade. Then the thought came to me that it was that black bastard's fault, what had happened to Dave, and I hated him, and wasn't afraid of them any more. I looked right back at them, noticing now that Baldy's moustache showed a scar on his upper lip where the dark hairs didn't quite meet.

'Did your brother wear a ring, something like yours?' Baldy asked me. So I told him we'd each been given a signet ring by Mum and Dad last March on our eighteenth birthday. Mine was inscribed J.L.B. for Jackson Lee Bennett, and Dave's D.L.B. for David Lee Bennett. The Lee part was from Mum's maiden name, Madge Lee.

'Was your brother wearing his ring when last you saw him?' he wanted to know, and I told him we never took them off, not ever, as far as I knew, since the day we'd got them. So he made some notes in his book and asked me other questions about Dave's height and weight, and if we'd had anything done to our teeth, and I said no, we'd never had any fillings or extractions or anything. Both of us had these riders, the two front teeth overlapping each other a little bit, but in the Juniors when the school dentist had wanted us to wear braces to straighten them out Mum had said no.

Then he asked me what had Dave been wearing when he left home last night, and if I'd seen him with the knife. And right away I thought I'd play it safe, so I said I didn't know because I was busy with some drawings I had to do and didn't see him when he went out, but if I looked upstairs in our room I could soon tell him what was missing, but he said not to bother for now.

Then Ginger said, 'Identical twins. Always went around together I suppose?'

'Most of the time,' I answered.

'And last night?'

Before I could reply, Mum asked him, 'You said there were two of them in the car. What about the other one?'

'Probably the owner of the car,' Ginger told her, 'We're tracing it. Black Morris saloon, registration GDX 409,' he said reading from his book. Then, to me, 'That ring any bells? Know anybody has a car with that number?'

I said I didn't.

'Any idea where he went last evening? Being twins and all I'm sure he'd say something about where he was off to, even if you couldn't go with him.'

Again Mum spoke up. 'Jack was upstairs in his room when Dave left. Said something about going to listen to a jazz club I think.' Remembering how earlier on she'd been shaking like a jelly, I felt amazed and proud of her. She sat there looking them straight in the eye, pale but calm as you please. Our Dad was staring at her, his mouth open and a look of surprise on his face. Baldy looked at him and he closed his mouth.

'What sort of drawing?' Ginger asked me, 'commercial art?'

'No. I'm doing industrial design at the Tech. Part time apprentice training scheme.'

Baldy asked if Dave did the same thing and I told him no, Dave was doing the straight course in Mechanical engineering. Then our Dad said if they were asking all those questions, then they weren't sure it was Dave, that he might have lost the knife and somebody found it. And Baldy said it was possible our Dad was right; after all, they were only checking, and with what we'd told them about Dave, the ring and teeth, they'd soon know. But anyway, where was Dave? Was he in the habit of staying out all night long? And we told him no, never before. So our Dad said nothing more, just sat there twisting his fingers and

34

looking at Mum. Baldy said they were really sorry to bring such terrible news, but as soon as they had any further information they'd let us know. He asked if we were on the phone, and I gave him the number. Then they left.

After they'd gone none of us said anything for what seemed like hours. Then Mum stood up. Not crying or anything, though her eyes looked dead in her face. She went up to our Dad, touched his face, then started off towards the kitchen.

Near the door she turned and said, 'Jack, you'd better tell your Dad about last night. I'll make us a cup of tea.'

I looked at our Dad. His face was still grey and drawn because of what he'd already heard. Now there was more. He sat with his shoulders hunched forward, elbows on his knees, the big hands twisting each other. Tell him about last night, Mum said. I waited until his thick grey eyebrows lifted at me. You could see the pain in his eyes.

'Well,' he said.

So I told him. Slowly. All of it. Funny thing, he seemed to be taking it so much harder than Mum. I didn't realize he was crying till I saw the tears where they'd fallen on his hands. In all the years our Dad was okay, but he'd never make a big fuss over us or anything, so it came as a shock to see him like that. I mean, I'd never have thought that anything could make our Dad cry. I told him the whole thing. Well, not exactly. I didn't tell him that I'd stuck the Spade. What was the use? Don't really know why, but I just didn't tell him about that. If Mum should mention it to him afterwards I could always say I thought I'd told him.

He didn't say anything. Not a word. No questions. Nothing. When I'd done he stood up in front of me, looking through me as if I was a stranger. For seconds. Then he walked off to the kitchen, me following. Mum watched us come in but went on with what she was doing. Dad sat at the table and me at the far end away from him, feeling tired, wishing that whatever was to be said would get said quickly so I could go up and get some sleep. Mum sat beside him and poured the tea.

'You knew about all this, Madge?' he asked her.

35

'Jack told me.'

'When?'

'Early this morning.'

It was all so ruddy normal, us sitting there talking as if we were figuring the odds for the pools or something.

Except that Mum and Dad never came downstairs in their dressing-gowns. This was the first time I'd ever seen either of them downstairs like that.

'Don't I count in this damned house at all?' Dad's voice was suddenly harsh. 'My son gets himself killed or something, you two damned well know what's going on but I have to hear it from the ruddy police. Don't I count at all in this damned house?'

Mum carefully put down the teapot.

'Before I could come to tell you, the police arrived,' she told him.

From somewhere outside myself I watched us. Me, somehow not worrying or upset or anything. Mum so small, redeyed and tired, but calm now as if she was prepared to deal with whatever turned up. And Dad. He sat there, big, angrily glaring at her, not at me, as if he resented her coolness and strength. I had the feeling that he was scared and the shouting was to hide it. His neck was getting red the way it did when he was all worked up, and I thought, Supposing he gets so mad that he bashes Mum? And I knew inside myself that if our Dad hit our Mum I'd tear his ruddy arm off. I suddenly felt strong enough to do just that. I drank off the cup of tea at one go, not giving a damn that it nearly burnt through my throat.

'What are we going to do, Dad?' Mum asked him, looking up into his face. She always called him Dad same as us kids did. Her voice was soft and sort of pleading, like a little girl, but not weak. And then our Dad reached out and grabbed her, pulling her to hold her tight, and began crying like a child. The way he pulled her I thought at first he was all set to bash her, and I was out of my chair and going for him when he started howling, and Mum was holding his head against her chest, protective like, and looking sideways at me. I left them and went upstairs to my room and lay on my bed. It was as if my whole body had stopped working. I couldn't feel anything, couldn't think about anything, except that Dave was dead. But all that meant was he was somewhere, not feeling or knowing, and he'd never come home again, never walk into this room kicking the door shut and saying 'Hi', which was mostly what he and me called each other. I'd never known anyone close, like family, who'd died, and it seemed strange that nothing should be changed, different, all his clothes and stuff hanging there in the wardrobe as if they were waiting for him. I wondered what I should be doing. Crying, perhaps. But I didn't feel like it, didn't really feel anything.

Later on they came up, both of them sitting on Dave's bed.

'Tell me, Son,' Dad said. 'What made you and Dave start this thing in the first place?'

'You mean last night, Dad?'

'I mean the whole damned thing, deliberately going where those coloured people live to make trouble.'

'We only did it for a bit of a giggle.'

'For a what? So it was some kind of joke. For whom? For the people you beat up, or for your brother who's lying stiff in the mortuary?'

I didn't answer that.

'I want to know what started it off,' he went on. 'If I hadn't heard it from your own mouth I wouldn't have believed it. That my own sons would do such a thing. Going around beating up old men and women for no reason . . .'

'We never hit any women,' I told him.

'Why? Didn't you catch any of them alone? By themselves? Look, Son, tell me. Why? What did those coloured people ever do to you? Any of them ever curse you or hit you, or . . .'

'Don't get yourself all worked up, Dad,' Mum said.

'I'm not getting worked up. I'm trying to find out what all this is about. My son has got himself killed and I want to know what's behind it, why they went around beating up helpless people.'

'They weren't so helpless when they beat you up and put you

in the hospital,' I burst out at him, talking as if he was on their side.

'So it was for me that you did it, was it? You hear that, Madge?' He stood up over me, looking bigger than his six foot one, the silver hairs long and stiff on his thick arms. 'So it was for me that your brother's dead. And the other man? Probably dead too.'

'Who cares about any bloody Spade?' The words were hardly out of my mouth before the whole world seemed to explode on the side of my face, and when the noise settled down I tasted the blood inside my mouth, hating him through the sudden tears which stopped me seeing him properly. I couldn't get up, and when my eyes cleared I noticed he was standing there looking at his hand as if it didn't belong to him.

Then he spoke, softly this time. 'You keep a civil tongue in your head when you're talking to me.' But he didn't wait for me to say or do anything, just turned and walked away.

'Your Dad didn't really mean to do that, Son,' Mum said, and she, too, went off downstairs, leaving me giddy and a bit sick in the stomach, my head ringing as if a bell was buried in it somewhere, thinking, If I'd only known he'd do such a thing, hitting me when I wasn't expecting it, not ready to defend myself. Sitting down and he hit me. Damned bully. If he wanted to hit somebody why didn't he have a go at those two detectives? He couldn't because he was scared of them, scared about them coming to the house and about what had happened to Dave, and about what I'd told him. That's why he hit me. He was scared. Just as he was scared of those Spades the time they beat him up. He wouldn't fight back or tell the police, but he'd damn well come home and switch off the TV because none of us could object. Asking if it was because of him that we did it. Heck, after the first time I don't suppose we thought of him at all. It was more the kick you got out of watching them standing there, too scared to run or shout or anything, knowing what was going to happen to them and waiting for it, watching you come nearer and nearer. Always go for their guts, Dave used to say. Always give it to them in their guts.

I was so lost in my thoughts that I didn't hear them come back until Dad said, 'To think my own sons were living here, under this very roof and doing things like that and I never knew, never suspected anything.'

I wished they would go away and leave me alone. What were we supposed to do, grow horns or something just because we did something he knew nothing about? He went on, saying something about how when he was our age he'd had to work too hard to be getting up to vicious tricks like that, but I wasn't really listening. My mind was on what they'd say over at the works when neither Dave nor me turned up there this morning.

'I suppose I ought to ring McGowan at the works and . . . ' I heard my own voice mixing with Dad's and I stopped.

He stopped too, looking down at me. 'You know something, Madge,' he said, 'I don't think he gives one little damn.'

What did he want, that I should burst out crying, for Christ's sake? They're both standing there looking at me as if I'm something that's crawled away from the zoo. Especially Dad. Going on at me because of a ruddy Spade, some fellow he didn't even know. And what about him, in spite of all this carrying on? Suddenly all sorts of things came back to my mind, things I hadn't even really thought of before. That time when Mr Fennicott and Mr Austin from down the road came to see him and they'd stood talking in the back garden, arguing for a long time. And after they'd gone Mum asked him what it was all about and he said they'd taken on some coloured men at the building site and some of the men were against it and were threatening to go on strike, old Mr Fennicott especially, and they were going to have a meeting about it next day at the site. And Mum said what did he think, and he said he didn't hold with that sort of thing, if there were jobs going why shouldn't the coloureds work, after all they weren't taking bread out of anybody's mouth. And Mum said suppose they called a strike what would he do? And he said he'd have to go along with it, whatever the others did. And now I was wondering why I hadn't thought of these things before. If he was against not letting the coloureds work why would he join with the others to strike?

And then a few months ago after Old Fennicott died and Mrs Fennicott put her house up for sale with the big red FOR SALE sign in her front window, because she said the house was too big for her to live in alone and she'd decided to go and stay with her daughter at Eastbourne. And these coloureds, Indians or something like that, went to see her about buying it and she told them she'd changed her mind about selling. Afterwards she'd come and told Mum and Dad, saying how she'd rather see the house rot to the ground than bear the thought of any nasty blacks living there. And Dave and me listening. Then Dave said, just for fun, there's nothing nasty about money no matter where it comes from. And Dad sat there and never said a word . . .

The phone rang and Mum went downstairs to answer it, then called to Dad to come down. Later on she came and told me it was the police telephoning to say they wanted to come and talk to us again. I followed her down to phone through to McGowan at the works, but our Dad was still on the phone, talking to someone at his building site it sounded like, so I went back to my room. My face was hurting like hell and felt stiff all over the right side. From downstairs I could hear the sounds of Mum busy in the kitchen and the rumble of Dad's voice, just like any day, as if nothing had changed. And there were Dave's things. Pin-ups on the wall beside his bed, and the Youth Hostel banner we'd got on that trip to Austria last year. Whatever Mum and Dad might be thinking, it was well after nine o'clock, and if that wasn't our Dave in the mortuary, then where in God's name was he?

Thinking about him, I felt the coldness creeping up inside me again. I couldn't think of him as being dead, not coming back here, to this room, not ever. What would I do, by myself? Just me, alone. It wasn't as if I'd any friends much, not real friends I could talk and do things with, the way I could with Dave. Sometimes not saying a word, just knowing we were there, with each other. We'd even talked Old Man McGowan into letting us work together in the machine shop and he'd said okay, he didn't mind. We'd lie awake in the dark some nights talking about how it would be later on, after we'd taken our City and Guilds exams and we had to split up, because I was hoping to try for a place with that firm of industrial designers in Manchester. Sometimes Dave would say he might even chuck Bradford's and come with me, but he wasn't sure. Everybody at the works was always saying how bright he was and there was a great future for him there. Those nights, just talking in the dark and seeing it all, the big things we'd do one day, probably having a go at working together as a sort of firm with our name BENNETT BROTHERS LTD. or maybe just BENNETT'S LTD. ENGINEERS. Seeing it all, making a packet and making Dad and Mum move away from this street to somewhere nicer. Perhaps even having Dad work with us. But not BENNETT & SONS. No, people had to know who was who. Just BENNETT'S LTD.

Now he was gone. I'd never really known anybody who died, anybody close, like a relative or good friend. You didn't count old Fennicott because he was only someone I knew from his living down the road all those years and just saying hello to him in the street. Never even went into their house once, though they were always coming over to talk to Mum and Dad. I wondered how it felt to be dead, not feeling anything. What about all the stuff you knew in your brains, all the thoughts and plans and everything! Whatever happened to them? Supposing it was possible to make some kind of machine which could record everything a person ever thought in his life. What I mean is, we remember things, so it's a way of recording them some-where in our minds. Well, if it was possible to make this machine and tap it into that part of the brain where the memory was and make it play back everything in it, just sort of reverse the process.

Thinking about that I remembered about the big diary Dave kept under his pillow that he was always writing in and wouldn't let anyone have a look. Perhaps it would be the same as finding out what he'd been thinking of lots of things, and it wouldn't make any difference to him now if I looked, so I fetched it out.

It wasn't a diary at all. Poems. That's what he'd been writing down. Poems, each one with a name above it and at the end his initials and the date he wrote it. I mean, if I hadn't seen it with my own eyes, right there in his own handwriting, I wouldn't have believed it. Not Dave, who was always saying he didn't give a damn for anybody, except me and our Mum and Dad. We'd never talked about poems and stuff like that. Not ever. At first I guessed he must have copied them out of some book or other, but then I remembered I'd never seen him with any other book, only scribbling away every now and then, and afterwards stuffing the book back under his pillow. Like this one:

Autumn Time   *October 16th 1956*

Cloudy afternoon
Drizzly damp afternoon
Earth breath steamy over dead leaves and yellowing wet grass.
Raindrop buds on naked branches.
Listen,
From the distant darkening,
In broken echoes light as falling leaves,
The scattered sound of rooks coming over.
Homing.
Calling softly to other.
Homing.
Quickly circling, impatient for the nests
Ragged and ugly as the naked trees,
Yet waiting,
Wing whispering, unwilling soon to end
The sweet delight of the last downward swoop.
Home,
And sway of slender bough in mute protest.
Rustle of feathers at the settling down.

D. BENNETT

Christ, he'd been writing stuff like this and keeping it all to himself. Even from me. While I shared everything I ever had

42

with him. Even my designs. Sometimes I'd have an idea and sketch it out roughly, then show him, telling him how I felt about it. And I'd always believed he felt the same way. Yet all the time I'd been shut out of this private place like some ruddy stranger. I couldn't even imagine how he got started on it. I mean, at Grammar School we did English literature, with poems and stuff like that, but we only did it because it was in the syllabus. We never really cared anything about it, never talked about it, at least he never let on that he was really interested. If it had been me who was keen on that kind of stuff I'd surely have said something to him. There was this short one:

Red Tie   *Birthday 1958*

Fragment of scarlet silk.
Jaunty trapping.
Colour of blood and courage
Ends wind-tossed, flapping.
In moments of despair,
Saddened, sorrowing,
You bid me raise a cheer,
Reach upward,
Towering.

D.B.

Now that I think of it, once or twice he made remarks which didn't seem to mean much at the time, and sounded strange coming from him. Like the night we'd gone up to this jazz club in Soho and a couple of fellows with a girl were singing American folk songs with guitars. Freedom songs they called them. About Spades in the States. I looked at Dave, the way he was watching them, and I could guess what he was thinking. The same as me. That, if they were so interested in the Spades and freedom they should be singing those songs somewhere in the Southern States. Little Rock or somewhere like that. Then one of them, a big fellow with a beard and a soft, girlish voice, sang something about an old Spade walking from Jacksonville to New York, on foot all the way, just so that he could have one day of real freedom before he died. And later while we were having a coffee and talking Dave said the words were okay but the fellow spoiled them by singing. Words like that should be spoken, softly, he said, instead of messing them about with his pansy voice and guitar. And I said what was he getting so excited about, after all, it was a song, wasn't it? And he said sure, it was a song, but some songs were not for singing, that people spoiled the music of the words when they tried to sing them. I mean what kind of a mixed up remark was that?

Looking through the book I noticed that the earliest poem was written in 1956. Nearly four years he'd been doing it, and not a word to me, and everybody believing we were like two halves of the same thing. Bloody selfish bugger. Christ, we'd done everything together. Same school in the same class throughout, even G.C.E. 'O' levels in the same subjects, and the same job on the same day. And I'd thought it was a diary, so even if I'd been a little bit curious I'd not have bothered to look because I'd have known beforehand what was in it anyway.

I lay there with the book on my chest thinking about Dave, and must have fallen asleep, because the next thing I knew was Mum shaking me and saying would I come down, that the police were back and wanted to talk to us.

They were the same two men. They said they found out about the other person in the car, somebody named Spencer. Dr William Spencer, from Leigh-on-Sea. A houseman or something like that at Guy's hospital. Young, really, only twenty-four. They'd been in touch with his relatives, a mother and sister at Leigh, and with the hospital. So it started again, the questions. And Mum said she didn't think Dave knew any Dr Spencer, but Baldy said perhaps as Dave and me were always together I might know. I told him I was sure Dave didn't know any doctor, but suddenly I wasn't sure, remembering about the poems in the diary. Supposing he did know this Dr Spencer but didn't ever tell me about him? Supposing after he'd left me at Whitechapel he'd gone off to see this bloke to help him and that was how he was in the car? How the hell did I know? What was I supposed to say?

Baldy must have guessed that something was bothering me,

because he suddenly looked at me and said would I think very carefully, try to remember if Dave ever mentioned knowing a doctor or meeting one. And I said no, he didn't, that I'd have known if he did. Then he wanted to know what we did, where we went, how we spent our time when we weren't at work. So I told him about how we liked listening to jazz, and collected records. And some nights we'd go up West to the jazz clubs, or if there was a jazz concert somewhere like at the Festival Hall or the Albert Hall. And Baldy's pal said he liked jazz too, and asked who were my favourites. And I told him I liked Ella and the Count and that fellow Monk and some others. And suddenly Baldy said how about the East End, which clubs did we like in the East End? And right away something clicked and I knew all the sweet, friendly talk was just to catch me with that one. It was so damned childish I could have laughed. I looked him straight in the eye and said we'd never been in the East End, didn't know they had jazz clubs there.

The way he and his pal were looking at me I could see they were wondering about my face, sore as hell and sure to come up a real beauty just near my left eye where it hurt most. Let them think what they liked, I couldn't care less.

Then Mum said why were they asking all those questions, what did it have to do with Dave being in an accident? And Baldy told her that they were trying to discover what had happened, because only the one car was involved and on a straight stretch of road there didn't seem to be any reason for the accident. So anything we could tell him might help them. He knew it must be painful for Mum and Dad, so what he'd suggest was that he and I had a chat together, so as not to bother them, and I could bring him up to date on Dave. Smiling his sweet policeman's smile all the time. But Mum said no, it was no bother, so go ahead and ask his questions.

Then Baldy's pal said could he see my knife? I told him I didn't have one, never owned one. And he said he thought Dave and me always got the same things, so if it was a Christmas or birthday present we might each have got one. Or perhaps we'd bought them ourselves. Watching him I wondered just how

45

clever he thought he was. If he wanted to play this silly game it was fine with me. So I told him Dave said he'd bought it off an American, just the one knife. He liked it because it was a lovely thing, especially the handle, the way it was made with alternating layers of ivory and silver, and the blade, double-edged, balanced. And Baldy asked where Dave had met the American. I told him I didn't know, which was quite true. It was the Saturday we'd gone with the works team to play cricket against a team at Dagenham, and I'd got hit with a ball on my elbow. Painful as hell, so I'd stayed in that night. Dave went off by himself but came back early, bringing the knife. We used to make up stories about the man who'd made it, a real craftsman he must have been. And the scabbard, hand-sewn and polished. We guessed it must have been made for a Spanish or Mexican prince, because of the design, with probably a sword to match. Dave had had the little shield specially put on the knife just near the hilt, so that he could have his name on it.

Baldy's pal said that he knew someone who collected old knives and daggers, but they were always kept as decorations, fastened on the wall. And why was Dave carrying the knife? Did we ever get into arguments with anyone when we went to jazz clubs or places like that? Did Dave always carry it about with him or only when he went off by himself? I told him I'd got so accustomed to seeing Dave with the thing that I couldn't remember when he wore it. Sometimes he'd have it and sometimes not.

Then Dad wanted to know why all the fuss and questions about the knife. They'd already been told it was Dave's, with his name and address on it. And Baldy explained, with his smile, that he realized it must be painful for us, but they had to check everything that might help them to establish the victims' identities without any possibility of doubt. He said they hoped to have the autopsy report later that afternoon and they'd ring us immediately, that Dad would be needed to come down and make a formal identification.

I went with them to the door to see them off, and there at her gate, inquisitive as ever, was Old Spotty Frock, her eyes boring into the car as it went past her. I didn't have much appetite, and I suppose neither did Dad nor Mum, but we went through the motions of eating lunch, and afterwards I helped Mum wash up. Usually Dave and I helped with the dishes at lunchtime Saturdays and Sundays, laughing and kidding with her, and talking to each other over her head, she was so small. This time she just washed up and passed the things to me, not saying a word, and when it was all done I went upstairs. The house felt strange; no jokes, no laughing, nothing.

Just for something to do I got out all my shoes and began brushing and polishing them. And thinking. About how something you did, just on the spur of the moment, could change your whole life. It wasn't as if we'd planned the thing the way it happened. We really meant to go up West to hear some jazz, then all of a sudden, at Aldgate East, we'd had this idea to get off the train. Just supposing we'd gone a couple of stations further, or even got off earlier, at Whitechapel or Mile End, for instance, we'd never have seen that Spade and none of this would have happened. Mum came in and sat on the edge of Dave's bed.

'Whatever happens from now on, Son, you know nothing.' Her face was white, the eyes red as if she'd been crying. 'You hear me, no matter who asks you, you know nothing. Just forget what you told me and your Dad. As far as anyone else is concerned, you never left this house last night, not since you came in from work. Whatever the police might dig up has nothing to do with us. I've lost one son through those damned people and I'm not going to lose another.' And she got up and went out.

4

BALDY PHONED SOON after four o'clock and said they'd be sending a car for Dad and to meet him at the mortuary. Mum said I should go with Dad so I got myself dressed. This time two policemen in uniform came and Dad and I went with them. We arrived at this place and one of the policemen led us into an office, white and antiseptic smelling, like a hospital waiting-room. Baldy and his pal were standing over by a window talking with someone wearing a long white overall coat. They nodded at us, but went on talking. The policeman told us to sit in chairs near one wall. Baldy and the attendant went off down a corridor opposite the main door, and in a few minutes Baldy came back alone with a flat glass ashtray, Dave's ring in the centre of it, clean and shining like a jeweller's showpiece. Just as well I'd come along with Dad. He took one look and went grey.

'That's Dave's,' I told Baldy, lifting my right hand to show him the matching one. He nodded, then said we could go in now to make the identification. I looked at Dad but he wouldn't look at me, just sat there squeezing his hands together.

'I'll go in alone,' I told Baldy.

'What about Mr Bennett?'

'Does he have to?'

'Not necessarily. In any case it's merely a formality now. The teeth formation, the ring, and the remains of the belt and scabbard found around the waist were enough.'

Dad said nothing. The attendant said I should follow him. Then Baldy moved in front of me as I heard the main door open and in came this girl. Baldy must have spotted her coming through the window. The way he was standing all I could see were her feet. Small, in plain black high-heeled shoes, the ankles sharp under the nylons, shaping nicely upwards.

I went off behind the attendant as she spoke, her voice low, clear, the way some of those students speak at the coffee bars and jazz clubs up West.

The attendant led me down the corridor with its heavy smell of disinfectant and cleanliness, into a large, chilly room with no windows, the bright overhead lights reflecting off the dazzling white tiled floor. One whole wall was like a huge filing cabinet, neatly squared off, with numbers. He walked right up and pulled a handle and this drawer came sliding out. He nodded to me to come closer.

In spite of what Baldy and his pal had told us about Dave being badly burnt, I'd somehow imagined he'd still look like Dave, expected to see the same face, even if he was dead. The thing in that drawer was ugly, faceless and sickmaking. Black. Nothing human about it. Nothing like Dave. Just a horrible black mass with the whiteness of teeth showing through where the lips had burned away. I felt my stomach heave but I swallowed hard, keeping it down. The attendant put his hand on my shoulder, pushing me to one side, then shoved the drawer back in. Even after the drawer was closed the smell of meat, like a butcher's shop, was thick in my nose. I asked the attendant where the toilet was; I couldn't hold it down much longer. Afterwards I washed my face and stood for a few minutes at the open window in the washroom next to the toilet. Dave, Dave. And all because of those bloody Spades. I'd make them pay, the murdering black bastards.

I walked out of there back into the waiting-room. Baldy was sitting at a table writing something. Dad was where I'd left him, but now he was talking with the girl. Her back was towards me, but the shoes and ankles were the same. She sat straight up in the hard chair, coarse black hair curled inward at the top of the high collar of her dark grey dress, pulled tight at the waist with a wide-shiny black belt. Nice shape. Nice legs, the way they were crossed. Dad saw me coming and said something to her and she turned her head to look. Christ Almighty! A Spade. A bloody Spade sitting there chatting with our Dad while Dave was in there, and all because of them. I felt like spitting in her face.

I said to Dad, 'Let's push off.'

He was saying to her, 'This is my son, Jack. The other, Dave, was his twin.'

I don't know what she saw in my face, and I didn't very much care, but right away her face began to close, the way the lights go low in the cinema just before the film starts. She stood up.

'I'm sorry about your brother,' she said, looking somewhere over my shoulder, then, turning to Dad, she said good-bye to him and walked past me to Baldy who'd stood up and was watching me. He and she went off down the corridor. I looked at Dad. His face was red as if he was working up to another angry session, one big hand grinding itself into the palm of the other.

'That young lady's brother was in the car with our Dave.' He said it as if he was accusing me of something. Well, how was I to know that? All that Baldy had said was that the car belonged to a Dr Spencer, but nobody had said who he was or where he came from. Maybe that Baldy had known all the time that Dr Spencer was a Spade. So, that was his sister! Well, tough ruddy luck.

'We'd better be going, Dad,' I said.

'We'll wait till she comes out, just to see she's all right,' he answered, his voice still angry.

'The police will see she's okay,' I told him, but it didn't do any good.

'I said we'll wait till she comes out.' He stood up. 'But if you're in such an almighty hurry there's nothing to stop you going.'

Well, why the hell not, I thought, and went outside. Even if her brother was a doctor, they were still Spades, and if it weren't for them Dave would be alive now, so why should I stand about waiting for her? The two policemen were sitting in the front of the car and one of them leaned over the front seat to open a door for me, but I told him I would be walking, but to wait for my dad. Felt like being alone a while to sort things out in my mind. Later on I'd catch a bus home. People were coming and going everywhere, riding in cars or on bicycles, people walking carrying shopping bags or pushing prams, talking with each other, smiling, smoke rising from chimneys, the brown leaves trembling on the trees waiting for the next sharp wind to put them out of their misery. Vapour trails high up against the blue of the sky. A long crocodile of schoolgirls laughing and chattering. Not a damned soul knowing or caring what had happened. Couldn't any of them feel that something had changed since yesterday? What was the use of all the working and studying and knowing things, if you could just suddenly not be there any more and hardly anyone would notice? This time yesterday Dave and me were standing side by side at the lathes, eyes behind our safety goggles, together in the pleasure of working accurately, machining the castings down to the same fine tolerance. Even Old Man McGowan used to say we were good, and he was not in the habit of scattering praise around. Where was it all now, the skill in the fingers, the thoughts in his head, even those he kept to himself like a ruddy miser, hidden in his book? The more I tried to think of things and sort them out the more knotted and jumbled they seemed to get.

I bought myself an evening paper, merely to have something to read, and decided to have a coffee. No need to rush home. The little café was none too clean, but the coffee was good, bitter and strong, from one of those Espresso machines. One thing was sure, the name Espresso didn't mean high speed, the way the coffee took its time dripping into the cup, too tired to reach more than three-quarters full. Strong and black. Black like that thing in the box which they said was Dave. Black like a ruddy Spade. If her brother was burned like Dave she'd really have something to see. What the heck did our Dad expect me to do? Talk to her? And looking at me like that. Well, let him try again. Just let him try.

Thinking about him I could feel where my face still hurt. To get my mind off things I started to read the newspaper. I nearly missed it near the bottom of the centre page. Not much. It said that the police were enquiring into the murder of Carlton Thomas, a West Indian aged twenty-four whose body was discovered late the night before near some condemned buildings in Willingdon Terrace, Stepney. They wanted anyone who had heard or seen anything that might help the police in their enquiries to come forward. That's all.

I read it twice and it didn't mean a damned thing to me. Odd that, because I always used to imagine that if somebody murdered someone else, they'd be scared out of their wits wandering around just waiting for the police to pick them up. But it was as if I was reading about somebody else. All I knew was that if it hadn't been for that black bastard our Dave and me would probably be at work today, happy as always. So to hell with the damned Spade. I caught a bus home.

Voices in the sitting-room, one of them different, so I went in. She was sitting in the armchair opposite Mum and Dad, who were on the sofa. First thing I noticed was the long legs, crossed at the knee but stretched out the way you see them do it in films. She looked up at me, then away, and went on talking as if I didn't exist. I wondered what the hell our Dad thought he was playing at. Bringing her inside our house. The tea trolley with the used things was near Mum, who had that stiff look on her face she gets when she doesn't care too much for someone. Our Dad looked at ease, even smiling a bit at whatever it was she'd been saying. Mum asked if I would like a cup of tea, and the way she said it was as if she wanted to have something to do, something different from making conversation with that Spade, but I said no, I'd had some coffee on the way. I was on the point of pushing off upstairs to my room when I took another look at her, the big grey eyes watching me as if I was dirt, and I thought to myself, no, she might get the idea I was scared of her. So I sat down. Near Dad on the sofa, right opposite her. I'd take a real close look at her. Dad had asked if I'd ever met one of them or talked with one. Well, here was one served up right in our ruddy front room, though I couldn't figure what the hell our Dad was playing at, bringing her home. Probably thought he'd show me how good he was, with no prejudice to the Spades, backing up the things he'd said earlier. Him and his bleeding heart of love.

For a moment after I'd sat down the conversation stopped. Then our Dad asked her, 'You were saying about your brother . . .' and she began again, talking about how, apart from his hospital duties, her brother had been working on something with two other doctors. A research project she called it, to do with a new technique for heart operations.

I must say she wasn't bad looking, for a Spade. Big greyish eyes, slightly slanted upward. Slim nose and a sort of cleft in her chin. And built for it. Now and then she'd move a hand making some point or other with this trick of rotating her wrist with the fingers spread wide. Long, pale brown fingers, the nails red like blood. But mostly the hands were quiet in her lap, one on top of the other, sometimes with a finger idly flicking the hem of her dress just over her knee. Funny about those grey eyes. I'd always figured that Spades had everything black, skin, hair, eyes, everything. Grey eyes, the lashes long and curving upward just like Maureen's.

'. . . he was in the habit of giving lifts to strangers at any time of the day or night. Anyone, no matter what they looked like. My mother and I were always fighting with him about it. Even so, I just don't understand how it could have happened.'

'You mean the accident?' Dad asked her.

'Yes. Bill liked to drive fast, but he was always very careful.'

'May have been just something went wrong with the car, you never know with these things.'

'But it was completely overhauled only a few days ago and Bill said it was working perfectly. I just don't understand it.'

Putting on airs like some ruddy duchess, just like those university types in the coffee bars and jazz clubs up West. They had this way of sitting near you and leaning forward to talk to somebody else on the other side of you, just as if you weren't there. And some of them looking like hell, with those awful thick stockings and their hair hanging down all over the place as if they needed a real good wash. And this one carrying on just like them, except for the colour.

'How long had he been at the hospital?' You could see our Dad wanted to get her off talking about the accident.

'Four years.'

'You interested in medicine, too?'

'No. At grammar school I'd thought of it, but changed my mind. I'm reading Marine Biology at King's.'

I wished I could think of something to say to put the bitch in her place. She wasn't the only one who'd been to grammar school. So had Dave and me.

I heard Mum say, 'Have you and your brother been in England long, then?' And I noticed that thing in the Spade's face, just as when I'd seen her at the mortuary, the mouth tightening and the nose twitching, and the way she answered our Mum as if she was looking down on her from a great height.

'We were born here, Mrs Bennett.' Cool, the snooty bitch.

'Oh, I'm sorry. I hadn't realized . . .' from Mum, and I noticed she was blushing, something I'd never seen our Mum do before. Our strong little Mum, embarrassed by a ruddy Spade, and all because Dad wanted to prove how big-hearted he was. I felt like belting her one across that stuck-up black face. Or better still, spread her out the way I'd had that Sandra, only this time . . .

She picked up her handbag, quickly uncrossing her legs without giving away even the smallest glimpse of anything, and stood up.

'I think I'll be going now, Mr Bennett,' she said to Dad. 'My mother will be anxious to know . . .'

'Yes, I understand,' he said. 'Will you give her our regards, please, and say how sorry we are about everything?'

'Thank you, Mr Bennett. I'll tell her. I'm afraid I'm not very familiar with this part of Upminster. How do I get to the station from here?'

'Oh, it's not far.' Then to me, 'Jack, will you show Miss Spencer the way to the station?'

I felt like saying no, but didn't want to embarrass him. Going down the path to our front gate I saw Old Spotty Frock peeping at us from behind her curtains. Probably wondering if it was some bird I'd brought home. That was a laugh. Me and a Spade bird! That would give some of those nosey neighbours something to think about. Could just imagine them carrying on about it. Struck me as so funny, I even wished Old Mother Fennicott was there to see me. Put her off her food for a year.

'Was your brother exactly like you?'

'What?' Came as such a surprise, her saying something to me.

'I asked if your brother was exactly like you.'

'Who, Dave? Yes. Exactly.'

Nothing more from her, walking straight up as if she was doing me a favour by being near me.

'Why?' I wanted to know.

'I was wondering whether he was as ill-mannered as you are.'

Straight out, just like that. I didn't say another word. Could have kicked myself for letting a Spade talk to me like that. Seeing the curtains flutter in the houses we passed. Then the people along the High Street staring at us. Mr Hardy where Mum gets her meat, putting up some notice in his windows and stopping to stare, his mouth a tobacco-stained fly trap. To hell with them. They could think what they liked. So I was ill-mannered, was I? And asking that about Dave. If he was alive and could see me walking along like that with her, he'd just about have kittens. What I should have done was leave her outside the station, but there I was standing with her on the platform, waiting for her train to come in. Not a word, her face looking up the line as if she didn't give a damn whether I was there or not. Then they announced the Southend train and there it was coming down the straight.

'Well, here comes my train. Good-bye, Mr Bennett, and thank you.'

The train stopped and she got in, took a seat and kept her face straight forward. I stood there watching her, hating her, suddenly thinking of all the things I should have said to her.

5

THEY TELEPHONED OR came around themselves, people from the street, to sympathize with our Mum and Dad. People I hadn't noticed for years since I'd grown up. You know, you went to school with their kids and, those days, you were in and out of their houses, even calling some of them Uncle this or Auntie that, just because they were grown-up and you'd always known them. But then you grew up too and you couldn't call them Auntie or Uncle anymore. Fact is you can't call them anything not Mrs this or Mr that, so formal like, and you can't suddenly call them by their Christian names like Jack or Bill or something like that, so, the best thing is, you keep out of their way. Especially if their kids grow up and move away or get different jobs or something.

Like Angie Lucas. She was okay even when she was at the grammar school. Then she got this scholarship to the university and after that you'd think she'd never seen the Bennetts before in her life. Even her Mum started to put on airs. Well, Dave used to say, Up theirs.

I mean, you walk up this street at least twice a day, not bothering with any of them, well, except for Old Mrs Collins. Nearly ninety if she's a day. Hair white as silk, but the way she skipped about you'd think she was a kid or something. Always busy doing something. Digging in her front garden, or pruning her rose bushes. Never forget that day Dave and I were passing by and she's on this little stepladder trimming her privet hedge and whistling. Not loud but real whistling, like a man. And Dave and me, we called out, 'Hi, Mrs C.' We always called her Mrs C, since we were kids. And she said, 'Hi, peas.' Same as usual. Always called us peas, like in a pod. Well, this day, Dave said that when she'd finished practising on her hedge, how about coming along and doing a real job on ours. And she started laughing at that, bending forward so she nearly fell off the ruddy ladder, we had to grab it to hold her still. Then, still laughing she said that that wasn't a hedge our Dad had planted around the house, it was a wall with roots to lock in his two young bulls. Always kidding she was.

Well, when I got back from the station I went up to my room, and I could hear Mum and our Dad on the phone, saying thank you to someone or other. Then the doorbell would go and I'd hear a familiar voice. The way they were talking about Dave and how shocked they were to hear of the accident, you would think they'd been bosom friends. I wondered how it would be if I walked downstairs and said I was Dave and what was all this talk about me being dead. Just for a giggle. Anyway from now on they'd have no problem sorting out the Bennett twins.

Around nine o'clock Mum called up to ask if I didn't want something to eat, and I remembered I was hungry. Mum fixed some supper and this time she and our Dad ate. They told me the police had telephoned to say Dave's body was now released, and they'd got on to the undertakers to collect it and fix it up. I asked our Dad if they'd be bringing Dave home and he said no, what was the use, nobody could see Dave's face. Then he said the police had told him there'd be an inquest on Thursday week and would I mention it when I went back to work so that I could have the time off to go.

After supper we sat around and talked, only this time it was okay – you know, easy, more like old times. Funny how something happens, something big and terrible and you think the end of the world has come and there can't be such a thing as tomorrow. Then without even noticing it, you live through whatever it is and things are more or less the same again. Except that now and then Mum nearly called me Dave.

Most surprising of all was Mum. You know, you read books and see flicks and things about mothers whose kids get into some trouble or get killed or something, and they put on this big act, crying all over the place and heartbroken, and lock themselves in their rooms and won't see anybody, not even their dearest friends, only the doctor. But here was our Mum, dusting and cooking and talking on the telephone and reminding me to put out my dirty laundry, just like any day when Dave was here. I figure Dad's right. You spend all your life with people and you never know what they'd do till the chips are down.

Before falling asleep that night I read some more of the stuff in Dave's diary. Amazing the things he had in it. After all, I guess he must have read some of that stuff somewhere else, because where did he know those words and how did those ideas get into his head. There was this poem called THE KING, all about a tomcat, and the way it uses people to get what it wants, but really despises them and prefers to move among the shadows at night, the same shadows that scare people out of their wits. Real creepy stuff.

Then I hid the book and lay there thinking about that girl, just wondering about her and the way she'd said I was born here, Mrs Bennett. Funny thing I'd never before thought of any of them as being born here. I mean they're supposed to be from somewhere else, Africa or the West Indies or wherever Spades come from. Old Simpson who was our teacher used to call them immigrants or something like that. Whenever you think of any of them you know they come from somewhere else. Like those cricketers, they're from the West Indies. And all those fellows on the Underground and buses. You don't see a Spade and figure that he's an Englishman. I mean it's not like those American Negroes. They belong there, in the States. But the way she'd said it, as if she had every right to be English, like Mum or me or anybody else. Wished I'd thought of something to say that would have put her in her place. Dave would have known how to fix her. Reading Marine Biology at King's. Putting on the same damned airs as that Angie Lucas.

Next morning Mum and our Dad said they'd talked it over and decided on cremation for Dave, and just the family attending. The funeral would be tomorrow, Saturday, at ten in the morning, with the service and everything taking place at the chapel in the cemetery. Funny thing the way we discussed it, so calmly, like where we'd go for the holidays. I couldn't help wondering if that's how it would have been if it had been me, instead of Dave. Don't suppose it would have bothered him at all.

Soon after I got in from work that evening they dropped in again, Baldy and his pal. Always together as if they were twins. And cute. Like how they said they'd brought Dave's photograph, but not to return it; they wanted to ask if they could keep it a bit longer as certain things had come up which needed looking into.

Then they said they'd had some information about Dave's movements. This conductor on a bus had recognized Dave from the photograph as the young man who'd got on at Whitechapel the night of the accident, and had jumped off at Leytonstone. Said he remembered the face because he'd thought the young man had been drinking, but afterwards he'd found

blood on the seat where the young man had been sitting. He'd
called his driver and showed him the blood. Lots of blood, as
the young man had been in a fight or something and was cut
stabbed. And the driver had called the inspector and they'd
telephoned the police to come before the bus was removed to
the garage. And the police had looked around for the young
man but couldn't find him. They figured he lived somewhere in
Leytonstone and had gone home. Anyway they'd made state-
ments to the police, the conductor and the driver. Baldy and
his pal didn't say how they came to hear about it but they'd
been up to Leytonstone and talked with the police there and
found out about the conductor. They'd got his address and his
bus depot, and gone to see him. Then they'd showed him
Dave's photograph and he'd said yes, that was the young man.
He was sure. Said he'd never forget that face. And he told them
he'd picked Dave up outside Whitechapel Underground and at
first had thought Dave was tight, him smelling strong of rum or
whisky. He'd never forget that face.

Baldy said it seemed to them that Dave had caught the bus in
Whitechapel and ridden to Leytonstone where he'd managed to
get a lift in the car Dr Spencer was driving. And they wanted to
know if I'd any idea what Dave might have been doing at
Whitechapel or thereabouts. Whitechapel wasn't the West End,
and they didn't know of any jazz clubs out Whitechapel way.
Clubs, yes, but not jazz clubs. And that business about the
blood the conductor had reported. That could mean that Dave
had been in some kind of trouble. So they said they were
checking with the East End police to find out if there was any
trouble reported on that night. Any fights or quarrels at any
of the clubs or anywhere else.

All of this time they were watching me, but I wasn't bothered
by any of it. All that friendly talk wasn't getting them anywhere
because I knew nothing about anything so they might just as
well save their breath.

Mum said, quietly, 'My son Dave is dead. What's the point
of asking all these questions about him now? What does it
matter where he was or who he was with?'

'I'm sorry, Mrs Bennett,' Baldy said, 'but we've got to look into everything which has any bearing on the accident. We don't know what happened or why it happened, so we're supposed to pursue our investigations as far as possible to learn the facts in order to present them at the inquest. We understand how unpleasant it must be for you, but we have no choice.'

'He's right, Madge,' Dad said.

'What about his friends?' Baldy asked. 'Did he go around with any special friend or group? These days most young fellows get together, sometimes three, four of them, go around together. Did you and your brother have any special friends you went around with?'

I told him that mostly Dave and me, we went around by ourselves. We didn't like going about in groups. We knew lots of fellows and girls but we met them places, at jazz clubs and things like that. Then he wanted to know why we didn't like chumming up with other fellows, so I had to explain it to him. Dave and me, we had this way of suddenly thinking of something and looking at each other and grinning. And if we were with fellows or even girls, they'd want to know what we were grinning at. But it wouldn't be something you could explain to them, and they'd get funny, you know, mad. Sometimes they'd imagine we were laughing at them. So it was better to go about by ourselves. I mean, we'd meet birds and fellows at the jazz clubs, or up at the Palais, places like that, but it was best to be by ourselves for going around.

While talking to him I was thinking of the times we'd decide to go somewhere and we'd wait for a train and while it was slowing into the station we'd see a nice-looking bird sitting in a compartment. Then Dave would go in one door and I'd go in the other and we'd sit apart, both of us watching her. Sooner or later she'd look up at one of us, then look away and see the other. Then she'd have to look again to make sure she wasn't seeing double or something. And we'd grin and she'd colour up, not wanting to watch us. Or sometimes we'd see someone watching us, curious because we're so alike, and we'd give them

60

the treatment, you know, both of us staring without smiling or blinking, till they looked away, embarrassed. Dave used to say we were giving them the Evil Eye, that in some countries identical twins like us would be killed at birth because the people would be afraid of our power.

Then suddenly Baldy asked, 'Why did you leave him and come back home last Wednesday night?'

I could have laughed. I mean, what did he think he was playing at, trying that one? So I asked him what did he mean? That last Wednesday night Dave had gone off by himself.

And he said, 'Oh yes, you told me,' or something like that, and dropped the matter.

6

I'D NEVER BEEN to a funeral before in my life. Around ten o'clock this car came and took us to the little chapel in the cemetery, our Mum and Dad and me. Inside were a few people we knew from our street. First time I ever saw Mrs Collins not smiling or whistling. Right in front was the coffin with flowers on it. Funny that, Dave had always hated flowers cut and now they were all piled up on top of him. Even in his book he'd written something about flowers!

Flowers
Flowers always taste bitter.
They're scared of people.
Come near and we die,
Whispers the red rose.
Tulips and daffodils
Turn away sighing;
The time has come for dying.

Cool and enticing,
The grass

Whispers, stay awhile,
When people pass,
Leaves always taste better.

D. BENNETT

From a side door the minister came in, white-haired and
tired looking, dressed in white robes over black robes, ribbons
hanging down from the book in his hands with blue veins like
a road map. He stood on this little pulpit near where Dave
was and I could see his shoes and the turn-ups of his trousers
under the black robe. Then everybody stood up and he began to
say prayers. At first I didn't get the hang of it, the words were
running into each other and he was sort of singing what he was
saying, but it wasn't singing. I was thinking what Dave would
have said about this old codger carrying on about his not being
really dead only sleeping; and all the time his face tired and
wistful and even the skin greyish as if he'd not felt the sun on
him in years.

Then everybody knelt down while he prayed some more, and
got up again, me doing whatever the rest did. They seemed to
know what to do without the minister making any signal or
anything. Then he stopped that singing voice and said, looking
up at the ceiling, that the day would come when there'd be this
loud sound of trumpets and all the graves would burst open
and everybody come out and fly up to heaven. I mean, what
kind of funny fairy tale stuff is that? If Dave could only have
heard him. And he went on about Dave being asleep in Jesus,
and the Lord giveth and the Lord taketh away. I wondered
what he'd say if he only knew what Dave had been up to. I
mean, if he'd known Dave had stuck that Spade, would he say
Dave was asleep in Jesus?

Anyway he was reading the stuff so I don't suppose he really
cared one way or another. After all he'd never seen Dave or
knew anything about him. And the way he was reading; he was
in a hurry to get it over. Can't be fun for anybody, even a
minister, being around coffins all the time. And through the
window these three men in working clothes waiting and smoking

behind their hands. And the way he said it, so sure, as if he could see Dave sleeping. Open that box and he'd get the shock of his life.

I looked at Mum and she was very pale, so I moved close to her, touching her, to let her know I'm there, in case she's feeling sick or something and she looks up at me and tries to smile, only she doesn't quite make it. I stopped listening to that old parson and all that stuff he was reading from that book and started thinking how none of this mattered one little damn to Dave and we might just as well not have come.

In a few minutes the service was over and somebody must have pulled a string or something, because this curtain came across the coffin. And suddenly it got me, and I couldn't stop the tears. There and then I knew that Dave was gone, for ever, and I was alone. My knees felt as if they couldn't support me, I had to hold on to the seat in front. Then Mum touched me, for me to go out. On the way home I couldn't help looking up at tall chimneys we passed and thinking that soon Dave would be just a wisp of smoke rising till it reached the clouds or even heaven, wherever that was, and that from now on some part of him would be floating away up there, and some part of him mixing with the rain and the sunshine, the breeze and the snow.

After we'd changed Mum said to our Dad why didn't he and me go over to the allotment instead of mooning about the place, and we said okay. Half-way up the street Dad said would I run back and fetch some string for tying up the bean poles, so I went in through the back door and there's our Mum sitting at the kitchen table, crying her heart out. She didn't hear me so I backed out and closed the door softly. Truth is I felt like crying myself. Down the road I bought some string at the newsagent's so I wouldn't have to say anything about our Mum crying to our Dad.

7

BACK AT THE works nobody came fussing around, but the way they'd nod and smile you knew they were sorry about Dave. Funny, when it was Dave and me the fellows didn't try to sort us out, they just called us 'Hi, mate' or Bennett. Now one or two began calling me Jack or Jack boy. First time one of them said Jack boy I thought of that Sandra, but she'd said it quite differently. Old Man McGowan asked me if I wanted to move to another part of the shop, I suppose because of me remembering Dave, but I said no, I preferred to stay where I was. Fact is I wasn't feeling upset any more about Dave. It was as if he'd just gone away for a while. I'd told Mum it was okay to leave his bed just as it was and she'd said why not take the record player up to my room, so now at night I could stay up there and listen whenever I liked.

A few nights later a funny thing happened. I was feeling restless and not wanting to sit around the house so I decided to go up West, not for anything special, just to walk around a bit. Going into the station, I don't know why but I looked around and there near by the kiosk where they sell fags and sweets and stuff like that is Baldy's pal. While I'm buying my ticket I watch him getting something from the kiosk and I get the feeling that he's following me, you know, like on the flicks. But it doesn't bother me, I'm not scared or anything. I mean, those fellows think they're so bright, like this Inspector Maigret on the telly. So I get my ticket and go down, but he's not following, even when the train leaves he's not on it. But you can never tell with those blokes, so up West I go over to the Kaleidoscope and sit around having a coffee and listening to some jazz and watching these birds. And there's one of them sitting by herself dressed up all in black with this black sweater, coarse knit and too big for her, and black hair hanging down her face with this whitish make-up, making her look a bit sick in that light. And I thought, One of those student types. And after a while she saw me looking at her and she sort of smiled and I thought, Well, why not? So I go over and sit beside her, she making room for me as if it is okay. And I begin chatting her up, but she's not a student at all. I mean she speaks quite ordinary. Lives up Willesden way and works in the city. Typist. I mean, she's not a student or anything and dressing up like that. But she's okay, nice teeth and she can take a joke. Ruth, her name is, Ruth Livingstone. And she asks me my name and I tell her it's Dave Bennett. Don't know why. It just came to me to say so. Funny, all the time I'm talking with her I'm thinking about that other one, and watching the way Ruth moves her hands, the nails bitten down to the quick on each finger. Miss Ruddy Spencer. Bloody snooty Spade. I wondered what her name was, besides Spencer. I had a couple of cups of Espresso with Ruth and later walked with her to Piccadilly Circus for our trains, going in opposite directions. I took her phone number and said I'd give her a ring some time.

8

THERE WASN'T MUCH to the inquest. The police read a statement about the accident, where it happened and what time, and showed photographs of it. Apart from the police there was our Dad and me and the coroner, and Miss Spencer all dressed in black sitting with a tall woman, coloured like herself, and proud looking too. And the doctor who had examined the bodies, and a few other people I didn't know. And all it boiled down to was the driver must have lost control or something. The doctor identified Dave's ring as the one he'd removed from one of the bodies. And the police talked about finding Dave's knife. Then I went up and identified Dave's ring and his knife. They called Miss Spencer and she said yes, her brother Dr William Spencer drove the Morris saloon with that number, and he was expected home that night but didn't arrive. Cool and calm she was. Even in that black stuff which didn't really suit her, she looked like some model, that long neck and the thin nose tilted up in the air. I sat there imagining how it would be to get close to that piece. After all the talk and questions, the coroner said that in the circumstances the only verdict which should be returned was death by misadventure. So that was it. Outside I figured Dad would want to talk to Miss Spencer, so I waited with him till the two of them came out. Dad spoke to the girl and she introduced him to the tall woman, her mother. Nearly as tall as Dad in her high-heels, and good looking like her daughter. I figured it must be because they lived in England. So I'm standing there and she has to introduce me to her mother too.

Her mother and our Dad get talking, so I say to her, 'Miss Spencer, I'm sorry you think I'm ill-mannered.' Really I didn't give a damn what she thought, but I guessed this was a sure way to soften her up.

'I wouldn't give it a thought if I were you,' she says, and I think that if I dropped dead that one would step right over me and not even notice. But now I'd started it and I suddenly made up my mind that, come hell or high water, I'd get close to her. We'd moved a few feet away from her mother and our Dad, mostly because she wasn't standing still.

'I don't know what I've said or done to upset you,' I tell her, 'but whatever it is I'm sorry.' Christ, if anybody could have heard me carrying on like that to a Spade, and she looking as if she didn't give a damn one way or another.

Then, without thinking I said, 'You know, you should never wear black. That other dress, the grey one you wore last time, suits you much better.' I was surprised, myself, to hear it coming out of my mouth; I mean, I hadn't prepared it or anything. She fastened those big grey eyes on me for a long time, as if she was making up her mind what to say, then they sort of crinkled at the sides and she smiled. Nice white teeth like Maureen's.

'Why, thank you kindly, sir,' she said, half mocking, making it like a joke. And we both laughed.

'No, really, I mean it,' I told her. And we stopped laughing, standing there looking at each other.

'I suppose I must have sounded terribly rude when I said you were ill-mannered,' she said, after a while.

'Well, you know how it is, I was upset about Dave. We being twins and that.' Dave wouldn't mind about that. She said okay, she understood and anyway it didn't matter so why didn't we forget the whole thing. Moving away towards her mother. Grabbing at straws, I said I hoped that the accident and everything had not interfered too much with her studies, and she said she hadn't been able to face a book since, and her mother was taking it really hard. Then she said well, they'd better be going and I said was there any chance of seeing her again. That stopped her cold, and those eyes got big again and watchful and I could feel her closing up against me.

So I said, 'I want to be sure you're not still angry with me, Miss Spencer.' Smooth and easy it came out, like how old Dave used to chat up a new bird. Watching her face, waiting to hear whether she'd swallow that one.

'I'm really not angry,' she said, the voice friendly again.

'Then can I see you again some time? Or even telephone you just to say hello?'

This time she smiled. I'd made it sound like I was ready to go down on my knees or something.

'Oh well, you can telephone if you like. We live at Leigh-on-Sea, and the number is in the directory.' And with that she walked past to her mother. I mean, after all this friendly talk it's natural for a girl to smile and look happy, but this one still wore her face serious, though just a little softer. Talking with our Dad, her mother reminded me of Mrs McIlroy who used to teach us in the Infants. Same kind of thin, kind face, but brown.

After they'd gone our Dad said, 'They're very nice people, Son,' meaning the Spencers.

9

A COUPLE OF evenings later Baldy dropped in, him and his
shadow, smiling the same old friendly smile as if the only thing
that mattered to him in the wide world was doing good turns
for people, like getting enough evidence on them to put them
away for at least a year. This time Dave's ring was his excuse.
He handed it to our Dad, but he seemed not too keen to take
it, so I took it from Baldy and signed the slip of paper for it.

'I'm afraid we'll have to hang on to the knife a while longer
while we pursue some enquiries into another matter,' he said.

Our Dad asked him why, because he thought that the inquest
meant the end of things.

'We've run up against a problem,' he said, putting on his big
brother act. 'You see, we've been following up on the report
from the bus conductor. He said your son had joined the bus
at Whitechapel Underground, so we had a chat with all the
people who were on duty at the station that night, just in case
anybody might have seen him coming out of the station.
Naturally we showed them the photograph you so kindly lent
us, but only one person thinks he remembers seeing him.
Strangely enough he feels sure that your son went down into the
station. The trouble with these investigations is that after a day
or two nobody remembers anything clearly. The fellow I'm
telling you about was the ticket collector on duty at the time
and he thinks he recognizes your son from the photograph, but
he's not positive about it. But he's sure that if it's the chap he's
thinking about he went down into the station. Says he saw him
standing near the door and gave him a shout, because a train
had just come in.'

Part of me was hearing Baldy, the other carefully retracing
my steps of that evening. I remembered the fellow calling me
about the train; and saw him leaning against the wall near the

barrier. He didn't seem interested in my ticket so I didn't show it to him, just rushed down the stairs. Lucky I had the return half. If I'd had to buy a ticket I'd have had it. At Upminster, that old fellow who collects the tickets late at night never looks at anyone; he only watches the tickets just in case you have to pay excess. There was a whole crowd got off that night so he didn't have time to look at anyone, even if he wanted to. Didn't see anyone I knew in my carriage. The ticket. Hell it was a return half Upminster – Piccadilly Circus. Didn't mean a thing. If they wanted to trace a ticket they'd be looking for one from Whitechapel. Anyway, if Baldy really knew something he'd not be sitting here making polite conversation. He'd have had me over to the police station in no time. Let him play cat-and-mouse if he wanted to, I couldn't care less.

'The strange thing about it is this,' he was saying. 'Although he can't be absolutely sure, the ticket collector at Whitechapel thought he recognized your son's photograph. He was the one on duty on the late shift. None of the other station personnel remembered seeing anyone like him. On the other hand the bus conductor recognized him as the lad who got on his bus and jumped off at Leystonstone. The point I'm trying to make is that, if both men are right, then your son couldn't have been in two places at once. Stands to reason.'

'Anyway, what's all this leading to?' our Dad asked him. I could see our Dad was becoming uncomfortable and I thought, please God let him keep his mouth shut. If he started any kind of argument with Baldy, chances are he would say something which would start the ball rolling towards me. Mum sat quiet, looking at Baldy without either interest or irritation, the way she sat through the rare occasions when she let Spotty Frock into the house. Boredom plus patience.

Baldy had left it to the last, but I'd had a feeling it was coming. 'On the very night your son was killed a young coloured fellow, a West Indian named (here he took the old notebook from his pocket and flipped through the pages) Carlton Thomas, was found dying in the street outside some condemned buildings in Hillingdon Terrace back of the London Hospital,

Whitechapel. He'd been stabbed twice and died soon after being admitted to hospital. According to the police from Leman Street, there seemed to have been a violent struggle. Samples of blood recovered from fragments of broken bottles indicated that Thomas's assailant was wounded in the struggle. There might even have been more than one assailant. From the nature of Thomas's wounds, the doctor who performed the autopsy described the weapon which could have been used. Its description closely fits the knife found at the scene of the accident in which your son was killed. Mrs Bennett, Mr Bennett, I hope you'll forgive me putting the matter so bluntly, but, as you know, I've got a job to do. If I don't do it someone else will. The strange thing about this is that Thomas was not robbed. His wallet containing more than thirty pounds was found intact in the inside breast-pocket of his coat. From all reports it would seem that he was a friendly fellow. From enquiries at the King's Head, a pub in Hillingdon Terrace, it was learned that earlier in the evening Thomas had been there drinking with some friends. He'd bought some liquor at the off licence and spoke about a birthday party he was having the following evening. He left the pub a little before closing time. He wasn't drunk, according to the report. Never was in any trouble. Worked as a clerk for a firm of hauliers at Lambeth. Highly thought of by everyone.

'Apparently nobody heard any sounds of a struggle. Most of the buildings around there are unoccupied, the place is scheduled for reconstruction; but a few people live in rooms here and there, you know, the diehards who refuse to budge until the bulldozers are on top of them. Nobody heard anything. Couldn't have been woman trouble because from all reports Thomas was a decent, quiet fellow. Lived in lodgings at Rexal Street, around the corner from where the murder took place.

'My problem is this. If I trace your son's movements backward beginning at the accident in which he was killed, I think he got a lift in Dr Spencer's car at Leytonstone. He arrived at Leytonstone in a bus which picked him up at Whitechapel Underground station. From the condition of the seat he used it is clear that he was badly wounded, somewhere in the back. He must have sustained that wound before taking the bus, which brings him somewhere in the neighbourhood of Whitechapel station. Now where do I go from there?'

Nobody spoke. Baldy sat there like some Sunday school teacher explaining a parable, looking pleased with himself, not like a man who had problems. Maybe he thought he was talking somebody into making a false move.

'As we see it, your son might have been involved in the attack on Thomas. I say might have, because we do not know for certain. I hope you'll bear with me in this. I'm merely trying to piece the bits of this case togther. If he was involved in the attack on Thomas, it might explain the blood on the seat of the bus. The police at Leman Street are having some tests made to see whether the blood found at the scene of the murder, other than Thomas's, and that found on the seat of the bus are from one and the same person. I expect to hear the result of their tests pretty soon.

'However, here's another point. Thomas's friends all say he was very strong, a very keen amateur weight-lifter and boxer. About five eleven and a half, weight about thirteen stone. The M.O.'s report says that he was in superb physical condition.'

Here he turned to our Dad. 'Your son was the identical twin of Jack here, so shall we say six feet tall and weighing about eleven stone, eleven stone four, five, thereabouts?'

'Eleven six,' I told him, just to be helpful.

'Thank you. Our guess is that there was more than one attacker involved. Thomas would normally have been more than a match for someone weighing eleven stone six or so. That is if the attacker was your son. Unless the attack was from behind. According to the autopsy, the wound which killed Thomas was in the abdomen, although there was another superficial stabwound in the back. Apart from these, there were several abrasions on the face and on the body, suggesting that he may have been struck with a blunt instrument or kicked while on the ground. As I mentioned before, it seems that he put up quite a fight.

71

'Another possibility is that Thomas was attacked by someone much bigger and stronger than himself. The local police are trying to trace his movements and associations to see if they can discover someone who had a grudge against him. We're not ruling out the possibility that robbery was the motive but that the attacker panicked and fled without attempting to rob the body. On the other hand, if robbery was not the motive, Thomas's attacker was some person or persons who hated him. Probably for some real or fancied wrong. Hated him enough to kill him.'

He stopped talking and let his sugary smile get some practice, while his eyes flickered to me, our Dad and Mum, then back to me. Nobody was arguing with him, he was playing his tune and dancing all by himself.

'There is, however,' he went on, 'one possibility we cannot overlook. That is that Thomas's attackers did not intend to kill him at all. Probably jumped him in the dark intending to rough him up a bit. We've been hearing one or two reports of that sort of thing happening lately. Groups of young men beating up individual coloured people. No complaints from the people themselves. Just rumours and hearsay. Could be that somebody, or a few of them, tried it on Thomas and he put up a fight so they used a knife on him.

'You know, in my experience, most of the killings we have to deal with are never intentional. Done on the spur of the moment. A situation gets out of hand, somebody loses his temper, or is frightened, or hurt or getting the worst of it and the next thing you know, he uses a knife or a gun or something and somebody dies. No murder intended. At least not in the heart or the mind. Can happen to anyone. I mean, who is a murderer? Before the act is committed such a person looks just like anyone of us. After the act we tend to think of him as some kind of monster.

'No, in my experience, and my colleague will support me in this, anyone can kill, provided all the circumstances conducive to such an act are present at a certain time, in a certain place. If it so happens that David Bennett was involved in the murder of Carlton Thomas, it may well be one of those occasions on which no murder was planned or intended. It could happen to you,' he looked at our Dad, 'or me or young Jack here.'

I looked him straight in the eyes; the smile around his mouth didn't reach up that high and his glance back at me was pure policeman. He had been idly turning his hat in his hands, but now he held it as if ready to put it on his head.

He stood up, his shadow imitating him. 'Suppose I'm breaking all kinds of official rules by discussing the case like this, but I wanted you to know a little of what's happening, especially as we're still holding some of your son's property. By the way, did you go out at all on the night your brother was killed?'

I suppose he thought he'd catch me napping by asking that one so suddenly. He must think young people were idiots.

'No, I didn't go anywhere that night,' I said, watching him. If he really knew something, well, out with it. Dave had gone into the station ahead of me and bought the tickets, then we'd gone through the barrier. That was the only snag, that the ticket clerk at Upminster might have remembered selling Dave two tickets. Then Baldy would be wondering why Mum and me lied about my going out. Well, the hell with him, he'd have to prove I was there. The fellow at the barrier had been reading a newspaper and didn't even look at us as we walked past him into the station.

Baldy said nothing more, and they left.

'Those fellows never give up,' Dad said, casual as you please. And I'd been worrying about what he might say.

I rang Miss Spencer three times that week but nobody answered the telephone. I'd checked the number in the directory and phoned the Wednesday evening; the line rang and rang, but nothing. I even checked with Directory Enquiries to make sure I was on to the right number and the operator rang it for me, but no reply. So I figured they were out visiting somewhere. Next night I rang again, soon as I got home from work, but still no answer. Tried three times, around seven-thirty, nine and ten-thirty. Same tune. The bell ringing its ruddy head off and nobody answering.

Told myself to hell with her, I wasn't ringing because I liked the bitch or felt friendly to her. I just wanted to get close to her to make her pay for embarrassing Mum, right in our own home, that's all. Just close enough to make her realize that she was nothing but a Spade, in spite of all her fancy airs. Probably knew they wouldn't be there, that's why she said I could telephone. Bloody spiteful bitch. If she didn't want me to ring she could have said so, instead of having me waste my ruddy time ringing and ringing. Just what one should expect from a Spade. Treat them decently like other people and what happens. They begin to pile on the ruddy agony. Well, to hell with it. Not any more. I'd only rung her because I promised I would. But not again.

However, later on I thought a bit about it while I was lying on my bed and figured that, after all, she couldn't know it was me ringing. I wasn't the only person who might want to ring her. Hell, she couldn't not answer just because it might be me. No, it didn't make sense. Probably she and her mother were doing something which kept them out late.

I rang again just before midnight, but still no reply. I went to bed feeling hurt and angry. Sleep was a long time coming. I rang from the call-box at work lunch time that Friday, but no luck. Tried again from the call-box near the station after work, but still no answer, so I guessed they must have gone off somewhere, well, to get over the shock of the doctor's death. People do things like that. They figure that if they go somewhere different, away from familiar things, everything will be fine. Forget that they take it with them inside, at least that's how it looks to me. I mean, wherever they go they'll be thinking of the thing they went away from, so what's the use? Better to stay where you are and get on with it.

Wouldn't have taken such a lot for her to have said they might be going away for a while though. I mean, I said I would telephone, so she couldn't imagine I meant next month or next year. Anyway, I telephoned twice next day, the Saturday, and still no answer, so I phoned Ruth, the bird I'd met at the coffee bar up West. Rang her at the Willesden number she'd given me, and her mother answered and said Ruth wasn't there and would I try another number at Kensington. So I rang this other number and this bird answered and I asked for Ruth and she came on the line. Said she was spending the week-end with a girlfriend from her office. Having a party that night, and would I like to come? Her voice sounded nice and friendly, as if we'd known each other for years. Said she'd recognized mine as soon as she'd heard it. Started kidding about how she knew I'd ring, that's why she'd left the number with her mother. All in one breath, you know, excited. Makes you feel good inside when somebody's so pleased just to talk to you over the ruddy phone. Funny thing. Talking to Ruth my mind kept switching over to that other one, wondering if she'd sound the same. Told Ruth okay, I'd meet her at South Ken station at seven-thirty.

While getting things organized to go and meet Ruth, giving my shoes the old spit and polish and pressing a suit, I got to thinking about things. Whenever I'm doing these familiar chores my mind seems to be better able to look around and examine all kinds of little details which normally I overlook. Like this thing with Mum. It suddenly came to me that since Dave wasn't there any more, Mum never stayed up nights. At least not so you'd notice.

Now I remembered that night I'd been up West and met Ruth I'd got home around eleven-thirty or so, anyway it was before midnight and the house was in darkness as usual, because our Dad and Mum always turned in around eleven except if someone came visiting and stayed late. I went in and was undressing when it struck me that something was different about the place, some little thing I couldn't put my finger on. Same thing last night. Went to the local flicks and got in just after eleven. Now, sitting there polishing my shoes, it came to me. The bedroom door. Our Dad and Mum's. Both times it was closed. That was it. The ruddy door was closed. I mean, in all the years since Dave and me had been big enough to stay out a bit late it was open. Not wide, just enough so Mum could hear us. And we sort of looked forward to it, like a signal or something. Used to kid each other about it. If ever we were held up anywhere at night and the time was getting on, one of us would say, 'Come on, let's hurry it up. Time our Mum was asleep.'

The way the thing hit me I must have lost track of time or something like that, because the next thing I know our Dad is standing beside me with his hand on my shoulder saying, 'Don't take it so hard, Son. It could have been any one of us.'

And then I felt the tears on my face. I didn't say anything to him, but put down the shoes and went up to the bathroom. Funny how a little thing like that can get you, deep down inside where all the big, terrible things can't touch you. It was as if Mum had said to herself, well, Dave's gone, so there's nothing to wait up for. Christ, I wished it was me who'd had the ruddy accident, then everybody would be happy. I hated myself for the weakness of tears, but they wouldn't bloody well stop, just pouring out of me as if I'd been wanting to cry for years and years. I sat down on the lav. wondering what the hell to do. Probably the best thing was to get out and find some digs somewhere. No point in hanging around when you're not wanted.

Mum knocked on the door to ask if I'm okay and I say yes. Our Dad must have said something to her. Let them think I was crying because of Dave, they'd never hear different from me. Wish I could write things down like Dave, poems and things, so I could put it down in a book just to tell it without telling it to anybody. Just for myself. Not for reading by anyone else. Like Dave once said. Some songs are not for singing. Funny that I didn't understand it at the time. I got dressed and was putting on my shoes but the left one wouldn't go on. The bloody handkerchief I'd stuffed in there. Christ, if Baldy could have seen that. I flushed it down the lavatory on my way down.

Getting my train I noticed how nobody looked at you. The ticket seller behind the perspex window with the little holes in it for hearing merely inclined his head to hear your destination and whether you wanted a single or return, then looked at the counter below the window to take your money. The ticket collector either clipped your ticket or waved you on, depending on how he felt. They must be really bored with all the people coming in and out never really noticing them. No wonder Baldy didn't get much change out of the fellow at Whitechapel. For all I knew he might have been here too to find out if Dave or both of us passed through the night of the accident. The way these fellows didn't notice anything. Must have made old Baldy want to tear what little hair he could still boast of combing.

10

THEY CHARGED THROUGH the still opening doors at Mile End and tumbled into nearby seats, a bunch of laughing, chattering teenage girls, overlarge handbags swinging as they jostled to sit beside one another. Real and dyed blondes, brunettes and a Spade, all pretty and excited, laughing and talking in the same breath. Reminded me of something I'd read in Dave's book, about Teds:

Teds

. . . Clad tight
In the resilient armour of their youth,
And bright contempt which threatened as it mocked
The wavering eyes of all who censured them . . .

Modishly dressed in various versions of the same stiletto-heeled shoes, swagger coats and hairstyles. Some chewing gum.

'Come on, Brenda, fetch it out.'

'Hey, don't mind me, it's only me leg you're crushing. Give over.'

'Yeah, Brenda, let's hear me stars.'

'That's the only thing me Mum reads in the Mirror. The other day after she finished reading the paper me Dad said to her what's that about a strike at Fords and she didn't even know what he was on about.'

'What's yours, Elaine?'

'Hey, wait a minute. Turn back that last page. Me new skirt's

77

just like that. Bought it up the Lane. Two quid. Five pounds at least up West.'

'Sagittarius.'

'What's it mean.'

'Pipe down and listen. An old friend will be prominent in your week's activities. Be decisive in your actions. You will find it will pay. Seek new and stimulating companions.'

'Crikey.'

'Hey, Doris, Bill still coming around?'

'That German boy staying over at Sheila's Mum's, he's ever so nice. Been out with him twice. I like him 'cos he always pays when we go to the flicks and things.'

'You coming hopping this year, Doris?'

A tight, closed group, the Spade as much a part of it as any other. And funny to hear the ordinary English voice coming out of her. Just to make sure I closed my eyes, and they all sounded alike, all the voices having that breathless urgency as if they were already late for living and had lots of catching up to do. And all that funny, meaningless talk. I looked at them again, and one or two looked across and smiled impudently, then giggled among themselves. When the Spade laughed her face dimpled and rounded until the eyes were nearly hidden. No break in their chatter even when the train reached Charing Cross and they rushed wildly out.

There was no sign of Ruth at South Ken station so I went into a phone booth to try again, meanwhile keeping a watch out for her through the glass. After a few rings and just as I was about to replace the receiver, someone answered. Mrs Spencer. So I told her it was me and could I speak to Miss Spencer, please? And she said she was sorry but Michelle had just gone out. Was there any message? And I said no, I'd promised to telephone her some time and I'd just remembered. Then I said I hoped she, Mrs Spencer, was okay, and she said yes, she was fine. They'd been down to the coast in Devon for a few days and it had been wonderful. And thank you for ringing and she'd tell Michelle that I phoned. So I said yes, please, and if she'd be in tomorrow afternoon I'd give her a ring. Then she said she was sure Michelle would be in, they usually were in on Sunday afternoon, and would I like to come over to tea? And I said yes, thanks.

Funny how a little thing like talking to somebody on the phone can affect the weather. I mean, a dull, cloudy evening suddenly becomes fine and wonderful, and you get the feeling you're big enough to do anything. Anything.

It was good to see Ruth. Without the dumpy sweater she seemed taller, slimmer, in a plain, close fitting sleeveless dress of tartan design, high-heeled red court shoes and her hair tied with a bright red ribbon, ponytail style. She seemed happy to see me, and tucked her arm under mine as if we were sweethearts or something, chatting about the party and all the nice people I'd meet.

We went down some stairs to a basement flat thick with cigarette smoke, talk and music. All young people, mostly student types, I thought. Ruth drew me in turn to several little groups standing about or sitting on sofas or the floor, who waved or said, 'Hi', and went on with their talk. The music was from a guitar played by a fellow with long hair and turtleneck sweater, sitting on the floor with several fellows and girls around him. They'd wait for him to get started on a song, then join in the singing if they knew the words. Some merely clapped hands softly. One of the fellows was coloured, thin-faced with large eyes and the beginnings of a beard. Ruth sat down with this group and pulled me down beside her.

The song died and the guitarman picked a few chords then started in on 'Swing low, sweet chariot', all of them taking it up, even Ruth. And the Spade not singing, but humming in deep tones while miming the playing of a double bass, puffing out his cheeks in mimicry of some musician whose antics were well known to the group. The song ended with lots of laughter. Sitting there I had a wonderful feeling of warmth, as if I'd known them all a long time. Even the Spade. His being there did'nt matter. I mean I wasn't bothered by it. They started another song. I shifted around till I got my back braced against a wall, my legs stretched out comfortably. Then Ruth wriggled

79

around to lean against my chest, her hair smelling clean of soap and health.

Somebody passed around a pretty strong punch in paper cups, and some little sausage rolls. The singing stopped and the talk began while we ate. About music and musicians, jazzmen, some of whom I'd never heard about. Mostly Americans. Coloured. And about their struggle in the United States, and the effect of their struggles on the music they made. And about the atomic bomb. And work. And where was Youth heading? And the importance of expressing one's personality and identity. You could tell they were educated types, I mean, the way they spoke and so sure of what they were saying. So I kept my mouth shut and just listened. Even Ruth would put in her tuppence worth now and then, as clever as any of the others. And Ron, the Spade. He had this deep, rumbly voice, and spoke slowly, carefully, as if somewhere in his mind he tested each word to make sure it was suitable to do the job of explaining the thoughts growing deep inside him. If you didn't see him you wouldn't figure that voice was coming from a Spade. Sounded just like that fellow who did the mystery voice on the BBC. Ruth said he was a student at RADA and I asked her what that was and she said a college where you learned acting and other things for the theatre. I just sat there sipping punch and letting the talk wash over me like tide on some warm beach where you didn't have to bother about anything. And wondering what old Dave would say if he could see me now, chumming it up with a ruddy Spade.

Michelle. So that was her name. I'd figured she'd have a name different from other girls. And the way her mother had pronounced it, making it sound foreign. Wonder what it would be like if she were beside me now, leaning close like Ruth. Don't suppose she'd condescend to sit on any floor eating sausage rolls. Wonder what she'd say when her mother told her she'd invited me to tea. She'd sounded friendly, that Mrs Spencer.

I'd missed the first part of whatever Ron was saying, then noticed that the others were quiet, listening to him.

'. . . and the Youth Employment Officer made a long speech to us about the wonderful opportunities awaiting us in industry and the civil service, because Britain was in urgent need of qualified technical personnel and the sky was the limit for anyone with drive, ambition and ability. You know the usual kind of drivel they shoot at you the last year at school. Well, there were two of us. Jackie Roberts and me. We'd gone up to Hale School at the same time. When the bloke had finished his speech he asked if any of us had any questions. And Jack stood up and said "Sir, do these prospects and opportunities you've described apply equally to us?" Meaning him and me, the only two coloured fellows in the class. You should have seen that bloke's face. He stammered something about when he spoke he was thinking of the English students, but, providing we attained the necessary standards he did not think we should experience any difficulty being placed. Funny thing is, though I was born here, my folks both came from Barbados, but Jackie's grandfather was born in Cardiff, and his father's been practising medicine in Hampstead ever since he qualified.'

The discussion warmed up. A redheaded fellow named Petty said it was the same attitude at the root of all the racial friction in the U.S.A. Native sons who didn't belong. You should have heard Ruth carrying on about everybody being the same under their skins. I wondered, How the hell would she know, she'd never had a different skin. Then one of the girls, a pretty little blonde with plenty of shape, called Hilary, said that Britain's youth had a responsibility to reshape the attitudes they had inherited so that the next generation would have a better chance to live in harmony with other people. I mean, a sweet little mouth coming all that stuff. I wouldn't mind if she tried out a little of that harmony on me, provided she didn't do any re-shaping on herself.

Then they got back on to the theatre and the flicks, and somebody talked about a Spade actor named Sydney Poitier. And Ron said that in the States and Britain the Arts provided an oasis where anyone could find shade and sustenance without reference to colour or creed, but why should it be the only place, because after all, only a very few people wanted to become actors or musicians or dancers. And it didn't make him feel any better to be able to move along easily, when he saw how badly other coloureds were treated. Then somebody said it wasn't all as simple as that, and look at the lousy parts most coloured actors were always given, flunkeys and servants and things. And I'm right there thinking if they knew the first thing about me they'd have me out of there in a jiff.

Now and then I look at the time because it's such a nuisance if you miss the last Underground to Upminster. Means having to get to Fenchurch Street and wait around for hours to get a steam train, or else get a train from Liverpool Street to Romford, then get a taxi from Romford all the way to Upminster. After all I'm not made of loot. Ruth caught me at it and put her hand over my wrist-watch, and after a while we're holding hands. Not only us. Ron has his arm around that blonde Hilary. Ruth says she's pretty bright and designs fabrics. Petty, the ginger bloke, is leaning against Ruth's friend Naomi, you know, as if they're good friends. Naomi is the one who has the flat.

Someone put on a record and soon everybody's dancing and I look again at the time and it's half-eleven and I tell Ruth I'd better be going and she says, joking, what's the rush, is Mother waiting to tuck her little Dave in. And though I know she's kidding, something starts up inside me, remembering that nowadays Mum doesn't give a damn whether I'm late in or not.

Ruth walked to the station with me and on the way I remembered. So I told her that my name wasn't really Dave, it was Jack. And she stops still in the street, asking, 'Why did you want to say it was Dave?' Her voice was angry. So I tell her it was just a joke, you know, you meet a girl and you figure you'd never see her again in your life, so a little kidding wouldn't hurt, I mean, no harm done.

'But I'm already thinking of you as Dave,' she said. 'How am I going to suddenly think of you as Jack?' I mean, what's she making all the fuss about. It's not as if we'd been friends for years.

Then suddenly she cheers up. 'You know, you're an odd fellow. Fancy doing a thing like that. How do I know your name is really Jack and you're not still kidding me?'

So I show her my ring with the initials and explain about Jack being for Jackson and L.B. for Lee Bennett. So we chat a bit and she tells me most of the people I'd met lived near by and the party would be going on for hours yet. She'd be spending the night at the flat with Naomi, and was hoping to team up with her permanently as soon as she'd talked her mother into it. Willesden was a long way to and from her job each day, and if anything was happening in town she always had to leave early to get trains home, and it was awful. Listening to her I was thinking I'd have to find myself somewhere too. She said she hoped next time I wouldn't have to rush off so early, and outside South Ken station we kissed. Holding her close, feeling the soft, willing warmth of her and the excitement of her sweet mouth. And suddenly who am I thinking of? Michelle. So I said cheerio to Ruth and I'd ring her soon, and rush into the station. A good thing people can't see inside your mind and know what you're thinking.

At home I get into my pyjamas and lie in bed reading Dave's book. It had become like a habit now, each night. Like listening to him say things I didn't even know he'd ever thought about. Sometimes I'd read aloud, but softly, hearing the voice and trying to imagine it coming out of Dave's mouth. If our Dad and Mum heard they'd think I was becoming a nutcase or something. Hell, they'd never hear, with the ruddy door shut tight. How did Dave know all those things?

Anyway, there were some things he didn't know. About Spades, for instance. Bet he'd never been to a do like tonight, with a fellow like Ron. Or talked to someone like Michelle. And that bird on the Underground with those others. Funny how I'd never noticed any Spades before except those fellows who worked on the buses or the Underground. I mean, you saw them but you never looked at them. Not really. Not like how you looked at somebody else, even for a minute, wondering what their name was or what sort of job they did or anything.

Going round with Dave I'd see Spades, lots of them, but all that happened was that, well, it sort of registered that there was a black face, but I didn't want to look at it, to see if it was young or old or handsome or ugly or happy or sad. Even when we'd knocked some fellow about I merely saw his blackness, not any feature. Christ, come to think of it, if next day I'd seen one of the fellows we'd knocked about the night before, I'd never have recognized him. Odd the way that, since Dave went, I'm seeing them popping up all over the place, looking and sounding like anybody else. Suppose if things hadn't happened the way they did I'd never have met Michelle. Sure if that bugger Dave had seen her he might even have made a play for her. I wouldn't have had a ruddy chance. And that Ron, talking about what had happened at his Grammar School. Wonder if there were lots more like him, going to Grammar schools and Techs and things, even to University. Him and Michelle.

Suppose lots and lots of them were born here, what would happen? I mean like the Spades in the States. They called them American Negroes, or Negro Americans, in those magazines like *Downbeat* and *Weekend*. What would they call fellows like Ron and that Jackie he talked about? British Negroes? English Negroes? Negro Britons? Negro Englishmen? Didn't sound right somehow. Oh, well, bugger the lot of them. Let them sort it out for themselves.

A gentle knock on the door and Mum came in and sat on the side of my bed. I get this funny feeling that something's wrong.

'What's up, Mum?' I'm getting ready to sit up, but she stops me.

'Nothing's wrong. Heard you come in and get into bed, but saw your light was still on, so I thought you'd be reading. There was a phone message for you tonight. To ring Miss Spencer early tomorrow.'

She sat looking at me, as if expecting some kind of explanation. I say nothing, thinking that perhaps I was wrong and although the door was closed she still listened for me coming in. Made me feel good, that did.

'She wanted to speak to you but I told her you were out.

84

Why does she want to talk to you?' So that was why Mum had been listening for me. To find out about Miss Spencer. Michelle.

'Oh, I don't know, Mum. Something or other I suppose.' I suddenly thought that perhaps she'd rung to tell me not to come tomorrow. Probably made a fuss with her mother for inviting me and now wanted to put me off with some ruddy excuse.

'Have you been seeing her, Son?'

'No, Mum, not since the inquest.'

'Then why would she be telephoning you?'

'Look, Mum, how would I know?' I mean, she's going on and on about it and I don't even know what's happening.

'Son, you know I never interfere where your friends are concerned, but I don't want to see you get mixed up with any of those people. We've had enough trouble with them as it is. If it hadn't been for them your brother would be right here, now. Well, what's happened has happened but I don't want to see you getting involved with any of them.'

'Look, Mum, I'm not involved with anybody. What are you on about? I don't even know why she telephoned.'

'Their ways are not our ways,' she went on. 'We'll never know what happened between that Dr Spencer and our Dave, but that's no reason for you to get mixed up with them. Had it not been for them my son wouldn't be in his grave tonight.' The way she spoke I wondered what she'd said to Miss Spencer. Christ, she must have gone and really mucked it up for me.

'What did you say to her, Mum?'

'All I said was that you were out.' Yes, I could guess how she said it, too.

'Okay, Mum, I'll ring her tomorrow.'

She stood up, looking down at me, then went out, closing the door behind her.

Hell, I wasn't a ruddy kid any more. Ordering me about. Don't do this. Don't do that. And that guff about the Spades being responsible for Dave not being here. Who does she think started the whole thing? Talking about getting involved. You

85

can't get involved with someone you can't get near to. From the way Mum had talked to her I guess she was just waiting to tell me sorry but they'd forgotten they were doing something else and couldn't have me to tea. Oh, well, to hell with her. She wasn't the only ruddy pebble on the beach. Lots of birds all over the place if I wanted one. But if she thought I'd give her the chance to snub me, she had another think coming. I'd phone and before she opened her mouth to make any ruddy excuse I'd say I was sorry but something else had come up and I couldn't make it after all. That would fix the stuck-up bitch.

After breakfast I waited till Mum was upstairs fixing the beds, then I made the call. Her mother answered the phone, her voice was nice and friendly, and then I could hear her calling, 'Michelle, it's Mr Bennett asking for you.' Then she was on.

'Good morning. Sorry I'm out of breath. I was out on the porch.'

'That's okay.' Waiting to hear her begin whatever excuse she'd cooked up, then I'd chip in and say my piece.

'About this afternoon. Do you know how to get here?'

I felt myself sweating. 'Well, I saw the address in the phone book and I figured I'd come down to Leigh and ask around.'

She laughed, still a little breathless, but gay, then said that many of their friends had difficulty finding the place at first, and would I take down the directions so they wouldn't have to send out a search party for me. She sounded just like those classy birds you see talking on the phone in the flicks to their boy friends. She held the line while I found pencil and paper, then told me. Our Dad came into the room while I was talking, looked around and walked out. After I'd written what she'd told me, I wanted to talk some more but couldn't think of anything to say. Then she said:

'Well, we'll expect you at five or thereabouts, Mr Bennett.'

'Jack,' I told her.

'I beg your pardon?'

'The name is Jack, short for Jackson.'

'Oh, well, see you at five.' And she hung up.

Our Dad must have heard the bell tinkle when I hung up. He came back.

'Mrs Spencer and her daughter are very nice people, Son,' he said. I waited to see what he was getting at. Maybe he and Mum had been talking about me.

'I expect they're going through a pretty difficult time just now, what with one thing and another. Mrs Spencer was really broken up over her son's death.' He stood there rubbing his chin, making that funny noise because he hadn't shaved yet, looking at me in that odd tone of voice. Anybody'd think I was planning to murder somebody or something, the way he and Mum were on to me.

Then he started to say something else but stopped, as if he'd changed his mind. He walked to the door, then said, 'Want to give me a hand over at the allotment?'

It was good to be out in the warm sun, the earth smelling clean with each spadeful turned, hands sticky from pulling beans and cutting rhubarb, hearing the birds chirping and the distant rush of traffic along the main road behind the far line of trees. Times like this when Dave was here we'd be nattering with our Dad and fooling around, kidding as we worked, happy in the nearness. Afterwards we'd step in at the Greyhound and have a shandy with our Dad on the way home to lunch. Now it was nearly the same, except we worked quietly, without saying anything. But it was okay.

Sometimes I looked over at our Dad, noticing the way his big hands did quick, tender things, feeling the strength and friendliness in him. Funny with our Dad, even as kids he didn't really like telling us off. Even those times when we'd do something wrong and Mum would tell him when he got in from work and he'd have to tan our behinds, he'd come up to our room afterwards and tell us some funny story about what he'd been doing on the building site, or give us some sweets he'd brought for us. Best of all was Sunday mornings when he'd take us to the allotment and we'd play cowboys under the trees, while he worked. I mean, he was okay.

'I'm going to have tea with Mrs Spencer and her daughter

this afternoon.' I said it before I even realized I was going to tell him.

He straightened up and turned to look at me, his eyes not smiling.

'Mrs. Spencer asked me to come,' I said.

'Is that why the girl rang last night?'

'Yes, Dad. What I mean is her mother had already asked me, but Miss Spencer rang to tell me how to get there.'

'How come Mrs Spencer invited you, in the first place?'

'Well, you know at the inquest? Talking with her daughter I'd said I'd give her a ring some time, you know, just to say hello and see how things were with them. So yesterday I rang, Mrs Spencer answered and said would I like to come to tea.'

Suddenly he smiled, but not as if he was amused or anything. More like if he was tired trying to figure something out. A sort of weary smile.

'You know, Son, I just don't understand you. I mean, the Spencers are coloured people, just like the others, aren't they?'

I knew what he meant. I didn't say anything to that. After all, what could I argue, seeing that he knew about everything that had happened. He sighed, shaking his head, and went back to what he'd been doing.

11

I'D SEEN HOW some of them lived when Dave and me went around, up Brixton and Notting Hill and places like that. Those big old houses with the paint peeling off them, and all those Spades standing about outside, and the way I'd heard people talk, they liked living lots together in one room. Going up to Leigh on the train I figured that, however it was, it wouldn't kill me for one visit. After all, I only wanted to get near enough to her to sort of find out how things were, you know, if I could make it with her. The way she dressed and talked they couldn't be too badly off. Probably lived in a little flat or something.

Just as well she'd given me such careful directions, or I'd never have found that house. I located the street easily enough, then there was this high hedge, not privet, another kind with little red berries and sharp thorns, and a low green painted wooden gate with the number '9' on it. A few paces inside the gate several flights of concrete steps, terraced, led downward between lots of apple trees on either side. A handrail of metal tubing followed the stairs and lost itself far below where the stairs curved away. I thought that if some poor bugger lost his footing and fell down that lot there'd not be much left of him to parcel up. From the top I could look out over the trees to the estuary and the outline of Southend pier in the distance. The tide was out and the late evening sun shone redly on the wavy mud and the little boats stuck fast at their moorings, some leaning over sideways to show their keels. Red, green, blue, yellow, all colours they were, some with masts sticking up naked like trees in winter, sleepy seagulls perched on the crossbar at the top. Way across the mud you could see the tall cylinders and circular tanks of the oil refinery at Grain Island, and the hazy outline of the Kent coast.

The apple trees were loaded with small reddish fruit, the ground underneath littered with windfalls. Probably didn't care for apples, these Spencers, or maybe they were maggoty.

The stairs ended on a wide concrete approach to the front door, spanking white with polished brass knocker and letter slot. Red bricks could be seen here and there through the thick ivy which covered most of the front of the house, except for two wide picture windows, one on each side of the door. Bungalow type, the house, built close against the hillside. That's why I couldn't see it from the top of the stairs, especially with all those apple trees in the way.

They must have seen me coming down. Before I could knock the door opened and there she was. The same, only different. Slacks, this time, in pale olive green, razor creased and showing off her long legs without hugging them. A loose-fitting long-sleeved blouse in flowered silk of green and bronze.

And that long neck rising soft and smooth from the V of her blouse, with the hair curling inward to tickle it. Each glossy strand in place as if it had been told to behave. I wondered how such coarse hair would feel if you ran your hand through it. High-heeled sandals in soft white leather against which the glossy red paint on her toenails shone like ten neat bloodspots.

'Any difficulty getting here?' she greeted me, opening the door wide for me to enter. I'd never been inside a house like that. Made me feel a bit uncomfortable, a bit scared that I might do something silly and embarrass the hell out of myself. This room I'd walked into, big, the carpet soft and cushiony, and no straight-up chairs, only armchairs and sofas and some low tables and fancy reading lamps. Everything in different colours. I mean, not like at home. One armchair was green, another off-white, another some other colour, mostly pastel shades, and the sofas the same. And no pictures on the walls. And those big windows with small flowering plants on the inner ledge and the drapes hung to make them seem more artificial than real. The carpet was like a deep cushion, soft and the colour of straw. In a far corner was a small piano, open, as if someone had been playing it recently. It was the only dark-coloured piece of furniture in the room. I mean, no wonder she was so snooty and stuck-up, living in a place like this. Must have pots of money.

We didn't stay in this room. She led me through into another room, at right-angles to the first one. Same kind of armchairs but no sofas and no rug. The floor was wood, parquet or something, and polished. But the thing about it was the view. One side was mostly glass windows looking out over the estuary, the late sun slanting in and glinting off the cutlery and china set out on a central low table for tea. I'd have to watch it, every move. Can't mess it up now that I'd got this far.

She invited me to sit. She curled herself up in a chair with her feet under her, easy and comfortable like a cat, her tailpiece and bosom roundly outlined. One thing I was sure about, it wouldn't happen like with that Sandra. Not ever. Not the way I was feeling right then.

'Mummy will join us in a minute,' she said. She had this way of looking straight at you with those big grey eyes which always caught me off balance. I mean, you don't expect to see grey eyes in a dark face. Looked very attractive, but strange, as if she wasn't really a Spade, but had put on some dark make-up. Like the time our school had this Christmas play and one of the fellows, Jerry Lindrum, had to be one of the wise men and have brown stuff all over his face, and his grey eyes shining through the same way as hers. I turned to look out at the view. The tide was coming in, already filling the shallow puddles in the mud around the boats. Tiny birds were darting about in the mud on invisible legs, stopping now and then to peck and gobble with a quick lift of the head.

'Here she is,' Michelle said. I'd expected Mrs Spencer to be like I'd last seen her, all dressed in black and sad-looking. If I'd never seen her before I'd have taken her for Michelle's sister. Well, older sister. She wore this long gown in pale green silk, only it wasn't really a gown because when she moved you saw that from the waist it was slit down the middle in front and underneath she was wearing slacks of the same material and slippers like Michelle's, but you could only see the very tips of the slippers because the gown was long, nearly touching the floor. Without any sleeves, and her arms smooth and firm all the way. No collar, but a big brooch with a dark green stone to keep the top together. And as much shape up there as her daughter. Or more.

I thought, Crikey, these people are supposed to be in mourning. At home our Mum was wearing black all the time since Dave wasn't there. And look at me. With my dark grey suit I was wearing a black tie. Must say that all these colours looked very nice on them, but it still seemed funny so soon after someone died to be dressed up as if nothing had happened.

She came and shook hands with me, her grip warm and strong. With her in the room I felt more relaxed and comfortable. It was so easy to talk to her, as if she wasn't, well, coloured. Mostly we talked about Dave and me and I told her about some of the fun we had, getting people all mixed up, other kids and teachers and even our Dad. And she'd laugh, deep and sweet inside her as if she was really tickled with it. We talked all through tea, her and me. Michelle mostly sat quiet, whenever I looked her way those big grey eyes would be on me, not staring, but looking me over, weighing me up.

After tea I offered to help with the washing-up but Michelle said no thanks, she preferred to do it herself, and so I stayed and talked with Mrs Spencer. About school with Dave, and the job, and how we'd started at the works at the same time, and we'd asked to stay together and at first the personnel man had said no, then he'd said okay but whether we stayed together would depend on how well we worked and no tricks. It was different there from at school. With all those machines whizzing around it was no place for tricks, and besides, we liked the job and wanted to learn. It was okay, and twice a week we'd have to attend classes, like school, and do maths and drawing and even English.

We talked about how Dave and me liked to go up to the West End and listen to jazz, and Mrs Spencer said she was a jazz fan herself, but mostly she preferred swing and blues. She didn't care too much for the traditional stuff. Ella Fitzgerald, Sinatra, Pearl Bailey, she liked singers like that. And her favourite was somebody named Ethel Waters who she said could sing the birds out of the trees. And she said would I like to hear some music? She went into the drawing-room and after a while the place was full of music low and sweet, saxes and a piano forming counterpoint to some terrific drumming. And she came back and asked me if I liked Gene Krupa and it was him and his sidemen. The 'gram was in the next room but her son had wired all the rooms for speakers so she could enjoy the music wherever she was. So we sat listening, quiet, and now she closed her eyes and you could see the sadness come over her face like a cloud, and I would have liked to say something to her, or hold her hand, but figured she might get me wrong. I mean, you never know. After all, she wasn't that old. With all that shape and not fat or anything. I wondered how it must be for a woman like her, nice looking and everything, and her husband dead. Supposing now and then she felt like having some of it, you know, what would she do? Don't suppose she'd just pick somebody up. Or perhaps people like her just don't think about it.

Watching her I wished I could say a word and make her son come back, you know, have him walk into that room right then and stand beside her and say 'Mummy' or whatever he used to call her. And she'd open her eyes and all the sadness would disappear and she'd smile like before. It probably wouldn't work, though. I mean, if someone's dead and then he appears right near to you, it's liable to scare the living daylights out of you and give you the screaming abdabs for days.

Michelle came back and sat down and when the music stopped Mrs Spencer said why didn't she show me around? So we went outside, the two of us, and behind the house, facing towards the estuary, was a kitchen garden sloping downward with everything neat, with the old paper packets pinned to little stakes so you wouldn't forget what seeds you planted. Different from how we did over at the allotment. And this greenhouse full of potted plants, some in flower. And she walked beside me and now and then my hand would brush against her, accidentally at first. Down the slope behind the house was a low wire fence which was the end of their land, and we stood there watching the tiny yachts now bobbing on the swelling incoming tide. They looked impatient, gently tugging at their mooring ropes and anchor chains. A little breeze sprang up, blowing the soft fabric of her blouse against her so I couldn't help looking.

'Your Mother told me you and your brother were very close,' I said, trying to get her talking about something or other, but she only nodded as if she wasn't interested in discussing it. Well, if we're going to play it this way I might as well try my luck once for all.

'Would you come out with me some time, to the cinema or something?'

I guess I said it in such a hurry that her mouth opened in a little 'O' of surprise. Then she laughed. You'd never credit what laughter could do to her face. I mean, normally she's not bad looking. Not bad looking at all. But when she laughs, her face goes all soft with little dimples by the side of her mouth and her eyes half closed and not staring at you.

'You don't need to shout, you know. My hearing's not the least bit defective,' she said.

I didn't realize I'd shouted. 'Sorry, but, will you?'

'I don't know. It depends.'

'What kind of answer is that? It depends on what?'

The laughter was gone, and those big eyes were back at it, sizing me up.

'It depends on how quickly I can make up for the lectures I've missed and the work I've neglected these past few weeks.' Then she went on to tell me about the examination she was taking in a couple of months and the reading she had to do, and sitting in reference libraries at the University copying stuff or checking on this or that. Most of the time I didn't really understand half of what she was talking about, but I didn't let on. When she got to talking this way I just liked listening to her.

'You know what they say,' I told her. 'All work and no play makes Jack a dull boy.'

'In which case my advice to Jack is that he play as much as he wants to, without bothering about me.'

She came right back at me, and I wished I'd kept my ruddy trap shut. I'd have to take it slow and careful with this bird if I hoped to make it. Going back up to the house we followed a path of crazy paving stones behind the little greenhouse, and along the other side of the kitchen garden. Here the path narrowed and I stood aside to let her squeeze past me. The pressure of a breast against my arm was a fleeting trigger to excitement. Where the path widened I took her hand, but she quickly withdrew it. Not roughly, but I got the message.

I wasn't in a hurry to go back indoors, so I stopped to look at the greenhouse, telling her about our Dad's allotment and the things he'd grown up there, and the way he was always reading stuff in the *Amateur Gardener* or listening to that fellow on TV then trying it out himself. And one time he'd tried this new system with the radishes and they'd grown big, with heads like little red apples, and Mum had told him off because she said they had no taste. And I asked her about the windfalls and she said that Mrs Spencer collected them for making jam. It was getting dark and cool so we had to go in, and I asked her again what about the date, and she said she had a lot to do that week, but maybe if I gave her a ring next week, she'd see.

Our Dad and Mum always used to tell Dave and me that we should never overstay our welcome, especially when visiting somebody for the first time, so I figured I'd better push off. Mrs Spencer said I should drop in to see them any time I felt like it and I said okay. She didn't look sad any more, and I thought I wouldn't say no to some of that, any time, but not really meaning it, just for a little joke to myself.

Michelle walked with me to the gate and near the top I wondered what she'd do if I sneaked a little kiss, but she was always one step above me, and at the top she stayed just out of range as if she'd guessed what I might do. We shook hands and she said good night, Mr Bennett, as formal as you please, so what the hell could I do but say good night, Miss Spencer?

All the way home I thought about her, but mostly about how she was playing hard to get, with all that Mr Bennett stuff and being so stuck up. Well, as Dave used to say, it's the snooty birds who can't stay away from it after they get it. Wonder what old Dave would have done if it had been him? The way she'd sat curled up in that armchair. Thinking about how my arm had brushed her breast it seemed funny that you could be that near to a person, I mean as close as that, and still there'd be miles between you. The way she behaved I'm sure she didn't even know my arm had touched her. And walking up those steps behind her towards the gate. It was all there, inches away, yet you couldn't reach out and touch it. Worse than a ruddy iron curtain.

12

OUR DAD AND Mum were watching TV when I got in so I sat with them looking at this play but not really following it because I'd come in after it started and didn't know what it was all about, and anyway I didn't really like that kind of stuff and my mind was somewhere else. Coming home, the train was full of fellows and birds, probably been down to Southend for the day or something and not had enough, so they were messing about, noisy and singing 'Sister Anna' and things like that. And two birds standing near the compartment door shouting their heads off and this couple, oldish, the husband a little fat fellow with glasses and his wife bigger than him sitting opposite me. She said to these two birds would they mind not making so much noise. And you should have heard what they told her. Get stuffed. And her husband jumped up, telling them off, and these fellows standing in the corridor came up beside the girls and pushed him back into his seat, laughing and saying 'Belt up, Dad,' and things like that. And I felt like having a go at one of them. I mean, suppose it was our Dad he'd been pushing. But I thought, what the hell, it's none of my business. And those two birds, laughing and showing off, and the man's wife looking white and scared. After all, some of those Teds carried knives. I couldn't see myself going with any of those birds. I mean, just look at them. And their voices. Flat and crude. 'Get stuffed'. Just couldn't picture Michelle behaving like that. Or Ruth, or any of those types I'd met at her party. Funny. I'd been over there and had tea with them, spent hours, and still I felt I was as much a stranger to her as before. Mr Bennett. That's all she'd call me. Mr Bennett.

The play finished and Mum said how about some cocoa and when she'd gone to fix it, our Dad said how had it been over at the Spencers, and I told him it was okay. Then I mentioned about the house and how they lived, you know, nattering with our Dad, and Mum came back with the cocoa and sat listening and she didn't say anything, but the way her face was set you could see she wasn't too pleased. And then our Dad said that now the thing to do would be to ask them both over to tea one of these days.

'No, I'd rather you didn't,' Mum said, her face tight. Our Dad asked her why not, after all if somebody invited you to their house, it was common courtesy to invite them to yours. But Mum said she was under no obligation to invite any of them into her house and she was not having another of them here. Never again. Her voice so bitter it shook me. As if something had been boiling up in her for a long time. So I said I'd already invited them to come over and what was I supposed to do now?

I hadn't really invited them. I mean, the way Michelle had kept me at a distance, and all she'd said about being so busy, I couldn't ask her out yet. But what Mum had said got under my skin. After all she was not the only one living in the ruddy house. There was our Dad and me, since Dave went.

'I don't care who invites who, but I'm not having any of those people in this house again,' Mum said.

'So what am I supposed to tell them, Mum?'

'What you tell your friends is your affair,' she answered, 'only don't bring them here.' She collected the cups and went off to the kitchen.

It was the way she said 'your friends' making it sound as if they were scum and I was just like them. Christ, I hadn't even thought of them as my friends. Maybe she was upset because I'd gone to see the Spencers, after what she'd said the night before. But that was no reason for carrying on at me like that. And calling them my friends. Friends.

I went up to my room, undressed and got into bed. After a while I could hear them arguing downstairs, our Dad and Mum, their words indistinct. I didn't want to hear, so I put on a jazz record, just loud enough, and got out old Dave's diary. Reading, I wished I could write some stuff like that, about Michelle especially. Friends, Mum had said. What did she know about it? You didn't have to be friends with a bird to, well, have a nibble. That Sandra, for instance. If I'd screwed her, that wouldn't have made her my friend. I didn't even really like the bitch. And calling me Jackie boy. If I ever caught up with her again I'd ruddy well give her something to laugh about. All seven inches. How the hell could anybody be friends with Michelle when all she did was look down her nose as if I was some kind of bug or something? Okay. But the day I got in between those legs she'd know what kind of bug I was. Friends hell. Perhaps Mum was sore because I said how the Spencers lived, their house and furniture and stuff like that. Well, that's how it was, so what was I supposed to say? That they lived in some ruddy cave like savages? Aw, to hell with it.

I heard them come upstairs, then close their door. Best thing to do was hunt around for a little flat of my own, then I could invite whoever I liked into it. Even Spades if I wanted to and nobody could tell me what to do. Just suppose Michelle softened up and I could make it with her, where the heck could I take her? Couldn't try anything with a bird like that in back of the flicks. Don't suppose she'd even let me hold her hand in their fancy house. Couldn't bring her here, even if Mum wasn't carrying on like she was. Best to have a place of my own, like Ruth's friend, Naomi, had up West. Suit myself what I did, then. Michelle. Suppose if she was a white bird, living in a house like that, the fellows would be hanging around all over the place. Don't suppose she gave a damn about fellows, anyway.

I got up and fetched a piece of paper and a biro. Maybe if I thought hard about it, I could write stuff like Dave did. After all, we were the same, so if he could do it, why the hell couldn't I? I sat on the bed, thinking hard about all kinds of things, birds and trees and flowers, things like that, but mostly about Michelle. And words came into my head, but hell, you couldn't write:

> I want to be with you.
> To take you in my arms and feel
> The sweet excitement in the touch of you.
> Like a wild moth, fluttering.

Just for fun I wrote it down as I thought of it. Funny the way things come into your head when you think hard about them. I read it over and over. Hell, you couldn't say that to a bird, especially one like Michelle, not if you didn't want to get your head knocked off your ruddy neck. Should change that bit, 'like a wild moth, fluttering'. Why the heck did I think of that? Suppose she were here right now. Michelle. In this room. Listening to some records. Would be fun to show her what I'd written. Only afterwards. And watch her face, reading it. Afterwards.

I tore it up. Didn't make any sense. Didn't even begin to express the things that were inside of me. I began reading Dave's stuff again, but she was behind every page, waiting for me. I began to wonder at myself, carrying on that way over a Spade. Normally I didn't spend much time thinking of birds, I mean, not any one of them specially. Think of them for a minute or so, if you've a date and you think there's the chance of something. Then afterwards you forget it. Sometimes even sooner than that. For instance you're walking along, down the High Street or even up West, Bond Street or Regent Street or somewhere like that, and just ahead of you is a bird with nice legs and a nice jiggly behind, a real sweet-looking piece. And you think to yourself how it would be to get into that. And just then you notice something in a window, a tie or shirt or a nice pair of slacks, tapered and with no turn-ups. Continental style. And right away you forget all about the piece. I mean, your mind starts figuring about whether you can afford a pair like that and if it will go with your sports jacket and shoes. And long after you've gone past the window you're still thinking about the stuff displayed in it. But this Michelle, thinking about her so much night and day. I must be going soft in the head.

13

ONE DAY DURING the week I saw a little piece in the *Evening Standard* about the police appealing to anyone who lived in the vicinity of Hillingdon Terrace and heard or saw anything which might help them in their investigations into the murder of the West Indian Carlton Thomas, to come forward. The piece mentioned the date in August and the time of night when the murder was supposed to have taken place. It was a dead give away that they hadn't a clue so there was nothing for me to worry about. After all, I didn't kill the Spade and Dave was dead and gone, so that's that. Wonder what Baldy must be doing, him and his shadow and all that stuff he was trying on.

Two evenings later I was watching the news on TV with Mum and our Dad, and before you know what's happening this announcer is talking about the murder and the police appealing to anyone who was in or near Hillingdon Terrace on that evening to get in touch with them. And while he's talking they show this photograph of the Spade, Carlton Thomas. Funny, looking at him, he seemed to be looking straight at me, but smiling and friendly. Perhaps it was taken a long time ago, the photograph, but he looked young, even younger than me. But somebody once said you can never tell about Spades, I mean, about their age. Twenty-four he was, but with a face like eighteen or so. Good-looking, like that fellow Ron, but bigger and with a round face. Made me nervous watching him. All this time I'd not felt nervous or anything, but now, watching that face I felt nervous and shaky inside. After all, Dave had killed him, not me. But if they found out I'd be just as responsible. But the thing was, all the time I didn't really know him, hadn't really seen him, so it didn't really bother me. But now, sitting there, and him smiling at me . . .

After the news our Dad said, 'They never give up.' Meaning the police.

For days after I could see that face in my head. I'd be doing something at the bench, or eating, or walking along, and thinking of Michelle, seeing her face in my mind, then her face would get mixed up with this other face. Or I'd be lying on my bed, reading or just thinking, and this face would come into my mind, smiling. But after a while I stopped thinking about it.

I didn't even try to telephone Michelle all that week. I wanted to but she'd said she'd be busy, so I didn't. The next Tuesday I rang her and she said sorry but she had a lot of work to do and I said I'd ring again at the end of the week and she said okay. Sounded as if she couldn't even spare the time to talk on the phone, and all that Mr Bennett stuff same as always. Why the hell did I bother with her anyway? Right then I promised myself I'd not phone her again. If she wanted to see me she'd ruddy well have to call me.

The following night Ruth rang me soon after I got home from work. She always sounds happy, her voice warm as if the most important thing for her in the world is talking to me. And always kidding. Said she needed to borrow a couple of strong willing arms to help her move her stuff over to Naomi's and did I know anyone who'd oblige? So I said sure, and what rate was she paying? Kidding her back. She could borrow somebody's car and if I felt like coming up to help, she'd meet me in town Saturday morning and we'd move her stuff from Willesden. Ron had promised to help her but he'd got this part in a television production so she was left high and dry. The way she spoke of Ron irritated me a little, but I said okay, I'd meet her outside Oxford Street Station at ten o'clock. Would mean getting up early on Saturday morning for a change, but I figured that once wouldn't kill me. I'd help Ruth and ring Michelle later. Or not ring her at all. Why did I have to go begging her for a date, anyway? Lots of other birds in the world.

Ruth was bang on time, I didn't have to wait more than a minute before she drove up in this big old Morris. I got in and she kissed me, her face smiling and happy. She was wearing that big old black sweater and slacks and no make up, but nice. It was hell driving up the Edgware Road, but it didn't bother her, people dashing across in front of the car against the lights. She kept chatting all the way, excited about moving in with Naomi and what they were planning to do at the flat, paint it over and buy new drapes and some plants and have lots of parties, everything in that breathless, laughing voice. And her Mum had treated her to a new divan bed which had already been delivered to the flat, and some new bedding. So she didn't have to bother about moving the old bed.

At the house her stuff was already packed in a big trunk and two suitcases, with a big carton full of books, all loaded on her bed. She'd been up early, packing things away. We were alone, her mother worked at the electricity showrooms. We humped all that stuff down to the car, into the boot and the back seat. Amazing how much there was when you saw it packed inside the car.

When we'd taken down all the heavy stuff Ruth said how about some coffee, and went into the kitchen to make it while I collected the little things left in her room, some photographs in little silver frames, and coloured shells, all shapes and sizes. She brought the coffee up to her room and we sat on her bed, drinking and talking. Then she had a cigarette and lay back, blowing smoke at me, her hair every which way over her face. I leaned over and kissed her, and now it was different from all other times with other birds, even Sandra. Long and exciting, with her arms going up around my neck, and the mystery of what the touch of another person can do to you down inside, the need urgent and compelling. And I'm a bit scared remembering that time with Sandra and not wanting Ruth to know it's the first time, really, for me. I mean going the whole hog. But helpless because everything is happening and I want to say something to Ruth but it's too much, and hearing sounds but far away. And feeling terribly strong and hearing her cry out then floating away for miles and coming back slowly, all my bones and muscles soft like water.

'You're dripping,' Ruth said. I opened my eyes and the

perspiration is pouring off my face on to her. We're naked, though I can't remember either of us undressing. Her body, damp against mine, breasts full and flushed, the rest of her amazingly white except for the thick black hair.

'Who is Michelle?'

I don't know what the heck she's talking about so I ask her what she means.

'I mean, who is Michelle?'

'You said that before. I don't get it.' I couldn't figure what she was driving at.

'Just now you called me Michelle, so I'm asking you who she is.'

That shook me. I must be going daft or something. I couldn't remember saying anything, least of all calling her that. Christ. I must be haunted.

'Just somebody I know.'

'Your girl?'

'I don't have a girl.'

'Don't lie to me about it, Jack.'

'I'm not lying. I don't have a girl.'

'Then why . . .' She suddenly turned her face away, the blush spreading up from her neck. I noticed the narrow crooked scar near her navel and gently touched it.

'What's this?'

'I had an appendix operation last year.' Still with her face looking away.

'Come on, turn around.'

Then those eyes on me, big, sad and accusing through the strands of hair.

'Why lie to me, Jack. If you have a girl why can't you just say so?'

'I told you, I don't have a girl. What are you on about?'

'This Michelle.'

'Look, I told you.'

'Are you in love with her?'

'What the heck are you on about?'

'Your friend, Michelle.'

First Mum, then her. Friend. What kind of crazy talk was that? I felt like laughing. In love with her? Hell, they should be there and hear us. Mr Bennett. Miss Spencer. In love? Everybody must be plumb crazy.

'Well, are you?'

To put an end to the ruddy talk I told her about Michelle. Well just that Dave, my twin, had been killed in an accident while hitching a ride with this Doctor Spencer, Michelle's brother. And I'd met this girl at the police station and she'd come over faint and my dad had brought her up to our place for a cup of tea, and a week ago her mother invited me over to their place at Leigh-on-Sea. That's all there was to it. And she's watching me while I'm talking, those big eyes searching for the truth behind every word.

'You're a strange person, Jack,' she said, after a while. 'Thinking about her while making love to me. Is she beautiful?'

'Look, she's a Spade.'

'A what?'

'You know, coloured.'

'What was that you said? A Spade? What does that mean?'

'Hell, nothing. Just the same as coloured.'

'And what difference does it make that she's coloured?'

The way she's looking at me as if she's getting ready to be angry. Like our Dad.

'What do you mean what difference does it make?'

'I mean about her being beautiful . . . Is she?'

'Well, yes, I suppose she is.'

'What's she like. Tall, thin, what?'

So the questions began until I'd told her all I could, about Michelle and her mother, where they lived, everything.

'Ever kissed her?'

'Are you daft or something? I hardly know her. Just met her those few times.'

She laughed, a funny ironic sound, and I remembered about her.

'Look, I'm sorry.'

'Why didn't you try? Because she's coloured? Some of them

are very nice.' She said it so simply, as if she knew all about it.

Then I remembered what she'd said about Ron, that he'd promised to help her move, and I wondered if he'd have been beside her now, instead of me. If she would, with him, all the way.

'What about you and Ron?' I asked, even before meaning to.

'Well, what about Ron and me?' she repeated.

'I mean, would you let him kiss you?' I couldn't ask the other thing.

'Why not, if he wanted to.'

'And suppose he wanted . . .'

'Don't bother to say it.' She interrupted. 'Ron goes with Hilary, so don't waste your time asking silly questions.' She rolled away, on to her feet, and began picking up her clothing, dressing quickly with her back towards me. Then she tossed mine on to the bed and I got up and dressed. Suddenly she was as distant as Michelle. We carried the cups to the kitchen and washed them, then took the pictures and shells to the car, locking the house. We didn't say much on the way to Kensington.

Naomi was in and helped us unload the stuff and they asked me to stay to lunch. When Ruth's room was straight with everything in place we sat around playing records and talking.

After two o'clock Naomi went out to meet some friends and I wanted to push off too, to get to a phone and call Michelle, but I also wanted to talk to Ruth, to see how it was with her and me. While Naomi was there we were talking about everything as if nothing had happened, but when she left Ruth would hardly say a word. I tried to kiss her but she wouldn't let me and after a while I got fed up with that and was leaving, but when I reached the door she called me back and said she was sorry and let's kiss and make up. But she didn't want to, again, so we sat around talking and I'm thinking it was much better being with Ruth, talking and I could kiss her if I wanted to and nobody being snooty and difficult.

She said why don't I stay and we could go out later, eat somewhere, then meet Naomi and some of the others at a coffee bar in Earls Court, but I felt a bit mucky, just in those old slacks, sweater and sports coat I'd worn to help her move. So she said that we still had the car so why didn't I wait till she fixed herself up then we could drive up to Upminster and I could change, but I'd have to buy the gas. That was okay with me. It was fun with her. The only thing was I wished I could drive instead of just sitting there while she did the driving.

When we went indoors I could hear Mum upstairs, so I went up to ask her and our Dad to come down and meet Ruth. Mum was putting away the clean laundry, sheets and towels and things in the big cupboard on the landing. I asked her if she'd come and meet a friend of mine, and you should have seen the way her face immediately changed, got tight and hard like something suddenly dried up. She asked who it was. Right away I guessed who she thought I'd brought home, and I had half a mind to say nothing more but just go down and hike Ruth out of the house. Anyway I said it was a friend of mine from Kensington, a girl, and you could see her face easing up, the tension going, leaving her mouth and eyes soft again. Heck, she must hate Spades worse than Dave and me ever did. Come to think of it we didn't hate them. At least I didn't. And Dave never looked like that even when we were going after them. With us it was a kind of game.

She came down and met Ruth and said our Dad was over at the allotment. You could see that she and Ruth clicked, right away. She said how about a cup of tea and Ruth said, fine, but she must let her help, and the two of them go off into the kitchen chatting away like old friends. I went up to wash and change, hearing their laughter coming up now and then, and thinking that I ought to give Michelle a buzz but Mum would be sure to hear me on the phone and it would spoil everything. Better wait until we were up town somewhere. Just suppose she said she was free and could I come over? I'd just have to say I couldn't make it as I was with some friends. Be a bit of a change from always having her say 'No, I'm busy.' Funny how every time I thought about her these days that vague photograph of that fellow Thomas kept popping into my mind. Didn't bother me much, though.

After I'd cleaned up I went down to the kitchen and sat listening to Ruth and Mum while they got the tea ready. Ruth was talking a blue streak about sharing the flat with Naomi and Mum asked didn't her mother mind about Ruth going off and leaving her on her own, and Ruth said not really, that she was the one who used to be left alone, her mother had all these friends and was always busy doing something or other. And Mum said what about her Dad, and Ruth said he'd walked out on them years ago when she was at grammar school and they never heard from him or knew where he was. He never wrote or anything and it was just as well, because he and her Mum had always been quarrelling and fighting.

To see Ruth in the kitchen you would have thought she lived there. She was wearing that Scots plaid dress she'd worn at the party, with her hair in a pony tail and bright red lipstick and smiling all the time. You could see that Mum liked her. Just when the tea was ready our Dad came in through the kitchen door and didn't want to shake hands with Ruth because he said his were mucky from digging in the allotment, so Ruth kisses him and says okay, you weren't digging with your face and you could see that tickled our Dad. And he washed his hands there at the sink and we sat down to tea, Mum telling our Dad he had lipstick on his face and he said what a pity it wasn't a working day, he'd give the fellows on the site something to think about.

After tea we were chatting in the sitting-room when the doorbell rang and there was Baldy, with his shadow close behind. Our Dad invited them in and they sat down. Baldy said they'd brought back the photograph and thanks for the loan of it. He put it down, face up, on the coffee-table and I could see Ruth looking at it, her eyes big and wondering. Our Dad said was there anything else, and Baldy said that the enquiries into the death of the fellow Carlton Thomas were still going on and he expected the police at Leman Street would come up with something soon. He didn't say anything about Dave's knife and our Dad didn't ask him. All I wanted was that Baldy and his pal would hurry up and go. I wasn't upset or anything, just bored with them coming around shooting the same stuff all the time. Now and then I could see him looking at Ruth trying to figure out who she was, but nobody introduced her to them. After a while they left and Ruth said we'd better be going as she'd promised to return the car before eight o'clock.

'They were policemen, weren't they?' Ruth asked while we were on our way. I said yes.

'They spoke about someone named Thomas. Wasn't that the name of the West Indian who was murdered somewhere in the East End?' She'd seen his photograph on television newsreel.

Then she asked about the photograph, but I was getting fed up with all these questions and told her our Dad had let them borrow the photograph and I didn't know why they wanted it, they didn't confide in me. She took the hint, though you could see she was itching to ask more questions.

We left the car at her friend's, then caught a tube to Earls Court and went to the coffee-bar to meet Naomi and the others. Ruth sat with me, holding hands as if she were my girl. I wanted to phone Michelle but didn't know where to find a phone. The others turned up, Ron and the blonde Hilary and every now and then I found myself watching them, wondering if she was in love with him, and if they made love. I felt sure they must do, the way she was all over him. He was okay when you got to know him; he knew how to take a joke and was not snooty or anything. I figured he must be different from those others, the ones who worked on the buses and the Underground. The way he spoke and everything. After all, I supposed that was natural because he was born over here.

I told Ruth I'd have to watch the time and she said don't be silly, I could stay at the flat. She could fix me up a bed on the sofa if I liked. Laughing when she said this, so I got the message. I said okay but I'd better ring home and say I'd be staying, so Mum would know where I was and not to expect me. I felt funny inside, telling her that while remembering that Mum would probably be asleep by then and not give a damn about where I was. Ruth said there was a phone box around the corner and why didn't I ring from there? Instead of calling home I rang Michelle. She answered and I apologized for ringing so late but said I'd been busy all day helping a friend to move. I said I was sorry I didn't call earlier and tried to make a date with her for during the week but she said she didn't think it was possible, then suddenly seemed to change her mind and said she had a late demonstration lecture on Monday and if I liked we could meet in town for a snack afterwards. We agreed to meet near the ticket office at Charing Cross tube station. We talked some more. She seemed really pleased that I rang. Funny thing, she didn't say Mr Bennett or Jack, but her voice had lots of laughter in it. After talking with her I didn't feel like staying up town at Ruth's, and on the way back to the coffee bar my mind was working overtime figuring out some excuse she'd swallow. Amazing how when you're in a room with everybody smoking and talking you never notice it, then you come outside and when you go back the place stinks of stale smoke and sweat and the perfume the birds are wearing.

As soon as I reached her Ruth began kidding me, asking if Mum said it's okay for little Jackie to be out all night, and right away I ask her if she thinks I'm some ruddy kid or something, that I can do as I please, I'd only telephoned to let them know where I was. Well, having said that I couldn't say I wasn't staying. We all left the coffee shop and went to a Wimpy bar near the Underground and had hamburgers and coffee and sat around talking till some said they had to be off and the rest of us walked up the road, Ruth, Hilary, Naomi, Ron and me. You know, after a while you forget that Ron is a Spade, listening to him talk and the way he behaves, so natural, like everybody else. But always sort of gentlemanly and well-mannered. I wondered what Michelle would think of him. We left Ron and Hilary at the top of Old Brompton Road and went on to South Ken. Indoors the two girls made a big production about fixing up the sofa for me to sleep on in the little sitting-room, fetching sheets and blankets and pillows. Then Naomi comes and kisses me on the cheek and says good night and sleep tight, then goes off to her room. And Ruth says good night too, and that she'll give me a shout when the bathroom is free. Hell, I didn't have a toothbrush or anything. Anyway, when she calls I have a wash in the bathroom and use the toilet then go back to my bed on the sofa, undressed to my vest and shorts, and sit there wondering what's up with Ruth. I mean, she didn't say I could go to her room. I sat there for nearly half an hour, listening to the strange little sounds which houses seem to make late at night when everything's quiet, as if they're relaxing and stretching themselves after the daily tensions from the comings and goings of people. Every time I heard a little creak I imagined it was Ruth coming to call me, but it's only the house making night noises, and after a while I realize I'm sitting on the edge of the sofa, tense and half frozen. So I get into bed and lie there listening. I must have fallen asleep, and the next thing I know is Ruth squeezing in beside me. I felt silly dozing off like that.

'I was waiting for you to give me a call,' I told her.

'Don't be silly. I couldn't have you in the room. It's right next to Naomi's.'

'So what?' All this in whispers.

'I don't believe in advertising everything I do. Do you always dress up when you go to bed?' I saw her point. The thing she was wearing hardly reached anywhere. No problem for me to slip out of mine.

'Don't forget this time,' she said.

'What?'

'The name's Ruth, remember.'

When I awoke next morning I was alone and the room was bright from the sunshine pouring in through a large window opposite my bed. I lay there thinking about Ruth and the night before and who they were, the other fellows before me. Not worrying about it but just wondering. Then I heard singing, and Naomi came out of her room calling wakey wakey.

We had breakfast, but it was funny the way they messed around in the tiny kitchen, making Nescafé and fried eggs on toast. They couldn't cook worth a damn, neither of them, but made so much fuss you'd think nothing but the fatted calf was being given the works. If our Mum could see what they did to those eggs she'd have a fit. Either Dad or me could cook spots off both of them any day. And yet, with talking and laughing, you ate up all the stuff without even noticing the taste. I left them around ten o'clock so as not to be late, because Mum gets a bit funny about Sunday dinner. Ever since Dave and me began working. Said it's the only day when the family was to-gether for the midday meal, as our Dad sometimes works Saturday.

When I got home I said we'd been to a party and as it was late I'd had a kip down on a sofa at a friend's house. Mum and our Dad didn't seem to mind. Mum chatted to me about Ruth, said she seemed to be a nice, steady girl. Dad said if he were me he'd be careful where he went and what he did, because he had a feeling those detectives were on to something and I should watch my step. I said okay but I wasn't worried. Old Baldy and his friends didn't fool me. If they really knew something which connected me with the Thomas affair they would have been on my neck long ago. They weren't paid to play cat and mouse with people. Besides, from that piece in the newspaper and what they said in the TV newsreel it was plain enough they hadn't a clue about what had happened. Anyway I told our Dad I'd be careful.

14

SUNDAY AFTERNOON I slept like a top. Figured it must have been because of what had happened with Ruth. Come to think of it, everything had happened in such a way I hadn't been worried or scared like I was that time with Sandra. It just happened. I wondered if Ruth realized that it had been the first time for me. Funny thing, some of those birds in the canteen where I worked, I was always cracking jokes with them and to hear the things they said I'm sure they thought I was an old hand at that stuff. But all the time I was thinking of what some of the older fellows said when they were nattering to each other in the workshop, about how some of those birds you saw swinging their tails about were really walking death traps. Stick your pecker into them and the next thing you knew you'd caught a dose of something or other. Dave and I used to talk about it a lot, but he said those old fellows were only spitting into the wind because they were too old to make it with those young birds. Sour grapes, he said, and he didn't give a damn but would lay everyone he could and take his chance. We'd talk about it and I'd agree with him, but inside I was dead scared. I suppose that's why I couldn't make it with Sandra. Kept remembering what those fellows said. But with Ruth I'd not even thought of it. Funny, that.

Sunday night I stayed in and watched television with Mum and our Dad. Ruth's visit must have done our Mum a good turn. She was easier with me, and when we'd done the washing up after dinner it had been nearly like old times when Dave was there, Mum talking, mostly about Ruth. I guess she figured that now I wouldn't be bothering with the Spencers. While the play was on I sat there watching, but really thinking about Michelle, impatient for the hours to pass quickly to the time when I was meeting her. After the play we're having this cup of cocoa and our Dad starts in again about Baldy and how the police never leave a case until they land somebody in the clink, and he's sure Baldy is on to something because he's so smug, just waiting for the moment to pounce. Listening to our Dad carrying on about it I realize he's dead scared.

Mum said, 'Let's talk about something else, Dad. The surest way to make something happen is to keep on saying it might happen. That's what the police are after. They want us to be so frightened that we'd do something silly to give ourselves away. Well, Dave is dead and none of us is mixed up in anything, so there's nothing for us to worry about. By the way, those horrible little black ants have somehow got into the scullery again. Don't know where they've come from. Will you have a look tomorrow?' And the conversation got around to the best way of getting rid of ants.

I felt sorry for our Dad worrying his head off and wondered

why it was the whole thing didn't bother me; just as if it had happened to somebody else. I just knew they couldn't touch me, in spite of Baldy dropping in and putting on the big act.

15

AFTER WORK ON Monday I rushed home to wash and change, telling Mum I wasn't staying to eat, that I had a date and would get something in town. I didn't explain. I suppose she thought I was meeting Ruth.

Rush hour traffic and changing trains made me late, but she was waiting. Wearing a plain beige linen dress under a tan-coloured coat and a gay many-coloured silk scarf loosely knotted around her neck. Her black, high-heeled sandals were no more than a few narrow thongs fixed to the soles. A little taller than most of the women scurrying about, she stood near the ticket office, calm, aloof, hugging some heavy-looking notebooks, caught sight of me and gave me a nice smile as I approached. We said hello, and I said I was sorry I'd kept her waiting, and how was she? Laughing, she said she was starving. I didn't know where we could go. Apart from a few coffee bars and some jazz clubs in Soho I didn't know much about the West End. Not about restaurants and places like that. Especially where to take a girl for a real meal. I told her I didn't know much about where to eat around there, and she said let's go to a place where she and her parents and brother sometimes went, a place called the Angus Steakhouse just off Leicester Square, but one thing I must understand, we were going Dutch. I asked her what was that, and she said we'd go halves on the bill. She didn't ask me. She told me. I didn't argue although I wasn't pleased with that.

We cut through Villiers Street and across the Strand to Charing Cross Road, me feeling the eyes of the world and his wife on me, and wishing that for the time being I could change my fair skin and blond hair to something dark. She walked along with that cool, easy stride, telling me about the lecture, seeming not to give a damn for the way people were looking at us. I didn't understand half of what she said, but it didn't matter. Near to that statue of Edith Cavell there was a bit of a crowd so I took her arm, holding it just above the elbow, feeling it soft but firm in my hand. After we passed the crowd I let go, remembering that she didn't like holding hands.

Somebody behind us gave a wolf whistle and she smiled, saying, 'He must be a tourist. Englishmen haven't yet learned the art!'

'Don't you mind?' I asked.

'Of course not. Last year Mummy and I were in Rome and the men tried to touch us all the time. Over there it's a kind of compliment, actually. Otherwise it means you're not worth noticing.'

Full of surprises, this one. Talking about foreign parts as if it was High Street Upminster, or Leigh or Southend. Crikey! Our Mum would just about do her nut if somebody whistled at her. Funny thing, after a while, the way some of the men looked at her, I had the feeling they wouldn't mind being me. I felt a lot easier.

In the restaurant there weren't many people and one waiter came up to us, smiling and saying how are you Miss Spencer, glad to see you again, and showed us to a table, handing us these menus like a Christmas calendar. I waited till she chose then I asked for the same. Avocado pears and then thin steaks with pepper. I'd never in my life been in a posh place like that, with so many waiters buzzing around you. Then they brought another menu for wine and I said to her she should choose something. Not the same waiter, another one with a black jacket instead of white. She was completely at ease as if she did this sort of thing every day. I couldn't figure it out. The way I'd heard it, Spades couldn't come into places like this, they wouldn't let them in.

'They seem to know you here,' I said. All the furniture in the place was dark and heavy-looking, and the carpet thick so you didn't hear the waiters coming till they were breathing down

114

your neck saying something you couldn't understand. And all those knives and forks and spoons in front of me, I hadn't a clue which to use first but decided to wait and see what she would do.

'We came here a lot when Daddy was alive,' she replied, 'Mummy and I sometimes lunched here with him when he came up here to demonstrate at the hospital at the corner.'

I didn't get it, but she spoke as if I knew what she was talking about.

'How do you mean demonstrate? What hospital?'

'The Royal Dental. Just a few doors away from here. The students would watch while he did something to a patient's teeth, explaining to them while he did it.'

'Is that what he was? A dentist?'

'Yes. He had a practice at Hampstead and came here twice a week.'

'Hampstead? That's a long way from Leigh. Did he have to make the trip both ways each day?'

I could never get over the way she laughed, that sweet, gurgling, fruity sound, the grey eyes darkening in the restaurant's gloom, the corners of her mouth slanted upward.

'No. At that time we lived in Hampstead, next to his surgery. After Daddy died we found the place at Leigh and moved.'

'You were lucky to find such a nice house.'

'Lucky? You should have seen it when we first bought it. Everything cluttered with weeds and rubbish like a dump, and the house nearly falling down. Hadn't been lived in for years. But we liked the site and the view across the estuary. We literally had to rebuild the whole house to get rid of the damp.'

We chatted about all kinds of things until they brought the avocado. I'd never had it before, and the thick, pale green meat tasted a little like soup, but I swallowed it down, encouraged by the way Michelle seemed to enjoy it. The last few spoonfuls were not bad. Probably have to acquire a taste for it. While we were eating the avocado the waiters brought a brazier and set it up near our table, and showed us the steaks for the second course, raw, then proceeded to cook them over the brazier, grinding pepper grains over the meat while it cooked. Thin steaks, which they served piping hot with sliced tomatoes and pineapple, nearly melted away in your mouth, they were so tender.

The waiter who knew Michelle came to ask if everything was satisfactory, leaning over her, and she smiling up at him. Funny how I suddenly felt like belting him one. Then I got to thinking, Hell, I must be jealous. But it wasn't that, really, just that it seemed strange him leaning so close to her like that. Few times our Dad and Mum had taken Dave and me out to lunch on a Saturday in Romford, it hadn't been anything like this. I mean, the waiters couldn't care less about us. They shoved the food in front of you and that's that. If you didn't like it that was just too bad. Anyway, the waiter asked me too if everything was okay and the steak to my taste, calling me sir every few words. I told him it was excellent. Nearly said it was the best I'd ever had but didn't see any point in laying it on too thick. I had the feeling he was being so nice to me on account of Michelle, probably thought I was her boyfriend or something.

Afterwards we walked around a bit, watching the lights and talking. Right then I didn't give a damn what Mum or anybody else might say if they saw me; anyway at night, walking around up West nobody looks at you, so there was nothing to worry about and we had a lot of fun. I wished I could take her arm the way some other couples were. Later we had coffee at a coffee bar in the Strand, then caught the District Line train at Charing Cross. In the brightly-lit compartment with everybody staring at us I could feel all the fun going out of me, the way they looked as if they were stripping us naked. Looking at us with their mouths tight, eyes swinging away when you looked at them, but only after you'd seen the shine of their disgust because we were together. Who the hell cared whether they approved or not, anyway? Michelle took one of her books from me, said 'excuse me' and began to read. Better than just sitting there feeling uncomfortable. I opened one, a big textbook, and began reading the chapter on Zonation of Marine Life. Like trying to read Chinese. That stuff about planktonic plants such as diatoms, photosynthetic dinoflagellates and other floating algae are known as phytoplankton – I could never get my tongue around any of those words. And to think that Michelle understood all that. Crikey!

I looked up at some people sitting opposite, their faces tight as if the muscles were long accustomed to unpleasant things, and wondered how many of them could read the book and understand a word of it. She was better looking and brighter than any of them. You could follow the women's eyes and see them taking in her dress and shoes, summing her up, then looking at me. Perhaps the silly buggers thought she was my girl and I'd bought her all that stuff. I laughed out loud, the idea was so funny.

They all looked up suddenly at me. Even Michelle. But she smiled, as if she could read my mind, while the others looked startled, as if they figured I'd gone daft or something.

Just to rub it in I asked her, loudly, 'What are dinoflagellates?'

'Marine animals with large, whip-like processes. Why do you ask?' Cool as a ruddy ice-maiden, her voice clear but not loud.

'That's what I thought,' I answered, laughing in the faces of those watching us and probably wondering what kind of funny joke we were pulling. And into my head came that thing Dave wrote in his book about the Teds:

> Clad tight, in the resilient armour of their youth
> And bright contempt which threatened as it mocked
> The wavering eyes of all who censured them. . . .

Right now I'd like to mock and threaten all their ruddy wavering eyes. Who the hell did they think they were? I wondered what they'd say if they could see where she lived?

We changed at Barking for her train to Leigh. She didn't want me to wait, because I could have gone through to Upminster on the same District train, but I said I wanted to. We didn't say much while we were waiting, and when her train came she didn't even give me time to try for a kiss but said good night and she'd enjoyed the evening. I said I'd phone soon

117

and she smiled without saying yes. Watching the train take her away I had the feeling that something had gone sour, you know, everything was going fine then something spoiled it, though I didn't know what. Perhaps it was the way people had been looking at us, making us self-conscious and uncomfortable. Well, that's how I felt and, in spite of the way she'd sat so cool and aloof, I wouldn't have been surprised if she'd felt the same way.

16

AT BREAKFAST NEXT morning Mum told me Ruth had telephoned. She said it not only to give me the information, but also to accuse me. You could hear it in her voice.

'I thought you were meeting her in town,' Mum said, then when I didn't comment, she added, 'At least that's the impression I got.'

I'd learned to keep my mouth shut if I didn't wish to get into an argument, and hurried through my breakfast.

'Some people like to go out and search for trouble,' she said, 'not only for themselves, but for others as well.' She was circling around, not wanting to come right out and ask me who it was I met in town, but hinting and hoping I'd bite, but I said nothing and bolted the rest of my breakfast to be on my way. During the lunch break I telephoned Ruth at her office. She hadn't called about anything important, merely to say hello. Then she said she'd heard from Mum I'd a date up town and didn't even wait for my dinner, and who was the lucky girl? I said it wasn't really a date, just some fellows I'd arranged to meet. I said I'd call her soon.

Most of the afternoon on the job my mind kept swinging back to what I'd told Ruth, asking myself why didn't I come right out and say yes I had a date. What was I afraid of? Was it because Michelle was coloured? Why was I getting myself into all this fuss and bother anyway? With Mum and having to lie to Ruth, and the Lord knows what else? Where was it getting me? So far I hadn't got as far as one kiss, not one ruddy solo kiss. Anybody'd think that after meeting and having dinner together, the least that would happen is that you'd get a kiss. At least one. But she'd behaved as if we were ruddy strangers. Why didn't I just call the whole thing off? So I didn't make it with her. Well, never mind, you can't win them all. If I didn't phone that would be the end of it, because I felt sure she wouldn't call me. All afternoon I argued it out with myself and finally promised myself I wouldn't telephone her again. Hell, I didn't have to crawl to anybody just to have a piece. After all, Ruth was okay and she was as nice as anyone else. Furthermore, no matter how she looked and dressed and talked, she was still a Spade. So, we'd had a date, and it had been fun. Well that was that. The rest of that week I didn't telephone anybody.

After dinner each evening I'd go for a stroll, sometimes up the lane to the Southend road, and sit on the grass verge watching the traffic rush past and thinking things out. Watching those cars and imagining who the people were driving them, and what they did, how they lived, making up things in my mind about them. Sometimes a big Rolls swished past, with some little old lady in the back seat and the chauffeur in the front with his peaked cap and his neck stiff looking straight ahead. Like a human machine. She was really doing the driving, the old lady, but by remote control; he was just a piece of equipment for pressing the starter button or brake lever and things like that. And he only had one name, like James, or Williams, or Burton. Stop here, Williams. Take me to Finch's and call back for me in an hour. And he had to touch his cap all the time and never look her straight in the face or argue with her the way he probably gave his old woman hell. And what was the difference between her and his old woman? Money, perhaps, and where you went to school, and the kind of house you lived in. Like that Michelle, talking about Italy as if it was around the corner, and those clothes and ruddy waiters breaking their necks to pull out a chair for her, and going around with her nose in the air as if she didn't give one hire-purchase damn who didn't like her.

Indoors, most of the time I stayed up in my room listening to records and reading Dave's stuff or sometimes trying to write some of my own but it never came out the same way as Dave's, easy and making sense. Sometimes I'd want to stay downstairs and have a natter with Mum and our Dad, but if the television was on Mum didn't want anybody to interrupt with talk, so what's the use?

On the Friday night Ruth turned up just before dinner time. She'd come directly from her office, just felt like getting out of the city for a change, she said. Mum was pleased to see her and we all had dinner together. Heck, I couldn't help noticing how different she was from Michelle, the way she ate and how she was dressed and everything. But she was always laughing and kidding around and lots of fun. You know what I mean. You didn't have to think about what you were going to say or if you were using the correct fork or anything.

After dinner we helped with the washing-up and I said let's go for a walk. There was old Spotty Frock sizing us up as we passed her gate and I suddenly gave Ruth the nudge and whispered 'look at this', then I turned as if I was going up old Spotty Frock's garden path, and you should have seen the way she disappeared from that window. Probably rushed to her front door, thinking we were coming in to pay her a visit or something.

I laughed till I cried and Ruth, half laughing, said I shouldn't have done it, it wasn't funny. Old Mrs Collins was in her front garden as usual, so we stopped to chat with her and I introduced her to Ruth. Then we walked around, through those little lanes and out towards the allotments, talking and joking. And on the way back we took a different route, not hurrying.

Back indoors we sat with Mum and our Dad talking a while, and you could see Mum was fidgeting to switch on the television, so I said to Ruth let's go upstairs and listen to some records. We sat on the bed, and now and then I gave her a kiss, but we didn't try anything, not with Mum and our Dad in the house.

'Last Monday night, was your date with your coloured friend?' Ruth asked me.

'What are you on about? I told you it was with some fellows.'

'Oh, come off it, Jack, I'm not that green. Look, you don't have to lie to me about it. What do you think I'll do, make a scene?'

Looking at me like that, she made me feel ashamed about lying.

'Well, was it?' she persisted.

'Yes.'

'I guessed it was. How did it go?'

'What do you mean, how did it go? We had a meal and walked around a bit. That's all.'

'That's all?'

'Of course. What did you expect?'

'Don't bite my head off. I just don't understand why you have to hide and lie about it. Are you ashamed because she's coloured?'

'No, it's not that. But, well, Mum's not too keen on my seeing her, so I didn't want her to start fussing me.'

'Oh, I see.' Then, after a few minutes of silence, 'What's she like?'

'She's okay.'

'Have you made love to her?'

'Crikey, what are you talking about? It's the first time I've ever been out with her. And anyway, she's not like that.'

'Isn't she?'

'No.'

'Then what does that make me?'

How the hell could I answer that one? She suddenly laughed and said, 'Every woman is like that, with the right man in the right place at the right time. Didn't you know? I'm wondering if I ought to be jealous.'

I said nothing.

'I think I'd like to meet her,' Ruth said.

'What for?'

'Just curious. Why don't you ask her to come up tomorrow

night. At the flat. Ron's celebrating the part he's got in a new TV play. Go on, bring her.'

'Look, I can't just bring her. She's studying for this exam and won't go anywhere. She had a late lecture on Monday. That's the only reason I managed to meet her in town.'

'Well, ask her, anyway. What difference would it make? She can either say yes or no.'

'She'll say no, that's for sure, so there's no point in asking.'

'You quite sure you're not making up excuses because you're ashamed to bring her? What was it you called her? A Spade?'

I'd have liked to belt her one for saying that. The way she was looking at me as if she half expected me to do something like that, but wasn't scared.

'Okay, okay. I'll ask her.'

'Well, go ahead, ring her.'

'You crazy? The phone's in the sitting-room and Mum's in there watching television.'

'Oh, yes. Well, let's walk down to the phone booth.'

'I'll give her a ring when I take you to the station.'

'No, that's too late. Let's go now.'

I didn't really like the way she was trying to boss me about, but I could see she wouldn't be satisfied until I made the call, so we went down the road. She even squeezed into the phone booth with me. Michelle answered, and her voice sounded pleased when she recognized mine. I told her that some friends were having a little party in Kensington and they'd invited me and said I could bring a friend, and would she go with me? Then I held my breath, waiting for the refusal I was certain would follow.

'When is it?' she asked.

'Tomorrow night,' I said.

'Will you come for me?' Just like that. I was sweating, but that was perhaps because it was warm in the phone booth, with two of us in it.

'Sure,' I told her. 'Around seven, seven-thirty.' Ruth began to giggle and I quickly put my hand over the mouthpiece.

'Fine, I'll be ready. Bye, Jack.' And she hung up. Jack, she'd said. JACK. I looked at Ruth and dumbly nodded my head affirmatively. We pushed out of the booth, but suddenly she wasn't laughing anymore.

'Boy, you've got it bad, haven't you?' she said. I'd had enough argument for one day so I kept my mouth shut. We went in and made a cup of tea, and soon after she said she'd better be going and I took her to get the District Line.

As she was getting on the train she said, 'You know something? I'm sorry I made you telephone her.'

17

MICHELLE AND HER mother were sitting on the concrete forecourt of their house when I arrived. As I approached them down the stairs I thought how right they looked, in harmony with all the colours around them, and though I couldn't hear their voices from that distance, by the action of their heads and hands it was evident that they were having a laugh at something or other. They both seemed pleased to see me and Michelle fetched a stool from inside for me to sit with them. Mrs Spencer carried on with the story, about the pottery class which she attended in Southend every Monday night, and funny goings on among some of her classmates. The way she took off their voices it was a real scream. Like this woman she told us about, calling the teacher to see some stuff she'd made.

'I think I'm getting it right, don't you, Mr Schuyler, I mean now that I've got the feel of the wheel, the shape's coming through, don't you think? I was telling my husband about it, and you wouldn't credit it, but he just can't believe that I'm really making a vase, after only two lessons. The thing is, it doesn't matter if you don't make anything, really, it's enough just to feel the thing growing in your hands, soft and silky, and just by squeezing a little you can make anything, any shape you like. Sort of creative, if you see what I mean,' and with her hands and face and voice taking this woman off to a 'T'. I couldn't help thinking, It's funny how she sounded just like somebody you know, like some of those women who come up to the house to see Mum sometimes and they get to nattering about things, what Mum calls 'dishing up the dirt'. Only Mrs Spencer was kidding, like some of those comics on the radio, only better.

When Michelle and I were on the way to the station you should have seen the way people were looking at her. The funny thing was I didn't give a damn. I mean I wasn't uncomfortable or anything. But you should have seen her. Wearing this dark blue silk dress under a coat of the same material and plain black shoes, and the single strand of pearls. I don't know much about those things, but I'd make a rough guess they were real. And the dress so plain and simple but terrific, and you didn't need to guess about all that shape inside.

On the way up to town we chatted about this and that, and I told her what little I knew about some of the people she'd meet at the party. Ron and Hilary, Naomi, Ruth and some of the others. Though I didn't let on about Ruth and me. Just said we were friends, and just to make conversation I said what a nice outfit she was wearing, and she said when she and her mother had been in Rome they'd just gone mad and bought more things than they should. Making it sound as if spending all that money was just fun. All the way the train was mostly crowded, and everyone opposite watching us, some in that sly way, but many of them staring and inside I'm laughing, sorry for all those poor buggers drooling both ends, the women jealous as hell about the way she's dressed and those long, lovely legs crossed like a film star and the men wishing they were me. Well, all except those others, the coloured ones who'd never look at us although you could feel that they saw us, saw everything about us without looking, not that they were mad at us or anything like that. They just kept their faces looking somewhere else. Made me think of what old Jelks, that teacher we used to have at Junior School, used to say about bats not needing to see where they were going because they had this radar thing in their ears which told them where things were so they could fly at high speed without banging into anything, even telephone wires.

We could hear the music from outside and when Naomi opened the door it was like the last time, only more people. Naomi took her off somewhere to leave her coat while I looked around for Ruth. She saw me and pushed through to give me a big kiss and ask where she was, meaning Michelle, probably hoping Michelle was near enough to see it. Don't know why but I didn't like her kissing me like that as if she owned me or something. We squeezed against the wall talking, and soon they came out and I introduced Ruth to Michelle.

The music stopped and some people came and said hello, and Ruth took over to introduce everybody, mostly first names only, and Ron came up to be introduced and started kidding, saying where had she been all his life and fancy England being such a small place and still they'd not met before, if it was Texas he could understand. And she laughing that gurgling laugh. And he asked her to dance. Then afterwards people sat around talking and before you know it there's this argument going on about South Africa and how there'd be a bloody revolution there if the government didn't change its ideas about apartheid. And everybody chipping in the way a few glasses of beer or punch makes everybody an intellectual, till the conversation got around to Britain and somebody said that probably if there were more coloureds in Britain, like millions of them, the same thing would happen here.

Naomi said come on, break it up, and somebody put on a record. I had brought her, and at last I got a dance. She had this way of half closing her eyes, yet you could see them shining with the fun she was having. Funny how she could do things, have a hell of a good time, without getting noisy or acting common, like some birds I'd met.

We had sandwiches and rolls and things. As soon as the music stopped people began talking and before you knew it we were sitting around on the floor, Michelle with her legs folded under her. I tried it but it made my legs stiff. This fellow Vic something or other began again on that business about South Africa, saying that all the trouble was because of the strange Boer mentality which could not conceive that the blacks were human beings and therefore would never accept them as equals. He said that if the first settlers in South Africa had been anyone else the history of that country would be vastly different. Ron said that was funny because the people who colonized the Rhodesias, the Southern United States and some other places he could mention were not Boers and their attitude to the blacks differed only slightly in degree. And again the talk came back to Britain and the coloureds here.

One girl said, 'At any rate any coloured person in Britain can find a job, and the pay is the same for everybody,' her voice fading away as if she wasn't quite sure that she knew that what she said was what she wanted to say.

'How many coloured persons do you know?' Ron asked her.

'Well, some,' she replied. 'There are two girls from Jamaica in our office, and everybody likes them.'

'And now Ron makes three,' he kidded her. He never spoke loudly or became excited, didn't even seem to be really serious, but there was something about him that made you listen to what he said, perhaps because his voice was so deep and clear and the words came slow and carefully.

'In any case,' he went on, 'you probably know three more than most people in Britain. After all, among a population of more than fifty million, there are just about half a million coloured, including Asians, Africans, West Indians and others. But that business about anyone being able to find a job is, to say the least, mere propaganda.'

'Does that include yourself, Ron?' somebody asked him.

'Whenever I say anything about coloured people, do me a favour and include me in,' he replied in that slow way of his, and smiling.

'But you're okay, you're at RADA and you do things, always getting good parts on radio and TV,' someone said.

'That's just the trouble,' Ron replied. 'The very way you said that accuses me, as if I should consider myself different from other coloured people, because of RADA.'

Vic joined in, waving a sausage-roll like an extra finger, with, 'Mary's got a point there, about equal pay for the job. After all, that's what most of the fuss is about, everybody not getting the same treatment. Doesn't matter if the bloke is an actor or some bus conductor somewhere, or even a road-sweeper, what he wants is equality with other actors or conductors or road-sweepers.'

'You think so?' from Ron.

'Hell, it's not what I think, it's what you see every day in the newspapers and on TV and everywhere.'

'I'm not interested in equality,' Ron said, then he went on, his voice serious, to talk about not liking even the sound of the word equality, because it had no real meaning for him, or for any other coloured person. Whenever anybody used the word it always indicated that coloured people needed something, some law or act of charity or faith that they could stand on to give them the same social or cultural stature as white people. He said that in his opinion the idea of equality started in America and was part of the great American myth, because all the time the coloured Americans were talking about equality, it kept their attention on the white American, on what he was, on what he had, on what he did. He became their goal, the focus of their hopes, ambitions and thinking. They wanted what he had, nothing more, nothing less. But all the time what was the white American doing? He was not standing still waiting for the coloureds to catch up. He could always think up new ways and means of keeping just ahead of them. So whatever gains the black American made, it didn't really improve his position because it didn't make him equal.

He stopped talking for a while and it was funny how quiet it got as if nobody could think up an argument for him. Perhaps because he'd got so ruddy serious, not smiling or kidding as usual.

Then he started again. 'The word I'm really interested in is freedom. That's a word that nobody can fool with, because it has the same meaning for everyone, black, white and every which who. Any of you ever notice that while most coloured people talk about equality, white people talk about being free, white and twenty-one? But the word free comes first, even before the whiteness. Listening to you tonight I realize that this conversation might well never have happened if Michelle and me weren't here. You'd most likely have been talking about something else. And the hell of it is that the fault is not yours. It's ours. We remind you of our inequality. And you remind me of your freedom. Your freedom to come and go, to fail or succeed, to do or not to do, to be decent or to be lousy without having to carry the whole weight of your race on your back.'

The way Hilary was watching him as if she could eat him up there and then, her hand on his sleeve, owning him and wanting everybody to know it. Couldn't see Michelle holding me like that, and looking.

'I want to be so free that, like you, I don't ever have to give a thought to being equal. I want to work and live with you, agreeing or disagreeing, liking or not liking, without having to qualify any of it by your whiteness or my blackness. I want to be like, like, well, the wind, big as big, free as free, reaching out to infinity without ever needing to measure myself against mere people.'

He suddenly laughed, reaching to pull Hilary's hair. 'You know something? The day we coloured really dig the freedom thing, the fireworks will start. Man, we'll take off right into orbit, the world will be so small for us.' Everybody was laughing, but not because they thought it funny, more as if they didn't know what else to do.

'What do you think, Michelle?' someone asked her. They were all calling her Michelle. With all the talking she'd said nothing, but had changed her position to allow more room for the dancers, and stood now over against the wall near Ron.

'I'd rather just listen,' she said.

'Oh, come on, tell us.'

'Plead the Fifth Amendment,' Ron joked.

I didn't get what he meant, but she smiled at him, then said,

'Actually I think all this talk is a waste of time, because it means no more than that, just talk. It rather amuses me to hear the way some of you condemn South Africa and the United States about their racial policies, because there's no way of knowing what your own behaviour would be if you lived there.' She paused, smiled crookedly at some stirring memory. 'One of my father's friends, a dentist from Dorking, emigrated to South Africa with his family, to set up a practice. Since going there he wrote only one letter to us, and in it he said that from what he'd seen of the way Africans lived, he didn't blame the South African Government for introducing apartheid. Some of you talk and talk, but I don't know how you would behave if you were in a place where every advantage and comfort was available to you because of your white skin, and you were encouraged to believe that you could continue to enjoy those advantages only if the black Africans were kept firmly in an inferior position.'

She turned to smile at Ron, a little smile as if they shared some special little secret, then her face became serious again. I felt proud, listening to her, but suddenly a bit scared. I wished Ron wasn't there.

'I was born here and I understand what Ron means about not belonging. But telling you about it doesn't mean anything, because I don't suppose you can understand. You're sympathetic, and you'd really like to understand what we're talking about, but it's not possible unless you were able to change skins with us.

'I shouldn't be talking like this. My mother says I'm still too emotional about it. But, you see, I know that when you look at me you see that I'm coloured, and immediately you expect me to think and feel and behave in some special way which you imagine to be natural for coloured people. What you don't see is that I'm English or British or whatever you like to call it. Both my parents were born here in London, and so was I. I don't know any more about what life is like in the West Indies than you do. When I hear a West Indian speak the first thing I notice is the unfamiliar accent, and I find myself wondering how it would be to live away from London, in those strange islands, among those strange people.

'It's very frustrating. When I've been in Scandinavia, or Italy, or Germany I've enjoyed it tremendously, but after a while I've longed to get back home. Here. In London. Just as any of you would do. And yet I know you expect me to be different from you. Isn't that why you asked me to tell you what I think?'

She raised her shoulder in a gentle shrug as if she'd said all she wanted to say, and was a bit sorry she'd bothered. Ron was smiling at her as if she was something special he'd found and wanted to get his hands on. I didn't give a tuppenny damn about all that talk, all I wanted was that he didn't get any ideas about her. As far as I was concerned, to hell with all that talk about coloured people. None of them meant a damn thing to me. Except her. Looking at her now, I felt my insides tighten up, with the loveliness of her, brighter, nicer than any of the other girls in the room. Perhaps Ruth was right. Perhaps I was in love with her.

They changed the record for a slow one, Sinatra singing You and the Night and the Music, and I took her arm to dance with her before anyone else asked her. We were dancing and somebody turned the lights low and I put my face against hers and she didn't draw it away.

I don't think I danced once with Ruth, and it was only when it was time for me to go that I thought about her, then I felt a bit uncomfortable, as if I'd somehow let her down. She was dancing with a fellow and I waited till they were finished and told her I'd have to leave to see Michelle home. Funny, but you can never tell about girls. She didn't act angry or anything, just said okay and would I give her a ring soon, and I said sure.

On the way to the station Michelle and I argued about me seeing her home, because of how I'd get back to Upminster from Leigh, and she wouldn't let me go all the way to Leigh. Said the best thing was for her to ring the private car hire number in Southend to have a car meet her train and take her to Leigh, and she would be okay. We could ride home together on the District Line to Barking.

Then she said, 'You know, Jack, you don't have to worry about me. I travelled around a lot with my parents when Daddy was alive. We spent nearly six weeks visiting my aunt in Chicago three years ago, and then eight days in Washington where Daddy had to attend a Congress, and I still think England is the only place where I always feel safe. You know what I sometimes used to do when we lived in Hampstead? Go for long walks by myself on misty, foggy nights. Just for fun, then go home and have a nice hot bath and a Martini. Just because even in the fog and rain and dark there's no feeling of menace. Do you know what I'm talking about? In spite of all the things that bother me because of people's attitude to the colour of my skin, in spite of the anger which often comes welling up inside me, I always feel safe. Oh, perhaps what I'm saying makes very little sense to you. I don't suppose you've ever been to the States. It's frightening at nights.' Talking softly aloud to herself as if remembering.

We were standing close together on the platform at South Ken, and without even planning it, I held her arm and turned her to me and kissed her. It was so wonderful I felt like crying. We didn't say much on the way to Barking. I felt excited but in a different way from what I'd always been expecting or planning. I wanted to stay close to her, to be with her, and yet it wasn't just to make it with her. I mean, I wasn't figuring how to sleep with her or anything. At Barking, while waiting for the South-end train I didn't try to kiss her again, for although we were standing close together, her head was turned away from me, as if she was occupied with thoughts in which I couldn't share. When her train came in she seemed to rouse herself, said, 'Bye, Jack,' and climbed aboard.

18

I HARDLY SLEPT that night, but lay thinking, trying to sort myself out. I'd never felt this way about a girl before. A date now and then and a kiss or a little playing around, but nothing to worry about. The birds expected you to try for a kiss, and sometimes back of the flicks you'd try to get your hand up there and they'd giggle and perhaps tell you off, but if you didn't try something they'd tell their friends you were slow or daft. Even with Ruth it was wonderful, both times, but I didn't feel this way about her. I mean, we were good friends. I liked her a lot, and wouldn't want to upset her or anything, but I just didn't feel this way. Mostly I was wondering what to do. I couldn't tell anyone about it, yet I wanted someone to know, besides me. I couldn't tell Mum or our Dad. If Dave was here we could have talked about it. But nobody else. Not even Ruth. I mean you couldn't start spouting off to one girl about another, especially after what had happened between Ruth and me.

I got to thinking about Ron and the way he'd been looking at Michelle, but anyway that didn't matter because he was going with Hilary. But just thinking of how they seemed to hit it off right away, smiling secretly at each other. Well, not to worry. But suppose he became interested and made a play for her. Would she prefer him because he was coloured like her? Not only that, but he was educated and talked in the same way, and he wasn't bad looking, even with that scraggy beard. Hilary didn't mind about the beard. She was a nice little piece, that Hilary, with her long blonde hair always shining.

Yes, perhaps I was in love with her. Those nights Dave and me would lie in the dark talking about falling in love with some beautiful girl whose dad had loads of money. Sometimes Dave saying he'd never get married and all that talk about love was a lot of mush and what was love anyway. And talking about old man Chalmers in the machine shop who was always on about women, and he'd once said that love lasted only as long as your pecker could stay upright. Dave said the old boy was only talking that way because he'd gone off women, and not surprising if you saw Mrs Chalmers. We'd seen them together in Romford High Road one Saturday morning. She was as tall as him but thin and flat as a board, with a face wrinkled up like a prune, as if she had too much skin. Funny how you could just lie there and feel that kiss all over again, her lips cool and soft and gentle.

I was a bit late home from work on Monday evening. Missed my bus to the station and after that everything was red lights all the way. From the moment I walked into the house I could feel the tension. Our Dad and Mum were in the kitchen, she getting dinner ready, and he sitting at the table reading the papers. I said hello, but only our Dad answered me. I went up and washed, then came back down. Usually he and me had a little natter while we waited for dinner. He passed over the sports pages without saying a word and I thought, What's up? Not a word from anybody until dinner was ready; Mum served it up and I'd just got the first spoonful in my mouth when she started.

'Mr Hardy told me he saw you Saturday night.' The way she said it, her voice tight, hard and accusing. For a moment I didn't remember who the hell Mr Hardy was anyway. Oh yes, the butcher. I didn't know where he'd seen me, or what he'd seen my doing, so I waited. From the sound of Mum's voice the least it could be was that I'd been raping some little girl somewhere. Dad went on eating, his eyes on the food in front of him. I was hungry as hell, but it suddenly tasted like mud in my mouth.

'He and his wife got on the train at Charing Cross, and they saw you.'

Nothing from me. The mouthful wouldn't move, felt like I'd choke.

'You and that nigger.'

Sometimes the fellows at the works would call one another all kinds of names. Even dirty names. But it didn't mean a thing. The way Mum said that word nigger, it cut into me, she made it sound so dirty. I let the food out on the fork and put it on the plate, pushing the whole thing away from me. I could see she was full to overflowing with it, and I didn't want to hear, the way the hate was boiling up inside me. I mean, I love my Mum, but what right did she have to say something like that? I stood up and she yelled at me.

'And where do you think you're going?'

I didn't answer. Couldn't, the way I was choked up. I moved my chair away and went upstairs, sat on my bed to settle myself. I heard her coming up the stairs and wished I could have locked the door to keep her out, but the lock never worked. It had been painted over years ago. She barged in, her face livid, and started in on me about not eating my dinner after she'd slaved all evening over a hot stove fixing it. I told her I didn't want any dinner, so she switched to the other thing, about since the day that nigger had come into the house there had been nothing but trouble. On and on. Not stopping. The niggers were the cause of Dave's death, and she couldn't understand how I could even stand to look at them, least of all going around with them. Every time she said the word nigger I felt I wanted to hit her. The more she went on the worse she became, yelling all kinds of things at me like someone I'd never seen before.

'Do your nigger friends know about you, what you used to do? You told them about the people you used to beat up? About the fellow in Stepney? Eh? They know that the police are after you? You think that stuck-up nigger bitch would even look at you if she knew what you are?'

I heard our Dad calling her from downstairs but she wasn't listening, just going on at me. I knew if she didn't stop I'd do something. Something. Then Dad came into the room and told her to shut up, pulling her out.

At the door she looked back and said, 'Don't say I didn't warn you.'

My own Mum. Long after she'd gone the words kept ringing in my ears and I could see her face, the mouth pulled back at the corners and a little bubble of spittle on her lower lip from saying nigger over and over. Hell, what had I done, anyway, that was so terrible? No, the best thing was to get to hell out of there as soon as I could, because if she kept on at me and calling Michelle a nigger like that I might do something that everybody would be sorry for. Just as well our Dad pulled her away. He was another one. Ruddy well sitting there stuffing his dinner while she carried on at me, and not saying a word. And he was the one always telling me what nice people the Spencers were. Why didn't he tell Mum that they were nice people when she kept shouting about niggers? Yes, better to get the hell out, then nobody would have to worry about what I did and who I went with.

I could hear the telephone ringing downstairs, then somebody answered, and hung up. That was a quick one. I put on some records, loud, to drown the echoes in my head. Lionel Hampton kicking up hell on the vibraharp. I lay on my bed, not really listening to the music, but letting it beat around my body. What the hell was happening to our Mum all of a sudden? Never in my life heard her carry on like that before. Never. As if she was going off her nut or something. I mean I could understand if Michelle had been rude to her that day when she was here, but all she'd said was that she was born here in England. Well, where's the harm in that? Why should me sitting with Michelle in a train set her off like that? I wondered what that old bugger Hardy had said to her. Must have dressed the story up good and proper. Well, up his. I didn't have to give a damn about him anyway.

I suddenly realized I was hungry, but I didn't want to go anywhere near the kitchen to give Mum a chance to start on me again, because as sure as hell if she said any more like that about Michelle I might do something I'd be sorry for later.

I slipped on my old suède jacket and went downstairs. From the darkened living-room I could hear the murmur of tinny voices from the television, just loud enough so nobody would hear the door as I went out. Our street had the heavy quiet of living going on behind thick curtains and the sly watchfulness of neighbours. Would be fun to be able to slice off all the fronts of houses and see what they were all doing. I headed for the High Street and that café near to Burton's which stayed open a bit late. Passing Old Man Hardy's shop I wished I was a small boy or didn't live around here, so I could bash his window in with a brick. Give him something to do besides shooting his old mouth off about things that were none of his ruddy business. What the hell did he care who I was with? On trains or any-where else. Old bugger was past it, so now he had to go sticking his nose into things which didn't concern him.

Not many people in the café. A few old boys playing dominoes in one corner and the waitress leaning against the counter watching them. God, I was hungry. She came over to where I sat, taking her time as if next year would do just as well. I asked her if I was in time to have a cooked meal, and without answer-ing she went back to the counter, and fetched a menu, so grease-spotted that some of the typewritten words could hardly be read.

'Steak and chips, with peas,' I told her.

'Steak's off,' she replied, her voice tired or bored or both.

'Well, make it chop, with chips,' I was too hungry to be fussy.

'Chop's off.' Still in the same voice. I felt the anger tightening my guts. Why the hell did they have the stuff down on the menu if it was all off?

'What's on?' I asked, feeling like hitting her or saying some-thing to wipe that stupid look off her face.

'Eggs and sausage. Fish. Beans on toast.' She couldn't care less, her eyes were looking over my head to something in the street outside.

'Sausage and chips,' I told her.

'No eggs?'

'No.'

'Tea or coffee?'

'Coca Cola.'

'No cokes. Seven Up or Pepsi.'

'Pepsi.'

She went away, leaned over the counter and shouted something to someone I couldn't see. Bitch acted as if it was the ruddy Ritz and she was doing you a favour to serve you. If I wasn't so hungry I'd walk away right now and let her stuff the ruddy sausages right up. While waiting I watched the domino players. The way those old boys hummed and hawed and pondered over every move you'd think it was a matter of life or death. Then they'd slam the domino hard down on the table before fitting it into position, taunting each other. Why did old people get so excited about something like a game of dominoes? I mean, all sorts of things happening in the world, in the street outside, and they're sitting there fitting pieces of wood together. Must be at least fifty or sixty, both of them. Half-way to the graveyard and wasting time in a ruddy café playing dominoes. What a hell of a way to live.

Either the food was okay or I was too hungry to care, but I cleaned it up. All of it. Then sat drinking the cold Pepsi and watching the old-timers. Now that I'd eaten there wasn't anything else to do but go home. Suddenly I missed Dave more than I'd missed him before. When he was here at least we'd be together even if we just sat around without talking. Just knowing he was there was enough. Funny how a little thought like that can grind you up inside. Wonder what he'd think of Michelle and the way Mum had carried on? Just suppose Dave was still here and somehow or other he'd met Michelle and got to know her? What would Mum have said? Her ruddy favourite and a nigger!

I couldn't sit around that dingy café all night long, and I was in no hurry to go home. I paid and left, undecided where to go or what to do. The red phone booth at the corner gave me an idea and I went in. Mrs Spencer answered. I told her it was me and could I speak to Michelle. She didn't reply for a moment, then, in a changed voice, cold and distant, she said, 'I don't think my daughter wishes to speak with you, Mr Bennett.'

I felt as if the whole world had fallen on top of my head. I don't know what I said to her, stammered something or other asking her why, what was the matter, what had I done, what happened?

'Your mother has been extremely rude to her on the telephone.'

I felt cold and weak. Just stood there holding the receiver but not thinking or saying anything, I don't know for how long, then I realized I hadn't said or heard anything and I said 'Hello, Mrs Spencer,' but there was no reply. She had hung up. The phone booth was hot and I was sweating, hating our Mum till I couldn't see straight. What did she want to do that for? God! I'd never have believed our Mum would do something like that, ring Michelle to tell her off. She must have asked Directory Enquiries for the number. Couldn't get at me so she had to try it on Michelle.

Jesus, God, what had she said to her? Clear as ever I could hear the words she'd said as our Dad pulled her out of my room, 'Don't say I didn't warn you.'

Without stopping to think I ran all the way to the station and bought a ticket to Leigh. As the train clanked along I tried to get my mind straight about what to say to them, Michelle and her mother, but all I could think about was what my Mum might have said about me to put Michelle off. Going down the steps to their house I suddenly felt scared to face them, dressed as I was without a tie and the zip on my suède jacket not able to close more than half-way up. I sat on one of the steps, looking down to where the lights from their house shone through the moving pattern of leaves, wondering about them, probably sitting there talking about me, hating me. I couldn't go down. I had to know what our Mum had said. I'd go back and find out and to hell with it. Whatever happened let it happen.

I could hear their voices in the kitchen. Mum was raising the cup to her lips when I walked in. Funny the things that stick clear in your mind, the brown cocoa mark at the edge of her mouth, her left thumb over the edge of the saucer on the table, and the thick grey hairs of our Dad's chest curling up through the V of his open shirt and catching the light in thin silvery gleams.

'What did you want to ring her for?' Although I'd planned to control myself and say it quietly, the anger spilled out with each word. 'What's she ever done to you? What did you have to ring her for?'

'What the hell's this?' our Dad said, putting down his cup and glaring at me.

'Ask Mum,' I told him, 'What's she want to ring Michelle for and tell her off?'

'What's he on about, Madge? What's he talking about?'

'Michelle. Miss Spencer.' I said. 'She wasn't satisfied with saying all those rotten things to me, she had to go and ring her. Why the hell can't you leave us alone?'

Our Dad jumped up and came towards me but I didn't give a damn, I wasn't scared of him. Just let him lay a hand on me again and see what the hell would happen. But all he said was for me to keep my voice down. Then he turned to Mum, his face confused.

'Madge, did you telephone Miss Spencer?'

'I telephoned nobody,' she replied, in that flat quiet voice which didn't give a damn.

'Jack here just said you telephoned that young woman. Did you?'

'I telephoned nobody,' she repeated, taking a long drink before putting the cup into its saucer and gently pushing them to one side.

'She's lying, Dad,' I said, 'I know she did. Mrs Spencer told me. I telephoned them and she told me. Now she's bloody lying.'

'You watch that tongue of yours,' our Dad said to me, his hands tightening into fists, but I couldn't care less.

'Well, what does she want to lie about it now for? Mrs Spencer wouldn't say it if she hadn't.'

'I telephoned nobody,' Mum repeated, like some ruddy talking mynah bird. 'One of his nigger friends rang here asking for him and I told her not to ring here again.' I felt the relief like a balloon inside me. She hadn't said anything to Michelle. Not anything about me anyway.

'But why, Madge?' our Dad asked her.

'I've said it once and I mean it.' Still in that flat, hard voice.

'I don't want them coming here or ringing on that phone either. They cause nothing but trouble and I'm not having it.'

'Okay,' I told her, 'I don't have to stay here. I'll find somewhere else to go.'

'You can suit yourself about that,' Mum said. Cool, as if she didn't give a damn if I dropped dead. I hated her so much I couldn't look at her, so I walked out and up to my room. I'd have liked to go and see Michelle but it was too late now. I could hear our Dad and Mum going at it downstairs, then our Dad came up to my room. He closed the door and stood there looking at me for a while, then sat on the bed beside me.

'Look, Son, don't let what your mother said downstairs upset you. She hasn't been herself these past weeks, you know.'

'I'm getting out,' I told him.

'Now, take it easy, Son. There's no call for that. When your mother gets upset she says things she doesn't really mean. We all do. In a day or so she'll have forgotten all about it.'

He could go right ahead and kid himself if he liked. Mum wasn't saying all that because she was upset or because of Dave or anything. She meant it. You could hear it in her voice, feel it in every word she said. She hated coloured people. Must have been hating them for a long time. Maybe that's where Dave and me got it from, without even knowing it. Couldn't be because of what happened to Dave.

'What's going on between you and Miss Spencer?' He switched off from talking about Mum.

'Nothing's going on.'

'Then why all the fuss with your mother? The way you carried on anyone would think something's up between you.'

'Well, nothing's up.'

'Look, Son. You can talk to me about it. After all, I'm your Dad, and that's what a Dad's for. This thing with your mother, I don't think she has anything personal against the girl.'

Like hell she didn't. Christ, that time Dave and me had gone up West and heard those people in Hyde Park talking about why didn't they send all the coloureds back where they came from, that Sunday afternoon. All those people talking and arguing, but none of them had sounded like Mum did. Remembering it, they'd all been standing around this fellow on a little box with a piece stuck up in front where he had some papers and things. And he'd been saying how the coloureds were taking all the jobs and all the houses and living off the women, and the best thing for the country was to send them all back where they came from. And the people listening had started arguments with him, some of them agreeing and some not. But none of them had sounded like our Mum, as if hating the coloureds was a personal thing. Did he think I was going to discuss Michelle with him so he could go and tell our Mum?

'Do you go over to the Spencers much?' he asked.

'Not much. I've been there a couple of times.'

'You serious about the girl?' he wanted to know.

'What do you mean, serious, Dad?'

'Look, Son, you know what I mean. You go there and you're seen all over the place with her. The way you carried on tonight I wondered if, I mean, I had the feeling you really liked the girl.'

'I like her.'

'What I mean is that you sounded as if it was really serious between you and her.'

What he was hinting at was that I might be in love with Michelle. Funny thing, I suddenly realized that I'd never heard our Dad or Mum talk about love or loving anybody. Here was our Dad, angling to find out if I was in love with Michelle, but he'd never use the word. He asked if I liked her or was serious about her, but all the time he wanted to know if I was in love with her. I wondered what he'd say if I asked him if he was in love with our Mum.

'You're not thinking of going courting with her or anything like that, are you, Son?'

Going courting. Michelle would get a laugh out of that if she could hear him. He sounded a little frightened and I had half a mind to say that yes, I loved Michelle, not really meaning it, but just to hear what he would say. Most likely he'd go and tell Mum and then the whole ruddy house would explode. Oh, hell, let him stew in his own ruddy juice. I didn't say anything.

'What about that friend of yours who comes here? What's her name, Ruth or something. Aren't you friends any more?'

'Ruth and me. Sure we're friends.'

'Don't you still go out with her?'

'Yes, Dad, sometimes.'

'I think she's a very nice girl. Very well-mannered and respectful. A very nice decent girl.' What the hell did he know about it? Because she was white she was nice and decent, no matter how easy it was to get in there. Don't suppose even Mum would mind too much if she knew what had happened with Ruth. She'd still think she was a nice, decent girl. Well okay, she's nice and decent. But what about Michelle? Wasn't she nice and decent too?

'She's okay,' I told him.

'You know, Son, I don't go along with your Mum the way she talks about coloured people. I always say that a man's a man no matter what the colour of his skin. In the war there were a few black fellows in our Company, and you couldn't hope to meet nicer chaps. Their skins might be black but they were whiter inside than many white fellows, I used to say. After all, the world's big enough for all of us, so I take people as I find them, black, white, tall, short, however they come. You can't say I've ever taught you different, can you?'

'No, Dad.'

'At the same time I can't say that I hold with black and white mixing too much, you know what I mean. It just doesn't work. I've seen a lot and I know what I'm talking about. Wherever they try it, it never does any good, only causes a lot of trouble, and you get the worst of both worlds. Look at what's happening here already to us, in this house. With your brother gone we should be even closer together as a family, not yelling at each other . . .'

Through the open window came the shattering, half-human screams of cats tangling up somewhere outside, and the thought came into my mind, What would it be like if human beings were like that, every time you tried to get a piece the bird started yelling the place down? Nights wouldn't be fun any more with everywhere like some ruddy madhouse.

'. . . Don't forget I was young too, Son, and I know what young fellows get up to. In my day we used to call it sowing our wild oats. After all, you're not a child any more. My old father used to say to me, if you can't be good, be careful. I can't say that I was always good, but I tried to be careful. So now it's my turn to give you a little sound advice. Anyone can see that Miss Spencer is a very attractive girl. Very attractive. But she's coloured. I keep telling your Mum that she's getting herself worked up over nothing. You're nobody's fool. Have your fun by all means, but don't put yourself in any position where you'd become involved. Yes, she's very attractive. Only wish I was about your age . . .'

He was half smiling, with the same look on his face as Old Man Chalmers down at the shop when he's talking about women. I got the drift of what he meant and suddenly felt like pushing my fist down his ruddy throat. I mean, it's one thing to hear an old lecher like Old Man Chalmers carrying on like that, but not your own ruddy dad. Made me feel sick. I got up and cleared off out of the room, downstairs and through the front door. I didn't want to hear any more, not the way he was talking as if Michelle was some bloody tart or something.

I leaned against the gate, feeling the cool of the metal through my slacks. Along the top of the hedge you could see wetness on the leaves reflecting pieces of lamplight. Funny thing about dew, falling all around you and you don't notice a thing till you see how wet everything is. Like when Dave and me were kids in the scouts. And this week-end we went camping way over the river in Kent, tracking and using a compass and making knots and all kinds of things. And chopping sticks for firewood. And singing around the campfire, all kinds of songs like John Brown's Body, then sleeping in the tent. And next morning all the grass around soaking wet with big silvery drops. And Dave said they must be fairy tears because nobody heard them fall in the night and they didn't splash and burst like rain. And this fat, dopey kid, what was his name, Leyland or something, he began to laugh because Dave said that and Dave got mad and jumped on him, punching him, and we had to pull him off.

I suddenly noticed that the lights in the houses on both sides of the street had gone out. Everything was quiet and a little breathless. A stray breeze started up from somewhere near the bottom of the hedge, blew some dead leaves along a short distance then hurriedly hid itself as if scared by the small commotion it was creating. I wondered if, for the moment, it had lived. Whether it felt the weight of the leaves as it pushed or carried them along. Crazy little breeze, now you hear it now you don't. Gone. Perhaps at this moment it was hiding among the hedge roots, building up another breath for the next little bash down the pavement. Must be okay to be a breeze, live, die, live again. Not like Dave. Dead and really gone. For good, always. No matter what that ruddy parson said.

I heard the door click and Mum's voice calling, 'Jack, what're you doing out there?' Softly, so as not to let anyone but me hear her.

'Nothing, Mum,' I answered, feeling the tightness come on. Why couldn't she leave me alone? I wasn't stopping anybody from turning in and locking their ruddy bedroom door. What did she want, to have another go at me?

'It's damp out there, Son, you'll catch your death.' I turned to say something and saw her tiny figure wrapped up in that old beat-up dressing-gown. Whenever I see her in that old thing, so big for her I don't know why she ever bought it, I get the feeling she's so little and helpless. What's the point of having an argument? I went in, she standing aside and locking the door after me.

'I'll make you a cup of tea. You've eaten nothing since you came home, and now I suppose you'll go to bed on an empty stomach.'

'I had something at the café next to Burton's.'

'So.' She sniffed. 'Leave your dinner and go to eat in a café. Go up and get into something warm and I'll bring you a cup of tea.' And she hurried off to the kitchen. I mean, what can you do? I was all tight inside waiting for her to start on me,

144

and she's thinking about a cup of tea. Hell, I must have the craziest Dad and Mum in the world. I promised myself next payday I'd buy her a really nice dressing-gown, woolly and warm, but more her size. I'd ask Ruth to go with me to one of those shops up West and choose something for her. Then hide that horrible thing she insists on wearing.

Dave was right. Dew falls so quiet you don't even feel it. Looking in the mirror I noticed the tiny drops in my hair. I went to the bathroom for a wash, then changed into pyjamas.

Mum came up with the tea in our Dad's big cup, and two pieces of cake. I was clipping my finger nails. She put the tray down on the dresser, hardly looking at me, and at the door said, 'Night, Son.'

'Mum.' I stopped her. She looked at me, not saying anything.

'I'm sorry, Mum. About tonight.'

After a little while, she said, 'Your Dad seems to think you're a man now, so I suppose you'll do what you want,' and left me, without another word, making me feel awful, like some ruddy bully or something. Oh Christ, why couldn't it have been me instead of Dave, then everything would be okay for everybody.

I ate it all, I was so hungry, then lay down, reading some of Dave's stuff. Like talking with him, only different, because the words were not like in conversation. But knowing Dave had written them made all the difference. I wondered what he'd have written about Michelle.

At breakfast next morning nobody said anything, but just as I was pushing off our Dad said, 'Son, your mother and me had a bit of a talk last night. It's okay if you want to invite any of your friends here. Any time.'

He was watching Mum, not me. She was watching him, quiet.

On the way to work I thought about it. What he meant was that I could ask Michelle home if I wanted to. Hell, he'd no need to say that about Ruth or anyone else. But the way Mum's face had looked, he was wasting his breath. Maybe she wouldn't exactly cut Michelle's throat, but she'd make her about as welcome as the plague.

19

AFTER WORK I hurried home, planning to get changed and go over to see the Spencers. I didn't telephone to let them know I was coming, just in case Michelle said no, she didn't want to see me. I had to think up some excuse for Mum and the way she'd behaved. Soon as I got in Mum said some fellow had rung up asking for me. Gave his name as Ron and left a number for me to call him back. She said it, you know, in just the same voice as she'd have told me that Ruth had phoned, and I chuckled to myself, thinking of what her reaction would be if she knew who Ron was.

When I got Ron on the phone he said it wasn't important, he'd been talking with Ruth and remembered meeting me and Ruth gave him my number, and how was everything with me, and it was crazy me living so far away, out of touch, and did I realize I owed it to my friends to be visible from time to time? Funny as hell, and I'm laughing my head off, then he asks, 'And how's the beauteous Michelle?' And right away I get the feeling that all the guff he's shooting is merely to find out about her. That's really why he phoned, who did he think he was fooling? I said that the last time I'd seen her she was okay, and he said, Come, come fellow, don't make it sound as if she's not always within kissing distance, laughing that laugh of his and saying that everybody had been asking about us, Michelle and me, so when were they going to have the pleasure of our company again? I laughed too, not feeling it, only making the noise. Saying I'd tell Michelle and we'd be coming up soon. Real soon. He said he had the idea of giving her a buzz but Ruth didn't have the number and they couldn't remember her surname or anything, waiting for me to tell him. Son of a bitch must think he's so ruddy clever. So I laughed, just the noise, and said tough luck and I'd tell her.

After he hung up I wondered about it. Bastard must imagine

that because he's coloured he can just ring up and everything would be okay.

Mum asked who Ron was, and I said a fellow I met at Ruth's when they had the party, and Mum said where's Ruth hiding herself these days, she hadn't been over. So I said something about her being busy, but I guessed she'd be over soon, and to stop her asking any more questions I picked up the phone and called Ruth. As usual her warmth and friendliness came bubbling out of the phone and she said, Well, hello stranger. So we nattered for a bit and keeping my voice quiet I said would she go with me to buy a dressing-gown for Mum and she said sure, when? So we fixed it up for Thursday because the places up West were open late. Then I told her Ron had phoned and she laughed and said did I tell him?

'Tell him what?' I asked her.

'Well, if you don't know, that means you didn't tell him, so don't worry about it.'

'Come off it, Ruth, what're you talking about?'

'Well, didn't he ask you for Michelle's phone number?' Her voice still had the laughter but now she was teasing.

'No, he only said he'd thought of ringing her. So, what's so funny?'

'Nothing. And how's she?'

'Okay. Mum's been asking for you.'

'Tell her I'll be over soon. And how's my boyfriend?'

'Who, me?'

'No, stupid. Your Dad.'

'He's okay.'

We arranged where to meet Thursday. Time was getting on. I washed and changed. Dinner was okay. Dad said how there'd been a bit of a do at the building site because some four by fours had slipped out from a sling while the crane was carrying them, and a couple of the men had been injured, one of them was in hospital, still unconscious. And there'd been this argument because the man in hospital had not been wearing his safety helmet. Dad said there was a notice that everybody should wear these helmets and safety boots when engaged on certain jobs, but the helmets were pretty uncomfortable, especially in the heat, so the men didn't like wearing them. The fellow in hospital, somebody named Doyle, had a wife and three children, the last one only eleven months old. The company wouldn't accept full responsibility because he should have been wearing the helmet. Mum said that was nonsense because something falling from a height didn't have to hit you on the head. And even if he was wearing the safety thing, he could have been hurt or killed just the same.

I left them talking about it and went for my train. I got into a compartment with these two women, pretty old, about thirtyish or something like that, talking about where they'd been for their holidays. And this one, fat in a dress, flowered with a low neck and the sunburn red on her arms and chest, thin flakes of skin lifting at the edges on her nose and cheeks, must have just come back from some place where it was blistering hot. Couldn't be anywhere in England, that was sure. Grey eyes with the lashes caked from the stuff she'd used, and her hair too black for that face, you knew it wasn't her real colour. Why the heck do women dye their hair, they never fool other women, nor even men. Specially when it's done black. Not shiny and alive like Michelle's or that kid who was in our class in the Juniors. Judy Fischler. Real black her hair was and blue eyes. We used to pull her hair, she had it in this thick plait, and call her Fishy, and she'd get mad and stand by the girls' toilet and cry. The other woman was not bad looking. Blonde, even her eyelashes, whitish, so that you had to look twice to see them. Why is it some people go brown so easily like this blonde, while some just go red and peel all over the place? The blonde was wearing a brown linen dress, plain and no sleeves, her arms brown and smooth to the red fingertips. A grey pullover was slung across her shoulders. And they're gabbing about some place called Ibiza and how wonderful the food was and the wine, and you could stay all day on the beach. And about some painter fellow who lived near the hotel.

'He's a bit of a one,' Fatty said, her voice making it seem as if she knew something.

'Bit of a lineshooter, if you ask me,' from Blondie.

'I'm not so sure.'

'Always saying how about coming up to his place to see his paintings? He'd have to try another, that one's got moss on it.'

I'm watching the way Blondie's eyes look naked till she blinks and you can see the lashes, then she looks at me, straight, still nattering to Fatty who says something to her and laughs, her mouth wide open and gold showing on a tooth way back on her lower jaw. Looking straight at me. I get this feeling of excitement sudden and strong, embarrassing the hell out of me, so I look away out of the window. I could feel my neck and face hot, blushing like some ruddy kid, and the two of them lowered their voices, whispering then laughing. Hell, you can't keep looking out of the ruddy window, so I look at them again, and there's Blondie's eyes on me, this time the lipstick shiny as if she'd run her wet tongue over it. And Fatty is looking at me and looking away. Smiling, as if they know what was happening to me and are getting a kick out of it. I was glad when the train reached Leigh.

Going towards their house I felt nervous. Kept repeating to myself how I'd say in a quiet voice that I was sorry for anything my mother had said but she didn't mean to be unpleasant, it was only because she'd been holding in about Dave all this time, and now it was getting to her, making her nervous and irritable, and she was sorry if she'd sounded rude.

Half-way down the steps I saw Mrs Spencer. She was under the apple trees collecting windfalls in a basket. Wearing grey slacks and a sloppy-joe sweater, with a blue scarf over her head and tied under her chin. Looking just like a young girl, bending over there, in the half-light of evening.

'Hello, Mrs Spencer.'

She hadn't heard me coming down, and straightened up quickly, looking at me. Not smiling, she picked up the basket and came towards the steps, leaving clear footprints in the soft earth. I reached to take the basket from her. She hesitated a bit before giving it to me, her face not too friendly.

'I had to come and explain about Mum, she's not feeling so good just now. That's why she was like that on the phone, but she didn't mean anything.'

All in a rush. Not like how I'd planned to say it, slow and careful. She was still standing there, a little below me because of the steps, this scarf around her face and the big brown eyes looking like a picture of some Greek women I once saw somewhere. All of a sudden she smiled.

'Extraordinary,' she said.

'How do you mean, Mrs Spencer?'

'You reminded me just then of my son. As a small boy whenever he became excited he had a way of gushing things out all in one breath.'

'Sorry, Mrs Spencer.' I meant about reminding her of her son.

'Did you tell your mother you were coming here to apologize?' Looking into my eyes.

'No, but I know she's sorry about last night. My Dad told me.'

She walked down the slope beside the steps and I carried the basket.

'Is Michelle indoors? I'd like to apologize to her too.'

'She's not in yet. She's got a late lecture tonight.' She didn't seem to want to say much to me.

At the door she reached for the basket, so I said, 'Can I wait for her?'

The way she looked at me, so different from the other times. Then she said, 'Yes, of course.'

I followed her through to the sitting-room where we'd had tea that Sunday. She said would I mind being on my own for a while because she wanted to prepare some of the apples, she'd already heated the stove to make some pies. She'd put on some records if I liked. I asked couldn't I give her a hand with the apples, I knew how to peel and core them, often helped Mum when she was fixing stuff. She said okay, but as if she wasn't too keen. I went with her along a short passage and into this big kitchen, everything white and shiny, and windows along one side looking over to the estuary, the lights from Southend pier blinking like stars.

Without waiting for her to say anything I took off my jacket and hung it over the back of a chair, rolled up my sleeves and emptied the apples into the sink. I turned on the cold water and began to wash them. She was so quiet I looked over my shoulder at her in the middle of the room untying the scarf from her head, looking at me. I asked her for a knife to peel the apples and she pointed to a drawer and went off somewhere. By the time I heard her come back I had them peeled and was digging out the centres because I couldn't find the thing to core them. She came behind me to see how I was getting on and I could smell the perfume she was wearing. She fetched a big china dish and without a word took the knife and apple from me and began slicing it away from the core into the dish.

'I didn't know you wanted them cut up,' I told her. She'd changed into a dress with a bright coloured pattern of small leaves, green and brown and blue, with a thick blue cord tight around her waist. She hadn't said a word, but the touch of her hand when she took the things sent cold fire all through me. I watched the strong fingers cupped around the apple, the skin shiny wet with juice, brown thumb of the other hand guiding the knife with quick sureness. Her perfume and the way she stood there, a slight ripple along the brown forearms. Then the eyes swung round at me. Large like Michelle's, but brown.

'Dry your hands. There's a towel by the door,' she said.

I dried my hands and put on my jacket, then sat watching her. She carried on as if I wasn't there. From the fridge she took two pyrex dishes all ready with pastry, and filled them with the sliced apples, adding raisins and sprinkling sugar and other stuff, before putting more pastry on top and bunging it into the oven. More or less the same way Mum did it. Funny, you never think of coloured people doing things like that, the same as anyone else. I couldn't help watching her move about, those long legs with no stockings, and little gold slippers without heels, like ballet shoes.

The look on her face must be because I'd got her started

remembering about her son. Wish I could think of something to say to make her smile or talk to me. Bet her arms would be smooth and cool if you touched them. Like silk, I'd bet.

The voice came singing through the house like a breeze, 'Mummy, where are you?' I turned around as she entered the kitchen door.

'Oh!' She stood still, eyes big, books and a string-tied package clasped to her chest. 'Hi, Mum!' She went over to kiss Mrs Spencer, then leaned against the refrigerator, looking at me, cold, as if I was something nasty crawled in from the bushes.

'Hello?' she said, with a question in it, expecting to know what I was doing there.

'Hello, Michelle,' I replied, 'I just popped over to explain about the other night. Mum didn't mean the way she sounded to you.'

'How would you know what she sounded like?' Her voice was spiteful and bitter. 'You weren't there.'

'I know, but I had a talk with her, and she didn't mean it like that.'

'Like what? And what's all this about? Are you apologizing for her? Well, let me give you a little message. Tell your mother I'm not interested in her apologies, not even if I heard them from her own lips.' And she walked out of the kitchen. I felt like a ruddy nit, not knowing what to say or do next.

'Go and sit next door while I have a word with her,' Mrs Spencer said, not looking at me, her head bent over whatever she was doing at the sink. I went into the sitting-room and stood at the window looking out at the winking lights along the slope and those reflected in the water from the stars above and the distant pier.

Behind the black silhouettes of chimneys and storage tanks the greyish skyline promised that it was still day, somewhere, if only one could fly straight out to it. Like a bird. Those swallows I'd noticed earlier on. Once I'd read in a book that they flew from thousands of miles every summer just to come to England and I used to wonder what for. We used to have to repeat it together in the Juniors. Went something like:

The swallows nest together,
Together in the eaves,
Waiting for the falling
The falling of the leaves.
They know the time is coming
The time when they must flee
Away to brighter sunshine
Far, far across the sea.

At the bottom of the slope a slow glow-worm of a train splashed light on the coarse grass and shallow bushes, then was gone, lazily chased by its own irregular echo. That blonde. The way that gold tooth glittered in the back of her wide, wet mouth.

'Now tell me some more about your mother being sorry.' I jumped. I hadn't heard her come into the room. She was wearing those little nylon things like socks without tops, just big enough to cover her toes and heels. Still dressed as when she'd come home, grey skirt and a long-sleeved white shirt with a little round collar like a small boy's. She came up to where I stood and leaned her back against the window, arms folded across her chest, her face still tight and angry.

'It's true, like I was telling your mother earlier on. She's not been really herself since Dave went, and gets worked up about the least thing.'

'Now isn't that touching? Aren't you forgetting something? I lost a brother at about the same time and my mother lost a son, her only son, but we don't use that as an excuse for insulting people.' The words were clear and deliberate, as if she'd been thinking them over a long time.

'Look, Michelle, I understand how you feel, but I know she's . . .'

'You do? You understand? Really?' She tilted her head backward and laughed, the light reflecting sharply on those eyes as she looked towards the ceiling as if begging God to bear witness to the load of rubbish I was saying. The laugh wasn't nice. Just like Sandra that time, stirring up the anger in me.

'What the heck's so ruddy funny?' I asked her.

'Not funny, Mr Bennett,' she replied, 'not funny at all. Only clever. Very clever of you to understand how I feel. Who's been telling you? Your mother?'

The corners of her mouth pulled down, making it look ugly for a moment. I didn't want to quarrel with her. If she wouldn't believe me then to hell with it. I didn't want to hear any more talk about my Mum.

'What I want to know is, why?' Her voice had changed suddenly, became softer, as if she was talking more to herself than to me. 'She answered the telephone and I asked if I might speak to you. She said you were not in at the moment, quite friendly, and was there any message? As friendly as ever until I told her who I was. What has she against me? What have I done to her?' Her whole face was soft and appealing, her lower lip trembling a little.

'Look, I told you . . .'

'Don't tell me, Mr Bennett. I understand. Believe me. I understand. I heard it in your mother's voice. I know exactly what she meant.' All I could do was stand there and look at her and want desperately to hold her and say I didn't give a ruddy damn what Mum or anybody said. Then again her face changed, hardened.

'Did she think I was chasing you? Was that it? A nigger, chasing her blue-eyed son?'

'I'm not blue-eyed.' I tried to make a little joke.

'I don't give a damn what colour they are.' In spite of herself she smiled, then wearily she added, 'Look, why don't you go home and set your mother's fears at rest. Explain to her that the reason I telephoned had nothing to do with you actually.'

'What was it about then?'

'Nothing important. In any case it no longer matters.'

'I'd still like to know.'

'I'm tired,' she said, and sat down, folding her legs under her. I sat opposite.

'Why did you phone?' I asked her again.

'If you must know, I told Mummy about the people I met at Ruth's, and we thought it might be a good idea for me to invite some of them over here as I've a birthday coming up soon. I telephoned you to talk to you about getting in touch with them.'

'Okay, I can tell you now.'

'I've told you it's no longer important. Those few kind words from your mother changed my mind for me.'

'Look, you don't have to worry about my Mum. Who did you think of inviting?'

'Can't you understand, or am I not making myself clear? I've changed my mind. I've decided not to bother.' Her voice had become hard once more. Curled up in that chair with her arms still folded and the skirt tight against her, showing her off, smooth and round. What was it that Dave had written in his book? Something about there was never anything wrong with clothes, only the people inside them, put the right person in the right clothes and everything was okay, even rags were okay on a dirty beggar, but a tie looked silly on the man behind the plough. Something like that, but the way he wrote it down it sounded okay. Michelle was fine in her clothes. Or without. She'd look good even in her skin.

Never forget that time there was this day trip from the works to Henley. By coach. A Saturday it was, and they'd fixed up a cricket match with some other works club up there. Dave and me were in the cricket team so we went, the coach full with lots of the men's wives and kids. And every now and then the coach would stop, always at a pub. The first stop Dave and me got down with the others and had a shandy. But afterwards we'd walk around to stretch our legs while the rest of them crowded into the pub laughing and singing their heads off, the kids hanging around the doors or peeping in the windows at them. Some places we passed had this notice up about not wanting coach parties, then you should have heard them carry on, calling the pub people sods and stuck-up bastards and some of them with young kids listening. Near Reading I think it was, a couple of the kids were sick, so the coach stopped by the side of some fields while their parents tidied them up and fetched some dust to clean the floor.

Dave and me walked down the road a bit to get away from the sour sick smell and coming back we could see these women stooping in a line by the hedge easing themselves. Back in the bus they began laughing and scratching themselves saying the driver was a clot for stopping the bus right beside the nettles. This fat woman, the backs of her legs were streaky white with ugly reddish patches from the nettles, and a fine network of blue veins like how a cabbage leaf looks after the worms have eaten off all the green stuff. I saw it and nudged Dave. He took one look and said that what she needed was a whole new skin. Now I was wondering how Michelle's leg would look. Nice, I'd bet, even with nettle blisters.

'If I really wanted to do something I wouldn't let anything anybody's mother said put me off,' I told her.

'It's not just what your mother said. After all, she's not the only bigoted person in the world. I've met others. It's what she implied.'

'Look, can't we just forget about my Mum?' I was getting fed up with all the ruddy argument. 'I told you it's nothing personal against you, no matter what she said on the phone. It's just that our Dave was sort of her favourite and she took it hard about his getting killed.'

She leaned forward, the look on her face as if she hated me, 'And I suppose she blames my brother and me for what happened, does she?' her voice rising. 'Well, you listen to me. Bill was a good driver. A damned good driver. He liked going fast but he could drive and he was always careful. Even my father used to say Bill was good. So I know that whatever happened that night wasn't his fault.' Her lips trembled. 'What he should have done was leave your brother wherever he was and let him either walk home or try somebody else, but Bill couldn't bear to see anyone stranded on the road. Especially at night. We'd tell him, Mummy and I, but he'd still do it. Well, you see what he got for being kind? And on top of that your mother blames him. Tell me, Mr Bennett, if it had been you or your brother driving, would either of you have stopped to give Bill a lift? Would you?'

I couldn't answer that. Not truthfully. Then a thought came into my head and the words were coming out, 'Now I would. Since knowing you I would.'

'Isn't that nice! But Bill didn't even know your brother. I'm sure of it. He was too decent, too kind. It doesn't pay to be kind. Not with you people. You're so damned sure and arrogant inside your white skin that you think you can say and do just as you damned well please. Any stupid half literate fool can be as rude and unpleasant . . .'

That set me off. 'Look, Michelle, if you mean my Mum, then that's enough. She's not stupid nor illiterate. I told you she didn't mean it on the phone, but if you don't want to believe me, okay, suit yourself.'

'Don't shout at me, Mr Bennett.' Making me feel shut out, like a stranger.

'I'm not shouting, only telling you. All right, so my Mum upset you. Well, I came and apologized, didn't I? She didn't send me. So, did you have to say that about my skin? What do I have to do, change it or something? You know what, right now you're carrying on just like my Mum, only you're saying white this and white that, but it's just the same. Would it be okay if I was black? Like that fellow Ron? Would that be okay with you?'

I stood up. Better to clear off before I said things I'd be sorry for.

'Who on earth is Ron?' Then you could see her face remembering, and she said 'Oh!' looking at me with her mouth open.

'He rang me tonight, trying to find out your phone number,' I told her.

'Oh, did he? And did you give it to him?' Smiling through her eyes.

'Why should I? How would he like it if I started asking him for Hilary's phone number?'

'And who is Hilary? Or shouldn't I ask?'

'His girl. The blonde with the long hair. You must remember her at the party.'

The smile died in her eyes. She leaned back in her chair, those big eyes as if they were looking right through me, and in the same voice as when she'd told Mum she was born here, she said, 'I think we'd better get something quite clear, here and now. I'm not your girl. Understand? Not yours, not anyone's. I went out with you because you asked me and I wanted to. But, don't get any ideas about me. I'm not your girl.'

'Because I'm white, isn't it?' I was all choked up at the way she was talking to me as if I was a stranger.

'If you want to put it that way you can please yourself. That's up to you. You're all alike. You take a girl out once or twice and then behave as if you own her. Well, I'm sorry, but you don't own me. And I wasn't thinking about your colour. I didn't go out with you because of your white skin, so don't you try to put words into my mouth. But, just the same, if you'd been coloured do you think your mother would have called me a . . . a Spade bitch.'

I felt as if all the stuffing had been drained out of me. I wouldn't have dreamed that Mum even knew words like that. And to say them to Michelle. Why? Then I thought of the way she'd been carrying on these past days. Jesus God. I felt embarrassed, ashamed.

'I'm sorry, Michelle,' I told her, 'I didn't know Mum said that to you.'

'Then why did you come to apologize?' I could see the tears filling her eyes. 'Look, why don't you just go away and leave me alone?'

'So now I suppose you hate me, just because of what Mum said.'

A tear ran down the side of her nose and into the corner of her mouth. She turned away, looking through the window, her lips trembling so I couldn't bear to watch. I said cheerio but she didn't answer. Outside I ran all the way up those steps, making myself go right to the top, cursing my mother all the way, hating her, with my chest near to bursting, wanting to get home, to tell her.

At the top I sat down to catch my breath, hating her so much

I was crying. My own mother saying that. My own bloody mother.

20

I WAS RUNNING down the slope to Leigh station, when I bumped into a man. I apologized.

'Jack Bennett, isn't it?' he said, and right away I recognized the voice, then him, and for no reason I suddenly felt scared. I said hello. It was Baldy.

'I'd like to have a little chat with you,' he said. I didn't wait, kept on to the ticket office. Don't know why, but the idea came into my head that meeting was no accident, he was following me. He stood aside while I got my ticket, then came along as I headed for the platform.

'How's everything?' he wanted to know.

I said everything was fine.

'Visiting friends around here?'

From the way he said it I guessed he knew where I'd been, but was up to his usual game, I didn't answer.

'Friendly with the Spencers?'

I said that I'd got to know them and dropped in sometimes to say hello if I was in the neighbourhood. He switched to asking how were my Mum and Dad, and the job, and how was the drawing getting on, but I knew he wasn't really interested in hearing about that.

'She's very nice,' he suddenly said.

'Who?'

'The young one, Miss Spencer.'

I kept my mouth shut, waiting to hear what was coming next.

'People like her and her mother, when you get to know them, you hardly think of their colour,' he said.

Nothing from me. I was wondering if he'd followed me all the way from home, if they were following me wherever I went.

'Pity about the doctor, though,' his voice trying to be friendly.

'Hell of a thing to happen to you when you're trying to do someone a good turn. Was something of a cricketer too, I hear. Pity.'

Still I said nothing.

'Life's funny, when you come to think of it. I mean to say, why should it have happened to him, of all the people driving along that road? Why not somebody else? Like Fate, don't you agree? Makes you wonder. I always say people are like straws in the wind. All of us. Things happen this way or that and there's not much we can do to change anything. Cigarette?'

He handed me one sticking out of a pack, then held his lighter for me, his hand huge and strong under the flickering flame. I told myself to take it easy, keep my mouth shut and not let him see I was frightened. He lit his own and blew a long streamer of smoke into the darkness.

'Funny about twins.' He sounded like he was smiling. 'They might look alike and all that, but I've got the feeling that inside they're different, like everyone else. One might be nice, easy going, while the other might be a real bugger. To be expected, I suppose. Natural balance if you like. Take you and your brother. From what they say at the works, he was a bit aggressive, wasn't he? Quick with his tongue, and his fists too.'

I felt like telling him to shut up about Dave, but decided to keep quiet. The train shouldn't be long. Perhaps you could get arrested for telling a detective to bugger off and leave you alone.

'Talking about Fate, the night porter at the hospital said Dr Spencer nearly didn't use his car that night. Had trouble getting it started. Battery low or something. Then just when he'd decided to leave it there and go home by train he gave it one more try and it started. See what I mean? One could say that if he hadn't made that last attempt to start it, he'd be alive this minute. Quite a thought, eh? The way I see it, if you boys had stayed at home that night at least three more people would be alive in the world today.'

I heard it. Every word. And nearly choked on the smoke. So he thought he'd catch me on that one, the stupid bastard. He'd have to try again. Let him shoot his mouth off to the breeze. To ruddy hell with him.

'Dr Spencer was merely what you might call a pawn on the chessboard of Fate. Expendable. I mean, if he'd left the hospital a few minutes sooner or later, everything might have been different for him. The other is more understandable. Been happening quite a bit lately. Not only in London, but wherever those Spades live. Birmingham, Nottingham, Bradford. We hear about it, you know. We've got our ways. If you see how some of them live, not much better than animals, it's not surprising that some people have it in for them. The way we hear it, they wait until they catch one by himself, usually at night, and give him a bashing. Nothing serious you know, more like letting off steam.'

His saying the word Spade started me up again, thinking about Mum, seeing how her face must have twisted up when she said that to Michelle.

'So far nobody's taken much notice. Even the Spades haven't made much fuss. But this time it's different. Knocking somebody about with your fists is one thing. But a weapon. That's a different matter. By the way, which one was the older? Him or you?'

'Me, by three hours,' I replied, without even thinking.

'Guessed as much. As I was saying, we can't let people get away with murder, whoever it is gets killed. And those who help us could make it easy for themselves. Meant to call around and see your Dad, but you can tell him for me we had a report from Leman Street. The knife we found at the accident, which you identified as belonging to your brother, could be the same knife which was used to kill the coloured fellow Thomas in Stepney. Fits the wounds. Now they're testing for blood type. Amazing what those C.I.D. boys can do these days, even though that knife's been through the fire.'

I felt cold hearing him talk like that, confident, as if he really knew all about it, but was in no hurry. The cigarette end burned my fingers and I threw it on to the rails. The burst of sparks when it hit the ground was like a tiny firework. The headlights from the train shone some distance along the track. I'd wait until I saw a compartment full of people, then climb in, unless he stopped me. But if he was sure of anything he wouldn't be talking like that, giving me messages to my Dad. Anyway, with other people in the compartment he'd have to stop talking. I didn't want to hear any more about it. I didn't murder anybody. Dave was dead, and I didn't go out that night.

'. . . always find them, no matter how long it takes . . .' The noise of the train pulling up cut off what he was saying. I walked away from him, down to the compartment near the engine, and got in, shutting the door behind me. Two other empty seats, but he didn't follow me, and when I got off at Upminster I didn't see him.

On the way home I couldn't help looking back every now and then, but there was no sign of him. I heard Mum and Dad talking in the living-room, but went straight upstairs, not even wanting to say anything to Mum. The word murder kept ringing in my head, making me really frightened for the first time since it had happened.

I undressed, fetched out Dave's book, and got into bed, but lay there thinking about Michelle, wondering if she really hated me. Maybe in a few days time I could write to her or perhaps drop around there and apologize for rushing off. If Old Baldy thought he could catch me like that, coming it with 'If you two boys had stayed home that night . . .' What did he expect? So that's why they'd kept Dave's knife . . .

I'm standing by the side of this road, wide and straight like a motorway, with cars rushing by at high speed, but I can't hear a thing, not even the sound of the tyres. It's daylight, but all the headlights are bright, rushing up the road, then the tail lights red, winking silently into the distance. I'm sick and my whole body in pain, standing there, far from everywhere and not knowing what to do. Then this car stops right beside me, the driver waving and I get in. It's Dave driving and he says Mum is wondering where the hell I've got to, and off we go racing down the road. I tell him, 'Take it easy, Dave,' but his face has changed. It isn't Dave driving but the coloured fellow

Thomas, and in the road, right in front of the headlights is Dave, and I shout to Thomas, 'Look out, look out,' but the car only goes faster, and when I look at him again he's changed to Michelle and she's laughing, steering the car straight for Dave, and right behind him, coming at us, is this other car, the headlights bright in my face, Dave there in the middle, not running, trying to tell me something I can't hear and those headlights right on top of us now . . .

I woke up sweating, the lamp full on my face, thankful that it was only a dream. It was nearly three o'clock in the morning. I switched off and lay there thinking about Dave, wondering what had happened that night, but my thoughts kept switching around to Michelle and Baldy, and the face of Thomas looking at me from the television screen. It was a long time before I dozed off.

At breakfast I told Dad what Baldy had said. I didn't mention where I'd met him, just that I'd seen him on the way home and what he'd said about the knife. Dad asked me what I'd said and I told him I'd said nothing, nothing at all, so he said that was all I had to remember, keep my mouth shut. If the police had anything to go on they wouldn't waste time talking, and I wasn't to let them fool me with any fancy talk. As far as the law was concerned if I was there with Dave at the time I was as guilty as he was, no matter who struck the blows. So all I had to do was say nothing. Dave had already paid for what he'd done, and that was that. An eye for an eye, not two for one.

Mum said the police ought to have other things to do than worry about some nigger and why couldn't they let her son rest in peace. I could only look at her, thinking of what she'd said to Michelle. But I said nothing. You could see that she was so full of hate that saying anything to her would be a waste of time.

21

ON THE WEDNESDAY night Ruth rang up to remind me that we were meeting the next day to buy the dressing-gown for Mum. It had really slipped my mind, and anyway, I didn't want to bother, not any more. But there was no point in talking about it to Ruth, so I said okay, and we arranged to meet at Knightsbridge station. I went there direct from work, didn't even phone home to say I wouldn't be in for dinner. Let her stew in her own hate juice.

Ruth and I had coffee before going to the shop. Now and then in the coffee bar she'd ask if anything was the matter, and couldn't I tell her about it? I told her nothing was wrong, but the way she kept watching me you could see she didn't believe me. We went into this big store. Just as well Ruth was with me, I'd never have had the nerve to call one of those shop women, the way they walked past, ignoring you. I told Ruth let's go somewhere else, but she said no, not to worry, let's wait. Then this woman came, saying yes, madam, to Ruth, and what did madam want, at the same time making it sound as if she was doing her a favour. I felt like laughing. Ruth told her she wanted to see some dressing-gowns, please, and the woman said would madam come this way, taking us to where lots of them were hanging from racks. Ruth didn't say anything to me, but began searching among those racks, the woman standing there, her face as if she'd rather be somewhere else.

Ruth took her sweet time examining all those racks, then she asked the woman if she didn't have anything nicer, because she was looking for something special as a present for someone. The woman said what price did madam have in mind and Ruth told her the price wasn't important, not looking at me. The woman took us to a counter, with shelves full of stuff behind it, and began reaching down these flat boxes and opening them for

Ruth to look at, dressing-gowns in lovely silk, and cashmere, and nylon. Soon the counter was piled up with them, Ruth handling each one as if her father's a ruddy millionaire and money's no object. Then suddenly she says no, I don't think any of them will do, come on, Jack, taking my arm and leading me off, the shop-woman not caring, already preparing the smile on her face for the oldish woman in the wide hat walking towards her.

Outside Ruth said that was the way to deal with them when they tried to treat you like dirt. We crossed the road and caught a bus to a shop in Oxford Street. It was different there, the shop assistant friendly and smiling at Ruth and me, and Ruth talking all over the place, so that I was glad we were buying it after all. We got a nice one, dark blue wool, with white piping around the collar and cuffs and pockets. Warm and not expensive either.

Afterwards we went to a little place Ruth knew in Frith Street and had dinner. Down some stairs into a cellar, not poshed up but cosy, and the food was good. Italian or something. I found myself thinking about Michelle, remembering the time we'd had dinner together near Leicester Square. If only Mum would mind her own ruddy business.

'Jack, what's the matter? Can't you tell me?' Ruth asked me. I told her I was okay, nothing was the matter, but she said I looked as if I wanted to murder someone and she hoped it wasn't her. She began telling me about some of the girls in the place where she worked and all the goings on, me listening but not really taking it in. Then she wanted to know had I seen Michelle lately and how was she? I said I guessed she was okay but I hadn't seen her, she was busy working for her exams.

'Ron seems to have a thing about her,' she said. I let that pass. The waiter collected our dishes and brought coffee in thick cups.

'You very keen on her, Jack?'

'Look, what are you on about?'

'Just asking you a simple question. Are you keen on her?'

165

'What do you mean keen on her? I've only seen her a few times.'

'That shouldn't make any difference.'

'Look, pack it up. Why can't we talk about something else?'

'You know what?' Stirring her cup slowly, watching it.

'What?'

She looked up at me. 'I think you are. Since that night you brought her to the party I've hardly seen you, unless I come over to your house. You don't ever phone me. And you got all hot and bothered when Ron asked about her phone number. Christ, Jack, if you're keen on her why can't you come right out and say so? It's not a crime. Wouldn't even surprise me if . . .' She left the rest hanging in the air.

I could only look at her. What the hell was happening to everybody!

'Well, have you?' she kept on.

'Have I what?'

'Been to bed with her?'

'Look, why the hell don't you pack it up. What do you think she is?'

She glared at me then lowered her head over her cup, her hair falling over one shoulder to the table.

'No damned better than me.' Hardly more than a whisper. I wondered if she'd start crying and have everybody watching us.

'Look, Ruth, I didn't mean anything, not about you. I only met Michelle a few weeks ago and saw her a couple of times. Heck, do we have to keep on about her? What's she done to you?'

No sign of tears when she raised her head.

'She's not done anything to me and I'm not giving her the chance. You think I didn't notice her at the party, carrying on as if she was better than anyone else. Who cares whether she goes to Italy and Spain and the States or, or Timbuktu? I've been to Spain too. So's Ron and lots of other people I know, and they don't make such a song and dance about it. Damned black snob.'

I grabbed her arm where it rested on the table, wanting to

166

smash her across the face. I squeezed as hard as I could before letting go, her eyes going big and frightened.

I got up and went to pay at the little desk, not looking back at her. I took my change and headed upstairs. She came running behind me near Shaftesbury Avenue.

'Jack, please. I'm sorry.'

I saw him standing on the corner, both hands stuck in his mac pocket, sideways to the lighted window, but looking towards me.

'Hello, young Bennett,' he said, coming in front of me. I stopped. Ruth caught up with me. I took her arm, leading her around him. He didn't say anything else, didn't try to stop us. Ruth looked back at him.

'Who's that?' she asked.

'I don't know. To hell with him.'

'But he knew your name.'

'So what? Lots of people know my name.'

We said no more, taking the side streets to Leicester Square station. I wanted to look back but Ruth would only ask something, so I waited until we reached the station and I was getting the tickets, before taking a quick peep at the stairs, but I didn't see him. The train was nearly empty.

'Jack, I'm sorry.'

'About what?'

'What I said.'

'Forget it.' I didn't want to hear anything more about that.

'Look.' She put the parcel and her handbag on the seat next to her and pulled up her sleeve, showing me the ugly bluish red finger marks on her arm. I said I was sorry. I really was.

'Well, I suppose I asked for it. Next time I'll know to keep my opinions to myself.' Gently touching the bruises. 'That's one disadvantage of having a white skin.' I could feel the anger coming back inside me, but she pushed her arm through mine, the same bruised arm, holding me tight.

'I wish you didn't live so far away, Jack.' Hearing her say that, I began thinking how it would be to find a place of my own, away from Mum and her ruddy interfering. After all, I was earning enough, and besides, I had nearly three hundred pounds in my Post Office book. Dave and me, we'd started with savings stamps at Junior school, and when we'd gone up to Grammar School Dad had made us change over to the Savings Bank and we'd kept it up each week since we began working. I was sure I was earning more than Ruth, and if she could afford to live in a flat, hell, so could I.

I asked her what it was like, living in a flat, and she began telling me. Funny, living at home, I never thought about things like rent and what stuff cost in the shops or anything. Mum wouldn't take any money from me or Dave. But the way Ruth talked it wasn't too bad, though I knew I'd rather have somewhere to myself than sharing with anyone. I told her I'd been thinking of moving for some time but couldn't find anywhere suitable. Making it up. She said would I want to live up Kensington way, seeing it was so far from my job? But I said I wouldn't mind. So she promised to look around, right away getting excited about it, saying it was better to search for yourself than through the agents.

At Earls Court she came with me to the District Line platform for my train which was in just as we got there. I said I was sorry about her arm but she told me not to worry about it and gave me a quick kiss before I got on. The doors were closed and the train moving when I noticed that she was still holding the parcel with the dressing-gown, there on the platform.

You should have seen their faces when I walked in, especially Mum, going for me right away about where had I been and why couldn't I have phoned if I wasn't coming in for dinner? Dad said he was worried, wondering if those detectives had picked me up or something, you never knew. I said I'd been up to town and forgot to phone. Mum wanted to know who I'd gone up to town with, but Dad told her it was none of her business. She didn't like that, you could see.

I left them and went up to my room. A few minutes later Dad came up and said I must remember that if any time it should happen that they wanted to talk to me, wanted me to go with them to the station, I was to say nothing, but insist that they

call him. I was still under age and if they wanted to do something they'd have to arrest me. Anyway I was to remember to
say nothing except that they must send for him. I was about to
tell him about seeing Baldy up town, but decided not to bother.
After all, he hadn't said anything to me except hello.

22

I'D HARDLY GOT in from work next day when the door bell
went. I heard Dad talking, then that voice. I'd got to know that
voice. I went down to find out what was going on. Dad took him
into the sitting-room, Mum and me following. Said he thought
he'd drop around just in case I'd forgotten to give Dad the
message, and he wanted to keep us in the picture. The Leman
Street C.I.D. were still checking. They were trying to find out if
the blood on the bus was the same as some of that found at the
scene of the murder. Then he said that in spite of it's being in
the fire, they'd know if bloodstains on the knife matched
Thomas's. Standing there playing with his hat in his hands,
talking, talking.

Suddenly Mum asked him was he trying to say that her dead
son had murdered somebody, and Baldy answered that he
really couldn't say one way or another, not at that stage. Then,
in that same soft voice he asked Dad, 'I hear you had a little
trouble at the time of the Notting Hill riots. Some coloured
men attacked you?'

Dad turned red and told Baldy that it had happened a long
time ago, and he failed to see the connection. Baldy said he'd
heard about the incident and was interested to know why Dad
hadn't assisted the police to prosecute. Still friendly, he suddenly asked me how Dave and me felt about what the coloureds
had done to our Dad. Before I could say anything, Dad asked
him what the hell he was driving at, and if there was something
on his mind why not come right out with it? You could see our

Dad was getting really worked up. Mum was watching Baldy as if she hated him, her face white and mouth pressed so tight as if she had no lips at all. The strange thing is that, listening to Baldy, I wasn't scared any more. What Dad said was true. Why would he bother to do all this talking if he really knew something? Nobody'd seen me with Dave that night or we'd have heard something about it ages ago. Right then I got the idea that Baldy was fishing, hoping Dad or Mum or me would say something that he could fasten on to. I could have laughed.

The doorbell rang again and I went to see who it was this time, and there's Ruth, with the parcel. Just as she came in Baldy walked out of the sitting-room with Dad, saying something about how he regretted causing any inconvenience, but in a case of murder the police couldn't afford to overlook anything. He stared at Ruth and me as he went out. From the surprise on Ruth's face, I was sure she recognized him. She looked at me but said nothing. For a while after he'd gone we were like a bunch of dummies, just looking at one another, the word murder still hanging about around us where he'd dropped it. Then Ruth said she'd had to come all the way over because I'd walked off and forgotten the parcel. Handing it to me. Dad and Mum went towards the kitchen.

'What was all that about?' Ruth whispered.

'What?'

'Him?' Nodding her head towards the front door.

'Oh, nothing. Go on, you give it to her.' I pushed the parcel back into her hands.

She walked past me to the kitchen and gave the parcel to Mum, saying here's a little present for you, Mum, calling her Mum, and Mum smiling, loosening the knots carefully to save the piece of string, then spreading the paper out and saying thanks, and it's lovely, and she shouldn't have done it. Ruth said it wasn't her it was me, and I deserved a special kiss. Mum standing there looking confused. I left them and went up to finish washing. That would just about kill her, kissing me. Couldn't remember her doing it ever since I was a kid.

Ruth tried her best during dinner to liven things up, talking a blue streak, but nobody felt much like fun, Dad hardly eating anything, and Mum watching him. I was hungry and so was Ruth. After dinner I went up to my room, leaving Ruth to help Mum with the washing-up. I played an MJQ and later on Ruth came up and sat listening, but every now and then I felt her eyes on me and I knew she was bursting to ask questions. Then she couldn't bear it and turned the volume down.

'That was the same man who spoke to you last night, wasn't he?'

'Yes.'

'I thought I'd recognized him but I wasn't sure. He's the same detective who came here with the photograph of you and your brother, isn't he?'

'Yes.'

'Jack, what's it all about? Are you in some kind of trouble? Can't you tell me?'

I said I was in no trouble.

'Then who, your Dad?' The look on her face so funny I couldn't help laughing. 'You think it's some sort of joke?'

'Look, who said it was any joke? All right. Those policemen found Dave's knife at the accident. He always carried it around with him, and they found it near where the car turned over. So, this fellow is killed somewhere in Stepney with a knife and they want to know if there's any connection, that's all.'

'Is there?'

'What do you mean, is there? Dave wasn't anywhere near Stepney. What would he want to go there for? What do you think he was, a murderer or something?'

'I didn't say that.'

'I know you didn't, but the way you keep on anyone would think . . .'

'All right, you don't need to shout.' She got up and turned up the volume, then came back and sat beside me.

'What's up with you and your Mum? Had a row?' I had to laugh. If she wasn't on to one thing it was another. And always the questions.

'You should have been a lawyer, not a shorthand typist,' I

told her, but she wasn't amused. So I asked what was on her mind now. She said she'd been wondering because she'd noticed we didn't say much to each other. I told her she was what my Dad called a chronic worrier, and if she kept on like that she'd give some poor bloke a hell of a time. Right away she asks if I didn't realize that it was she being given a hell of a time and not the poor bloke as I called him.

Anyway she stopped the questions and we nattered about this and that, mostly about finding a little flat or room somewhere. She began telling me about how lots of fellows like Ron and Ginger Petty lived in flatlets and did all kinds of things for themselves, even taking stuff to the launderette. She asked me if I knew how to make a bed or cook or iron a shirt. I said no. She laughed, for the first time that night, telling me she'd have to keep an eye on me or I'd starve to death and go around like a beatnik.

When it was time for her to leave we went down to find Mum and Dad. Usually at that time of night they were in the sitting-room watching television, but we heard them in the kitchen, and when we walked in they were sitting there, serious as judges. Ruth went and kissed Mum and said good night to her, then the same with Dad, me looking and wondering when all this kissing had begun anyway. And you could see that, for all his serious face, Dad was as pleased as anything.

As soon as I got in from seeing Ruth off on her train Dad called me into the kitchen. He wanted to know if I'd mentioned to Baldy about Notting Hill. I told him I hadn't. He sat there wondering aloud who could have told him. Not any of his mates on the site. Only a few of them knew anything about it and if the police had gone there asking any questions they wouldn't have got much change out of any of them. Then Mum said perhaps the police had been talking to some of the neighbours. One by one they ticked them off, all those they thought might have known about it, till they came to Spotty Frock. Mum said she was sure if it was anyone it was that woman.

Funny thing, but right after that Dad cheered up, said he didn't give a damn what she'd said. He seemed to feel better, thinking it was not one of his mates at the site. But all of a sudden he got serious again and said did I realize how everyone had to suffer for what Dave and me had done. Innocent people. Him and Mum and others. He didn't name any names but I knew who he meant. He said that ever since Dave was killed neither he nor Mum had known a quiet night, especially Mum, crying in bed most nights. Christ, the way he carried on I felt sorry I was alive. I just sat and listened to it.

Then Mum had a go, telling Dad not to waste his time talking to me, didn't he see I was all taken up with those niggers, even after what they did to my own twin brother. I could have killed her. I lost my temper and asked her if she thought I didn't care about Dave, just because I didn't go around moaning all over the place and being unpleasant to people I hardly knew. What did she want me to do, hate everybody just because he was dead? Okay, if I was making so much trouble for everybody, I'd clear out. Find a room somewhere for myself then I wouldn't be bothering anyone. Crikey! You would have thought I'd dropped a bomb or something the way Mum jumped at that.

'So that's it, is it? You're such a man now that you think you can just walk out of here when you please,' her voice screaming at me.

'Since when is this house not good enough for you? And your brother not cold in his grave? Tell me.' Dad told her to quieten down and told me I should stop talking damn rubbish, that I had a good, comfortable home and whoever heard of such nonsense. Inside I felt quite calm, and suddenly I made up my mind. I said to Dad that I meant it, about leaving. I'd had enough of being treated like a child.

Mum was watching me, her mouth thin and tight, then she said, 'I think it's those niggers that put you up to it.' Just like that, as if she hadn't listened to a single word I'd said.

'Now, Madge,' Dad warned her. 'There's no call for that, no call for that at all.'

I couldn't say a word. I know it's not right to hate your own mother, but who says anybody's mother has the right to say things like that. I was pushing my chair back to get up and shove off upstairs, but she was up in a flash and standing with her back against the door.

'Yes, it's those dirty Spades that put you up to it.' The voice was quiet but full of spite. 'All of a sudden you think you're a man and you can leave home. I don't know what's been going on between you and them, but all of a sudden you can't be spoken to. You should be ashamed of yourself. After those dirty niggers killed your own brother. Taking up with that black slut and carrying on God alone knows what. They've no shame, the lot of them.'

'Now see here, Madge.' Dad tried to shut her up.

'Don't see-here-Madge me,' she spat at him. Then back to me. 'If you think your brother's in his grave and you'll get off scot-free, you're damn well mistaken. So you'd better watch out, I'm warning you. You'd damn well better watch out.'

I could only stare at her, like someone I'd never seen before in my life, her face twisted with hating me, the corner of her mouth whitish with spittle. My own mother. I just couldn't understand it. What had I done? What was there so terrible about wanting to be on my own? From what she'd said she probably had it in her head that the Spencers had put me up to it. Christ, how daft can you get?

She left the door and came back to the table. The dressing-gown was lying on the table near where she'd been sitting. Grabbing it up she threw it at me.

'That's why you fetched that in, was it? To soften me up? Well, I don't need anything from you. Take it and give it to that nigger slut, with my compliments.'

The parcel hit me in the face, the corner catching me in the eye. The sudden pain brought tears, and millions of words came crowding into my head which couldn't be said to my mother. I let the parcel fall on the floor, pushed the table to one side and went through the door, upstairs into my room. I pulled my bed around against the door so nobody could get in and lay on it while the things inside me tried to tear my guts to bits. I stuffed my mouth with the sheet to stop the sounds I couldn't help making, helpless, as if I'd lost something for ever. When it stopped I lay there, feeling tired and really alone. In my mind I called Dave to come and change places with me, be here instead of me, then all would be fine. For Mum. She hated me for being alive while Dave was dead. All the talk about niggers and Spades was just her excuse for hating me.

I heard somebody stop outside my door, as if they were listening, then walk away. Sounded like Mum. I cursed her in my mind. Later, when everything was quiet I got up and put a few things in a canvas holdall Dave and me used for our kit when we went swimming, my razor, comb, brush, Post Office savings book, small towel, a pair of socks, my new copy of World Sports, and Dave's book of poems. Then I moved the bed away, not even bothering to be quiet, and went downstairs and out of the house. Only when I was on my way to the station did I make up my mind to go to Ruth.

23

WHEN SHE OPENED the door and saw me, her eyes became big and scared. Before I could say a word she grabbed my arm and pulled me inside, then stood looking at me as if I was a ghost or something.

'What's happened, Jack?' Keeping her voice down, probably not wanting Naomi to hear us. Her hair was in curlers and she was wrapped up in a thick white towel robe. I told her I'd had a row with Mum and walked out, and could I stay there just the night?

'Is that all, Jack? Nothing else? Please don't lie to me.'

I said of course that was all and what she she acting so funny about. Right away she sat down and began crying, hiding her face in her hands. I sat beside her, not knowing what the heck to make of it.

After a little while she told me. She thought perhaps the police were after me, because soon after the train left Upminster he'd come and sat near to her, the same man she'd seen at our house, Baldy. She'd recognized him at once. Said he was a police officer and could he have a word with her? Then he'd wanted to know how long she'd known me, and if she'd known Dave, and what I was like, if she knew any of my friends. All kinds of questions. Did I ever talk to her about my brother and the things we did and where we used to go. Most of the time she said she didn't know because she didn't. Then she asked him why was he asking all those questions and he said because of a little matter they had to clear up. He asked her if I'd ever mentioned going to Stepney with Dave and she said no. Then he asked how did I feel about coloured people, and did we ever talk about them? She couldn't remember all that he'd asked and what she said, but she hadn't said much really because she didn't know anything. He'd got off at East Ham after thanking her for her help, but she didn't see how she could have helped him, not knowing anything. She was frightened, remembering the remark he'd made about someone being murdered, and when she got in wanted to ring me and tell me what had happened, but Naomi was in the sitting-room with some friends and the phone was there, so she couldn't. The friends had left only a few minutes ago and before she could ring me, here I was.

Again she wanted to know what was going on and if I was in any trouble, otherwise why would that policeman ask her all those questions about me? And what did he mean about Stepney? She'd read in the newspapers about the man being killed in Stepney. Did that have anything to do with me?

'What is it all about, Jack? Tell me, please.' I repeated that Dave had always carried a knife with him, a fancy thing in a sheath, just for fun, and the police had found it at the accident. Now they were wondering if it was the same knife that had killed the fellow Thomas in Stepney, and if Dave had been anywhere in Stepney that night.

'Had he?' she wanted to know.

'Look, Ruth. Dave left home to go and listen to some jazz in the West End that night. At least that's where he said he was going. I don't know anything about him going to Stepney and can't think of any reason why he'd want to go to Stepney?

'Why did the detective want to know how you felt about coloured people?'

'How should I know?'

Question after question, till I got fed up with it and said look, is it okay for me to stay? She thought it would be, but she'd better have a word with Naomi. She was back in a few minutes with Naomi, both of them telling me I could stay as long as I liked if I didn't mind bunking on the divan, and they fetched blankets and sheets and some cushions for pillows. I felt sorry about imposing on them like that but they said it was okay and they'd help me look around for a place.

Funny about waking up in a strange room. For some minutes you're wondering why familiar things are not where they're supposed to be. Slowly you realize where you are and the whole thing starts up again, as if sleeping is only like a one-minute rest between three-minute rounds, and they're waiting to have another go at you. Broad beams of sunlight were streaming through the open window shades on my feet where they'd pushed out from under the covers, and it was nice to feel the warmth. From somewhere outside birds were chirping, sparrows probably, making this excited noise as if they were quarrelling and fighting among themselves and I thought, crikey, even the ruddy birds! My watch said seven o'clock and I got up, dressed quietly and began folding the blankets and sheets, figuring on slipping out before the girls got up, but before you knew it, there was Ruth in her dressing-gown, hair every which way. Made me remember Mum's old one still stuck under my bed. Wonder what she said when she couldn't find it. She'd have to go and pick up the one she slung on the floor. I didn't give a damn.

While I washed and shaved Ruth made coffee and toast. Naomi was still asleep and Ruth said we shouldn't make any noise to wake her up. Saturday mornings they usually slept late, not having to work. Most Saturdays I didn't work either, except like today when we had something special to do at the works.

Ruth said that she and Naomi would try to find a room or flatlet for me and I promised to phone them around noon, as I was only working half-day.

24

WHEN I CAME off work I saw Dad standing near the bus stop, waiting for me, then remembered I'd told him I had to work that Saturday.

'Well, Son.'

'Hello, Dad,' and we stood there embarrassing the hell out of each other.

Then Dad said, 'Well, let's get on home.' So I told him I wasn't coming home after what had happened last night. He said I shouldn't be a damn fool, that two wrongs didn't make a right, and where did I think I'd go anyway? I said not to worry about me, I'd find some digs somewhere. He said that digs and places like that were for people who had no real home and family and if that was really what I wanted to do nobody would stop me, but it was never any good doing things in anger on the spur of the moment, so why not come home and let's talk it over quietly together. And about what Mum had said, I shouldn't take any of it too seriously. She got these crazy ideas in her head and wild horses couldn't drag them out. I should know by now that her bark was much worse than her bite, and underneath it all I was her son and blood was thicker than water.

Standing there listening to him I didn't know what to say, especially with him talking like that.

'Well, Son, we can't stand here all day,' he said. I told him I didn't want to come back to have Mum carry on at me like she did, throwing my present in my face and cursing people she didn't even know. Then he got very serious and turned as if ready to walk off and leave me saying,

'Look, Son, you're a man now, so it's up to you what you do.

If you've decided to leave home and go your own way, at least do it right. Tell your Mother what you aim to do, then do it, but don't sneak off in the middle of the night and have her wondering where you are and what's happened to you. In spite of what she said and did she's still your mother and entitled to be treated with respect. Well, there's the bus. Are you coming?'

I went along with him, thinking to myself, Okay, but she'd better not start, not again. On the bus we talked about all sorts of little things till we got home.

Going through the kitchen door with Dad, I saw Mum doing something at the cooker. She looked over her shoulder at us. All she said was, 'Hurry up, you two.' Then she went on with what she was doing.

Hardly a word while we were eating, but as soon as we were finished Dad told her that I'd said I was moving out. She shrugged her shoulders.

'That's up to him, isn't it?' she said, and right away she got up and began collecting the dishes as if she didn't want any further discussion.

Dad put an old newspaper on the table and began cleaning out his pipe with the big old stag-handled scout knife he'd had since he was a boy. When Mum had cleared all the dishes into the sink he told her to come back and sit down.

'At least we can discuss it like a family,' he said.

'There's nothing to discuss,' Mum said, 'if he wants to leave let him leave. But whatever it is he's running away from he'll find it waiting for him wherever he goes.' She sat straight in her chair, arms folded across her chest. Dad got up, went around the table, carrying his chair with him, and sat beside her.

'Now listen, Madge, what's happened has happened and we can't change anything, least of all by quarrelling amongst ourselves. Our Dave did something wrong, very wrong, come to think of it, and what happened to him was, in a manner of speaking, some kind of, well, rough justice, if you like, what people call retribution. Anyway, he paid for what he did, so there's no reason to take it out on Jack here. Best thing . . .'

She didn't let him finish.

'How do you know that Dave did anything? Tell me that. How do you know?' pulling away from Dad's arm which he'd put around her shoulder, her mouth tight. We were both staring at her. Dad asked her what in heaven's name was she talking about.

'Just what I said. How do you know that Dave did anything at all? How do you know he hasn't paid for something he didn't do? You weren't there, were you?'

'But Jack here said . . .'

'I'm not interested in what Jack said.' She turned to look at me, cold, like a stranger. 'I've been thinking about it. Every night I've been thinking about it. Dave is not here to defend himself, so anybody can say what they like about him . . .'

'Now, look here, Madge,' from Dad, but I could only look at her, not knowing whether to laugh or cry.

'You said the nigger was on top of Dave hitting him, didn't you? Well, what about you? Not even a scratch. Not one little scratch. What were you doing when all that was happening? Running? Hiding?'

She leaned across the table, spitting it out at me.

'You ran away and left him, didn't you? That's why you got here first, sneaking in with your lies. You didn't stay to help him, your own brother. Oh Dave, oh Dave.' And she sprawled on the table, crying, her fingers trying to dig into the wood. I felt afraid, without knowing what I was afraid of. Christ, I'd told her everything, exactly as it had all happened, and I'd thought she believed me. What was she trying to do, make me feel like a criminal or something? How could she think I'd run off and leave him? Dad helped her back into her chair, looking at me as if he too suspected me, believed what Mum had said. You could see it in his face.

'Look, Dad . . .' I began, wanting to tell him again how it was, make him understand I couldn't do that to Dave, not Dave, no matter what Mum said. She must be crazy or something. But he hushed me.

'I don't want to hear any more. Your mother's upset enough.'

But Mum straightened up, and pushed him away, nearly knocking the table over, Dad's pipe and knife sliding down so that I had to grab them from falling on the floor. She came around the table at me.

'Maybe it was you who stuck the knife into the nigger. How do I know it wasn't you? How do I know you didn't stab him then run off? Dave could have picked up the knife where you dropped it, and now he's dead you let him take the blame. I don't believe he did it, you hear? I don't believe my Dave killed anybody. I think you did it, you, you . . .' Crying and coming for me. I jumped up, backing away, and Dad dashed around and held her. Then both of them were staring at me, down at my hands.

I must have dropped the pipe. I was holding the knife, gripping it tightly, the blade sticking out at one end, the thick spike at the other.

'Put that knife down, Son,' Dad said, his voice soft. It was as if my hand belonged to somebody else. I closed the knife, afraid of it, and put it on the table. I wanted to explain that I didn't mean to do anything with it, not against my own mother. I'd only stopped it from falling on to the floor.

Mum turned around, holding Dad tight, saying over and over, Jesus God, oh, Jesus God. Dad looked at me, telling me with his eyes to go, leave them alone.

I went and sat in the sitting-room, unable to think straight. I saw Dad leading Mum past the door and up the stairs, talking to her, telling her not to worry, everything was going to be all right. A few minutes later he came down, not even looking at me, and telephoned Dr Wishart. From what I heard the doctor was out somewhere, but his wife said she'd tell him to call at our house as soon as he could. After he hung up Dad went back upstairs. I didn't know what the hell to do. What had happened to Mum all of a sudden? A couple of minutes ago she was ready to tear my eyes out, now Dad was carrying on as if she was really sick. The whole thing was like some crazy nightmare.

I don't know how long I'd been sitting there before the door-bell went and there was old Dr Wishart, looking the same as ever. Dave and me used to call him Dr Five-by-Five because he was so short and fat, always smiling, his thick white curly hair always neat like Mr Brylcreem himself.

'Well, what's your Mum gone and done this time?' he asked me as he came inside, but Dad had come down and he and the doctor went up to Mum. I stayed downstairs and after about fifteen or twenty minutes Dr Wishart came down and handed me a prescription to take to the chemist. He gave me a funny look, not smiling, and I wondered what they'd said to him.

When I got back from the chemist the doctor had gone. I gave Dad the stuff, three small boxes. Sounded like pills.

'What's up with Mum?' I asked him.

'The doctor says it's her nerves. He gave her something and she's sleeping now.' Then, after a bit, he added, 'Perhaps it's just as well if you clear off.'

'Look, Dad, I wasn't . . .'

'I'm not accusing you of anything.' He wasn't even looking at me. 'But I think it's best if you clear off for a while until your mother is more herself.'

'Dad, if you mean about the . . .' But he wouldn't let me say anything.

'What's happened is over and done with, whatever it is, and we're having no more talk about it. I had a word with the doctor and he agrees that it would be best if she was kept quiet for a bit, not allowed to get excited about anything. I'll ring your Aunt Beth and see if she can come down and help out.'

It's funny, but hearing him talk like that, telling me to get out, made me feel different about going. Planning it with Ruth I was excited, wanting to do it. But now, it was as if I hadn't made any plans at all and here was my own Dad kicking me out of the house. And for what? I hadn't done anything, anything at all. I hated them, both of them.

'Okay,' I said. 'Do you want me to clear off right now?' To hell with them, I'd find somewhere to go. I wasn't some ruddy kid. Even if I had to sleep on the streets I didn't care.

'Don't you take that tone with me,' he said. 'You're the one who started it. You said you wanted to clear out. But you couldn't do it quietly. You had to get your mother all upset.'

I couldn't listen to any more. I got up, went upstairs, and began to put my stuff on my bed, suits, shirts, everything. Then I realized I didn't have a suitcase. Never had one. Well, Dave and me had never been anywhere to really need them. Times when we went off to scout camp we put our stuff in one of Dad's. I'd have to go out and get one. He came into the room quietly and said someone was on the phone for me. I thought it might be Ruth. With all that had been happening I'd forgotten to ring like I'd promised. She'd chew my ear off.

It was Naomi. She sounded a bit angry, saying they'd been waiting for me to ring and were worried, wondering if anything had happened to me. I knew what she meant. Just to keep her quiet I said I'd come over home because Mum was ill. She asked what had happened, and I told her it was something to do with Mum's nerves and the doctor had been over and given her something to make her sleep. She asked had I seen Ruth and I said no. Then she said that when they hadn't heard anything from me, Ruth had left saying she was coming up to Upminster to find out what had happened. So I said okay. I'd be here when she arrived. I asked if they'd had any luck and she said they'd been looking around all morning but hadn't found anything. Either the places were dumps or they were much too expensive. They'd heard of a room in Earls Court Road and she was going to see it later in the afternoon, and if I'd be at home she'd ring me and let me know. I said okay. I didn't tell her that Dad had thrown me out. To hell with it. I just didn't give a damn what happened.

'You don't have to clear off today.' Dad had come in and was standing by the door. I didn't want to hear any more about anything. Just let them leave me alone.

'I'm not turning you out,' he went on, 'but the state your mother's in it's best if she's not, well, upset. There's your job, so you can't, like, go up and stay with Beth and Andy, and anyway I've phoned Beth and she will be coming here to look after your mother. Perhaps for the time being you could stay with a friend or something. No need to shift all your stuff. After all, it's only till your mother gets over this . . .'

'You said to clear off so I'll clear off.'

'You started it, don't forget that. You just walked out of here without a word to anyone, your mother was in such a state not knowing where you'd got to . . .'

'What does she care?' I could hardly speak, all choked up inside. 'All she thinks about is Dave. Now she's saying that it was me who killed that . . .' I couldn't make myself say any of those names, not even coloured; Mum had made them all sound so dirty.

'Your mother is not herself. You should know that. Ever since your brother went she's been brooding over it, keeping it inside, wouldn't even talk to me. Most nights I'd be lying there, she thinking I'm asleep, but I know she's crying her heart out. Well, now it's got a bit too much for her. Don't suppose she really means half of what she says.'

'Oh, she means it all right.'

'Now just you shut up. Just you damn well shut up. You've got a hell of a lot to learn, young feller. A hell of a lot. After the doctor gave her the injection, when she was dropping off, do you know what she said? Where's Jack? . . .'

I didn't want to hear, it didn't mean anything to me. Maybe she just wanted to know if I'd cleared off yet.

'All right, suit yourself what you do,' he said, turning away. 'Clear off if you want to. But suppose your mother takes a turn for the worse, what then?' Christ, what did they want from me? A little while ago he's telling me to get out, now this. As if everything was my fault.

There was a ring at the door and he went down, then came back, opening a telegram. I guessed it was from Aunt Beth, but after he read it he gave it to me. It went

PLEASE COME SEE ME EARLIEST CONVENIENCE.
URGENT. DENISE SPENCER.

I turned it over and saw it was addressed to me, Jack Bennett. Right away I felt as mad as hell. It was my telegram. He'd seen it was addressed to me and yet he'd opened it and read it. The first ruddy telegram I'd ever had in my life and he had to open it, as if it was for him.

'What's it about?' he wanted to know.

I folded it and put it in my pocket. None of his ruddy business.

'What're they sending you telegrams for?'

'Did you have to open it?' How would he like it if it was for him and I'd opened it?

'I'll open any damn thing I please.' You could see he was getting all worked up. I began folding my ties.

'I want to know what it's all about,' he asked again.

'I don't know.'

'Then you'd damn well better get over there and find out, hadn't you?' and he went out of the room.

I read the telegram over and over again, wondering what it was she wanted. Denise Spencer. Mrs Denise Spencer. Not bad. Not bad at all. Better than Madge and Ruth, names like that. What was so urgent that she wanted to see me about it? It could only be about Michelle and the way I'd rushed off, not bothering to say good night or anything. But what was so urgent about that?

25

I DIDN'T PHONE to say I was coming. Michelle came to the door, looking a bit surprised to see me.

'Hello, I thought it was Mummy,' she said, opening the door wide for me to go in past her. She was wearing tight grey slacks and a fluffy V-neck sweater. Lipstick red as her shiny toenails.

'I had a telegram from . . .'

'Oh, yes.' She led me through to the room looking out on to the estuary.

'The telegram said it was urgent.'

'Yes, I know.'

We sat down, her face serious as hell, curling up her legs under her.

'Any idea what it's all about?'

She just sat watching me, as if seeing me for the first time. Not even smiling.

'Look, is it something I said the other night?' I was beginning to feel a bit uncomfortable with her sitting like miles away and watching me, as if I was some ruddy stranger.

'Would you care for a drink?' As if she didn't hear what I said. I told her no, I didn't want a drink.

'How're the studies going?' I asked. Just talking to make conversation.

'Very well, thank you. And your work?'

'Same old drag. Nothing to get excited about.' Silence for what seemed like ages. For no reason at all she pulled her chair further away under the window.

'What's it all about?' I asked her.

'Meaning what?'

'The telegram. What's up?' I was getting sick of just sitting there, waiting.

'You know, the very first time I saw you, when I was speaking with your father, I thought you reminded me of someone, but I couldn't think who. Now I remember. Not so much a physical resemblance as the same look on your face.'

'What look's that?'

'Oh, just the way you look. As if you hated everybody.'

'I haven't a clue what you're talking about.' Sitting way over there as if she thought I would try something. To hell with it.

'Doesn't matter.'

'Who was he, a boyfriend of yours?'

'No. Just someone I met. A really nasty, horrible person.'

'Well, thanks for telling me.' I got up.

'I wasn't referring to you. Look, you asked me who he was and I told you, that's all. No need to take it personally. Please sit down.'

She went and fetched a box of cigarettes and offered me one. I said I didn't want to smoke. She took one and lit it, the way she held it I could see she wasn't a regular. Puffing like somebody sending out smoke signals.

'What did he do?' I wanted to hear about this fellow I reminded her of. I sat down.

'What did who do?'

'The nasty, horrible person like me.'

'He struck me.' The way she said it, as if it had happened only five minutes ago, her face going tight and sharp, just like Mum's when she's mad about something. All of a sudden I wished I knew who he was, the bastard who'd hit her. I'd have liked to bash his bloody head in.

'What for?'

She crushed the long cigarette in the ashtray and got up, leaning her head against the window, looking down at whatever was happening outside. I'd have liked to touch her neck, so soft-looking, the hair shining with a brownish tint from the sun on it. Those legs. I'd bet she could run like a bullet. Somebody once told me they could all run, fast.

'Nothing,' she said.

'How do you mean nothing? What did he do, just walk straight off the street and hit you?'

'It was at a dance.' Still looking out of the window.

'Look, can't you just sit down and tell me what happened?'

She turned around, looked at me for a while as if making up her mind, then sat down.

'Okay, now tell me,' I said, to get her going, 'So he took you dancing and he hit you.'

'It was last summer.' She curled her legs up under her, talking, pulling at a curly thread in the sleeve of her jumper. 'A friend of mine from King's lives at Southend and she invited me to spend a week-end with her. On the Saturday night we went to a dance at the Palais. I wasn't particularly keen on dancing there, but a band from London was on just for the night, and we wanted to hear it, especially the vocalist. He'd been on television several times and I liked the way he sang, smooth and easy. Usually I only went dancing with Bill, to his hospital do's, or sometimes he'd take Mummy and me up to town, mostly to Edmundo Ros's club. That used to be wonderful.'

The little smile on her face seemed to come from some far away place and it didn't stay long.

'Penny and I got there early but it was already crowded so we had to stand, but we were quite near the stage and we could watch the band and the vocalist when he came on. People asked Penny to dance. I didn't mind. It was funny watching the drummer. As he played he kept talking to himself, not really saying anything, just miming words, his eyes closed and his head cocked to one side as if listening to the sounds of the other instruments.'

The way she was telling it, as if she was there again, living it, reminded me of Dave. Same way he had of telling you about something that happened as if it was happening again, now. Like that Sunday when Mum had made us some buns for tea, but something or other made her forget about them and they came out half burned. Mum was so mad she wanted to dump the lot, but Dave said no, let's cut off the burnt parts. Then he began messing about, saying how the same thing happened once upon a time to a bloke named King Alfred, better known as Alf King, and right away he began making up a story about how Alf had dropped in to have tea with this bird and she asked him to keep an eye on the stuff in the oven while she popped out for a jiff to get an evening paper to check if her pools entry had come up. While she was out Alf got so excited watching wrestling on TV that he forgot all about the stuff in the oven and the next thing you know smoke is all over the place, and this bird just beats the fire engine back to the house. Telling it so he had Mum in fits, saying only royalty could burn stuff just so.

While Michelle talked, her eyes were looking somewhere over my shoulder, through the wall and away, and I could nearly hear the drummer talking to himself, and see the spotlight on the vocalist when he walked on to sing.

'He was just as I'd seen him on television. Relaxed, you know, as if he was full of music and he only had to open his mouth to let it out. And the way a bit of his hair kept falling over his forehead and he'd push it away with his left hand. Most of the people had stopped dancing to listen to him, crowding up around the stage, yelling and whistling when he finished each number.

'Right behind me were three young men, shouting a little more loudly than anyone else. I tried to move away from them, but it wasn't possible. But soon the band started again, and they went away. I found seats near by, sat down, and put my handbag on the next one to save it for Penny. I sat there listening until the band went off for a break. Penny was a bit concerned because I wasn't dancing, but I didn't mind, I was enjoying the music.

'After intermission two of the young fellows who'd been so noisy came up and asked us to dance. The one I danced with was tall, thin and blond, rather like you, only his hair was wispy and straight, not curly like yours. He was a good dancer, but a bit silly, you know, dancing but looking bored as if he didn't really care much about what he was doing . . .'

I was seeing it, seeing her with him, whoever the hell he was. Seeing her grey eyes shining, moving as light as a feather the way it had been when we'd danced at Ruth's, eyes closed and her whole body as if the music had got inside her like fire.

' "Hey, you're good," he said, or something like that, when the music stopped, and we were standing there waiting for the encore. There was hardly any wind left for replying. I just smiled and turned to go, but he held my hand.

' "Hey, wait a sec, they're starting again. How about it?" Before I could say anything the music began again. I must say this for him, he could dance. This time he began to improvise instead of just standing there leading me. Smiling to himself, you know, as if he was really enjoying it. Till the dance ended.

' "Say, you're some cat," he said to me. I didn't know whether to be pleased or not.

' "What I mean is," he said, "you're good, see, know what I mean?" I wanted to get back to my seat, and moved ahead of him, but he held my arm, following me, talking. "Never seen you here before. I know just about all the cats who come."

'I told him that it was my first visit, that my friend and I came really to hear the band.

' "Oh, the chick old Phil's been dancing with. Phil's me mate. Okay for the next?"

'I said I'd have the next dance with him and he went off to talk with his friends. Penny was sitting there, looking absolutely furious. I asked her what was the matter.

' "That fellow you've been dancing with."

'I said I thought he was pretty good. Then she told me.

' "He did it for a dare. Danced with you. Him and his two friends saw you standing listening to the band, and they dared each other to dance with you. His friend Phil, the one I was dancing with, told me about it. They drew straws, got them with the coca-cola, and the blond one got the long straw. You know what that Phil said? They wanted to know what it felt like to dance with a Spade. That's what he said. Damned filthy morons."

' "With what?"

' "That's what he said. With a Spade. Meaning you. I was so mad I felt like slapping his damned face. So I walked off the floor and left him. Look, let's get out of here."

'We picked up our bags and were going to the cloakroom when the band started another number and he was coming towards us, smiling. Without a word we walked right past him to get our coats. When we came out he was standing there, barring our way.

' "Hey, what's up? You said I could have this dance." Pointing his face at me.

' "She's changed her mind," Penny spat at him.

' "What for? What did I do?"

'His voice was squeaky, he was so surprised.

' "Just get out of our way," I said, "Just clear off and leave us alone." We pushed past him and left. It was too late for the buses so we walked the short distance along the front to where she lived. He must have followed us. A few yards from her house we heard the running footsteps and he caught up with us, blocking our way.

' "What did me mate tell you?" His voice sounded loud out there in the stillness.

' "Will you get out of our way and stop bothering us?" Penny said to him.

' "I want to know what me mate said to you. He told me you walked off and left him on the floor. And anyway, she promised me the next dance."

' "Will you get out of our way?" Penny wasn't scared of him. I was.

' "Go on, tell me," he said to me, "Why'd you shove off? Why'd you promise me the dance and then shove off? Think you're too bloody good to dance with me?" I was so scared, wondering if his friends might be following too.

' "Look here," Penny told him, "do you realize we're standing just outside our house? If you don't clear off this minute I'll scream and get my father out here to deal with you." That would have been some trick because her father died when she was three and we were still about fifty yards from her house. But the boy probably believed her. He moved aside, then suddenly punched me in the face and ran off, shouting "dirty bloody Spade".'

Her voice was tense with remembering. I felt the tightening inside me, the quick hatred for the fellow, wishing I had a face for him, for finding him and hurting him even more than he'd hurt her. Then, in the same moment, the thought of Mum using the same words, and the memory of a wet, windy night and the other faceless man kneeling in the road and slowly, falling over.

She uncurled her legs, drawing them up until her face was hidden between the knees, her hands over her ears as if trying to shut out sounds I couldn't hear. I wished I could go and sit beside her, put my arm around her and tell her how I felt. But I couldn't. There was this thing, like a wall of glass around her. Then I wasn't thinking any more. I was beside her, holding her. She turned around, her face wet and streaky, her mouth open to say something and I kissed her, holding her tight, feeling my heart near to bursting inside me, and her giving in, kissing me.

'I love you,' I told her when at last I could speak.

She loosed my arm from around her, pushing away. I was surprised at how strong she was. She moved away from me.

'You're covered in lipstick,' she said, not smiling, and going somewhere inside. I wiped my mouth, the wide red smears on the white cloth reminding me sickeningly of another time. She came back and stood by the window, facing me.

'It was I who sent the telegram,' she said. Before the words really sank in she went on, 'I didn't want to phone your house again and I wasn't sure who'd open the telegram, so I used Mummy's name.'

'Okay.' I understood. 'What's it all about?' The sun came out from behind a cloud and shone full into the window around her head, so I couldn't see her features clearly.

'I wanted to explain something. Last time you came you rushed off before I could say it.'

I could still taste the bitter tang of her lipstick and remember the feel of her soft warm tongue in the little moment before she struggled away from me. I crossed my legs, hoping she hadn't noticed what had happened to me.

'Look, do you have to stand there?'

She left the window and sat on the couch facing me, her face serious as hell, all the lipstick wiped clean from her mouth.

'What I want to tell you is that in spite of what your mother said I don't hate you. I'm not forgetting what she said, but I don't hate you for it, and I didn't want you rushing off like that, thinking I hated you.'

When I didn't say anything she went on, 'I had it all thought out, what I was going to say to you, I'd gone over it in my mind until it was quite clear, but now . . . what I mean to say is that I don't think I want to go out with you any more.'

'Why, because of what my Mum said?'

'No, your mother has nothing to do with it. Not really. The

truth is, I'm not in love with you and when we're out together I'm not comfortable with you.'

'Look, what are you talking about?' I asked her 'What have I done now? Is it because I kissed you just now? Christ, I wasn't trying to rape you or anything. You don't have to feel uncomfortable because of that.' Talking to her I could still taste her lipstick in my mouth and wished I could spit it out or wash my mouth or something. She sat there, not smiling, but cool and easy, not giving a damn.

'I don't mean sitting here with you, or . . . I'm talking about when we've been out together. Walking along or on a train. The way people stare at us. And I can feel that you're uncomfortable too.'

'I don't give one little damn about them.'

'Most of the time I don't either. When I'm by myself. Or when I went out with Bill.'

'So what's the difference?'

'With Bill I never noticed if anyone stared. Probably because I didn't care if they did. It's the same when I'm with one of the girls from college. People look at us. You can see them looking, not staring. Not the way they look when I'm with a man. A white man. Staring. Hating me with their eyes. And hating him for being with me.'

Her voice had gone hard and nasty. Just like Mum's when she's worked up about something. She went on, 'When I'm by myself I don't care who stares at me. By myself I'm at ease, looking them straight in their face, proud because I am who I am and I know what I do and what I'm going to be. I can look at them and not care a damn who they are or what they're thinking. I don't want to change places with any of them. Ever. Sometimes I despise them. Not because they're white. It's what I see in their faces when they look at me.'

'What's all that got to do with me making you uncomfortable?'

'Don't you see?' she asked me, making it sound as if I was some kind of ruddy idiot for not understanding. 'When you're there you sort of get in the way between me and them, and I have to tell myself that probably you're not thinking what they're thinking, and you're not like them. It's as if I have to look at them through you, and that makes me feel helpless against them. Do you see what I mean?'

'No.'

'Well, I'm sorry, but I can't explain it any better. Mummy understood when I told her, but she said the reason I felt that way was because I'm not in love with you. Perhaps if she was here she could explain it much better, but I asked her to go out because I wanted to tell you myself.'

'So you don't want me to come here any more?' She looked away, her voice going so soft I could barely hear it.

'I didn't think you'd still want to.' Then, turning back to me, 'I suppose it would be best if you didn't.' Looking down at me the same way like that time over at our house. Like some queen. Yes. Just like some effing black queen. Well, to hell with it. If she thought I'd come crawling to her . . . I stood up.

'Okay, if that's how you feel about it.' I fished the telegram out of my pocket and dropped it on the chair. She followed me to the door and opened it.

'Good-bye, Jack.' She was holding out her hand. After telling me all that, she was holding out her hand for me to shake as if nothing had happened. The things I wanted to say to her, but I kept my mouth shut and went through the door, not looking at her.

Going up those steps my insides felt like water, my head full of all the things I should have said to her. Bitch. Sending me a ruddy telegram. Urgent. Just so she could tell me to bugger off. Bitch. Just because my skin was white, that's why. Comfortable. Balls. If I was black like her ruddy brother or Ron then everybody would be comfortable. Bloody bitch waited till I'd made a damned fool of myself telling her I was in love with her.

All the way home I could hear her voice saying 'Good-bye, Jack.' Standing there, waiting to shake hands. Let her ruddy wait. Bitch. Bloody Spade bitch. I spat to get the last taste of her lipstick out of my mouth, then lit a cigarette.

26

INDOORS I SAW Dad in the sitting-room but didn't want to say anything to him. I started upstairs, but he called me down, whispering so as not to wake Mum. He asked what Mrs Spencer wanted to see me about and I said I didn't know because she wasn't there when I arrived and I didn't wait. He looked at me as if he didn't believe me, then he said that someone had been on the phone to me a couple of times and left a number for me to call. He handed me a piece of paper with Ruth's number. I wondered what the hell he was playing at, carrying on as if he couldn't recognize Ruth's voice. I made the call.

Naomi answered, right away wanting to know what on earth had happened with Ruth and me. She sounded excited and angry. I could hardly get a word in edgewise. I said I hadn't seen Ruth all day long, but she asked me what the hell was I up to, that Ruth had left to go to my house and she'd come back and locked herself in her room and would not open the door or talk with her, and I'd better get over there right away. Slamming down the phone. All I could think of was that perhaps Ruth had come and Dad had told her I'd gone to see Michelle.

He was sitting there, pretending to read the newspaper, but you could see he'd been listening to every word. I asked him if Ruth had been over while I was out, and he said no, she hadn't called. Looking surprised at me.

'Her flatmate says she's been over here,' I told him.

'Not here, she hasn't,' he said, 'I haven't moved from here since you went out, and nobody's been here. What's up with her?'

I said I didn't know, but her flatmate said she was acting funny, locked herself in her room. The look he gave me, then right out asked me if I'd gone and got the girl into trouble.

Right out. I didn't know what to say. Just hearing him say it made me scared as hell.

'At your age you ought to have had more bloody sense,' he said.

When I got to their flat my finger had barely touched the bell before Naomi opened the door saying, 'Oh, it's you,' as if she didn't expect me, yet half pulling me inside. Right away asking me what did I say to Ruth to make her behave like that. Not really believing me when I said I didn't know what she was talking about.

I left her and went to knock on Ruth's door, saying, 'It's me, Jack.'

She opened up and you could see she'd been crying, her face red as ever, her eyes all puffed up. I asked her what was the matter, but she wouldn't answer, just went and sat on her bed, looking at me as if she thought I'd hit her, or something. I shut the door. Whatever it was I didn't want Naomi to hear it, especially if it was what Dad had said.

'Look, what's up?' I asked her again. But she just sat there looking at me, her eyes scared, twisting a hankie in her fingers. I went and sat on the bed near her, asking her what was the matter. When I got near she drew away, still not saying a word. So I thought, Right. First Michelle, now you. To hell with it. To hell with all of you. I'd just had enough of it.

'Look, Ruth, what's going on? What the hell's up with you?'

'Nothing,' she said, making it sound like she was accusing me.

'Then what did you want to lock yourself in here for? The way Naomi was carrying on on the phone, I thought something had happened to you, for Heaven's sake.'

'Nothing's happened to me.'

'Then what's the big idea?'

'Don't ask me. You tell me what's the big idea. You tell me.' She straightened up, pointing her face at me. 'Only don't tell me any more lies. I don't want to hear any more lies.'

It couldn't be what Dad thought, or she wouldn't be saying this, so I got the idea that somehow or other she must have found out that I'd been to see Michelle and was all steamed up about it.

'If you mean about me going to see Michelle, I had a telegram from her mother asking me to go over there.'

'I'm not interested in where you go or who you see.'

'Then what are you making all the fuss about?' Smiling at her. Reaching to tickle her chin. Sure that she wasn't in any trouble, so I wasn't worried any more. After all, I didn't have to explain anything to her, about Michelle or anything else.

'I heard about it,' she said, dropping her voice.

'Heard about what?'

'About what you did. You and your brother.'

It was as if I couldn't breathe, everything going weak.

'What the hell are you on about?'

'I was over at your house at lunchtime. Wanted to surprise you so I went round to the back door. It wasn't closed. I was just going in when I heard your mother. The things she was saying about you killing that coloured fellow.'

She was looking at me, her eyes scared again. I was cold all over, my heart banging away so I could hear it.

'It was horrible. I just stood there. I didn't really want to listen. I couldn't help it, all of you screaming at each other. So I came home.'

I couldn't say anything.

'Why couldn't you just tell me the truth when I asked you, instead of all those lies? Why did you do it, Jack? Why did you?'

'Do what?'

'What your Mum said. Stab that man?'

'You're barmy as hell. What are you talking about? I didn't stab anybody. If you want to go around sticking your nose in other people's business you'd better damn well make sure that you hear right.' I was mad as hell, her calling me names and telling me I killed somebody.

'But I heard her, Jack. I heard her.' She was watching me with her mouth open like some crazy goldfish.

'I don't know what the hell you're talking about. All I know is I didn't stab anybody. If you wanted to know something why didn't you come right in and ask and get the ruddy story straight instead of sneaking about the place and getting yourself all screwed up?'

'I don't want to listen to any more of your lies,' she said, her voice quiet, 'I'm not crazy. I heard your mother. She wouldn't say something like that if it wasn't true. Not about her own son. God, it's horrible. And you can sit there and say it's not true.'

'Look, I told you. I didn't stab anybody.'

'Then who did? Your brother?'

'I don't know what you're on about. My brother went out that night and got killed in an accident. That's all I know. I don't even want to know anything else.'

'Then why have the police been asking all those questions? Why?'

'Why don't you go and ask them?' Suddenly I didn't give a damn about anything any more. Or anyone. Not her or Michelle or Mum or Dad. Anyone. And I didn't care what the hell she said.

'Look, if you think I killed somebody why the hell don't you go to the police? Eh? Why don't you?' I got up. She pulled backwards as if afraid I was going to touch her, still watching me with her ruddy mouth open. I left her sitting there and passed Naomi in the hall. She must have heard it all. I didn't give a damn. To hell with them. To hell with all of them. To hell with the whole ruddy stinking world.

The house was in darkness. I went quietly up the stairs thinking to myself, What the hell? Passing their room I heard the voice, softly, 'That you, Jack?'

I couldn't believe my ears. Stood still to listen. Seeing the door half-open. Again, 'Jack?' Softly. Sleepy.

'Yes, Mum. You okay, Mum?'

'Yes, Son. Night, Son.' Sleepy. And the ruddy tears in my eyes, I could hardly see my way to my room.